MATTHEW RIEF

REVENGE IN THE KEYS
A Logan Dodge Adventure

Florida Keys Adventure Series
Volume 3

Logan Dodge Adventures

Gold in the Keys
(Florida Keys Adventure Series Book 1)

Hunted in the Keys
(Florida Keys Adventure Series Book 2)

Revenge in the Keys
(Florida Keys Adventure Series Book 3)

If you're interested in receiving my newsletter for updates on my upcoming books, you can sign up on my website:

matthewrief.com

MAPS

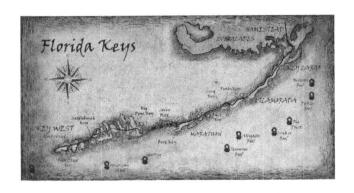

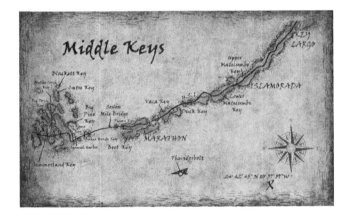

PROLOGUE

Keroman Submarine Base
Lorient, France
July 16, 1944

There was a strong easterly breeze through the humid evening air, carrying the smells of the ocean mixed with lingering gunpowder. Vice Admiral Heinrich von Gottberg stood atop a tall fortified spire, wearing his midnight-blue double-breasted jacket and matching peaked cap. His gray hair was barely visible as he stood against the concrete railing, holding a pair of binoculars in his right hand and a half-burned cigar in his left.

The night sky was dark as a crypt and deathly quiet, but Gottberg knew that the stillness would not last for long.

With dreary eyes, he looked out upon what remained of the city and the concrete bunkers below. The base was comprised of three main bunkers, aptly named Keroman I, II, and III. He stood atop Keroman III, the largest and newest of the bunkers, which was 170 meters long, or just short of two football fields, and 138 meters wide.

Allied raids against the base and the surrounding city had become common. The bunkers had withstood over thirty bombing raids during the past two years, but the city of Lorient was in shambles. With the successful invasion of Normandy by Allied forces, Gottberg knew that it was only a matter of time before Keroman was surrounded.

He took in a deep breath, sighed, and set his binoculars on top of the concrete ledge in front of him. Moving his right hand up to his face, he tilted his head down, closed his fishy blue eyes and squeezed the bridge of his nose. *Three months*, he thought. *Three months of sleepless nights. Three months of waiting.* He felt the sagging, rippled skin that formed dark bags under his eyes.

A moment later, the sound of the distant humming of propellers ripped a hole in the quiet night air.

"Where is the shipment?" he said to a dark-haired seaman named Theodor Franke, who stood stoically behind him. His voice was stern and low, hardened from years of giving orders and inhaling tobacco fumes.

"They are five minutes out," the young, energetic man replied.

Looking out at the cloud-covered night sky, he inhaled and let out a deep puff of smoke, knowing that five minutes would be too long. As if to solidify his thoughts, a bright yellow flash illuminated the blackness, and the loud ground-rumbling sound of an explosion rattled the air.

"Man the flak guns!" he barked to Theodor. "Concentrate on protecting the supply trucks."

The young man turned, grabbed a radio headset that was resting on an oak table and relayed the orders. As he set the radio back onto the tabletop, a loud, high-pitched siren rang out over the air.

Through occasional breaks in the clouds, Gottberg could see them. A swarm of B-17 flying fortresses soaring high above. Soon their payloads would rain down in waves, destroying everything that wasn't protected within the bunkers. But Gottberg knew that the shipment had to reach the base safely at all costs.

"Send two platoons out of the bunkers," he ordered. "Assemble them at the northwestern outpost."

Theodor's eyes grew wide and his mouth dropped open. He couldn't believe what he was hearing. The northwestern outpost had been all but leveled, and no soldiers had left the safety of the bunkers during a raid since he'd been ordered to Keroman over two years earlier.

"Sir, I—" the young man stammered.

Gottberg shot him a stern gaze and cut him off. "That's an order, seaman! And have them bring heavy machine guns."

Trying to stop his hands from shaking, Theodor grabbed the mouthpiece and relayed the order. It pained him to do it. The soldiers inside the base had grown close, and he knew that he would be sending many of his friends to their certain deaths.

Gottberg understood the magnitude of the order that he was giving, but he had his orders as well, and they were directly from the Führer. The cargo being transported was vital and was to be loaded onto the most advanced U-boat they had at Keroman and sent underway as soon as possible.

Karl Dönitz, the commander of the Kriegsmarine, had one final plan against the Allied forces. An attack on US soil with a biological weapon deadlier than any ever produced. With the end of the war dawning upon them, they would strike the Americans right through their hearts, bringing the war to their soil.

Only seconds later, the dark sky came alive with activity as B-17s swarmed high above like a kicked hornets' nest. The German soldiers manned their heavy-caliber flak guns atop the bunkers, riddling the sky with holes. They hit an occasional B-17, causing it to retreat or rain down towards the ground like a falling meteorite. But every time the German soldiers hit one, it seemed as though five more took its place.

Bombs fell from the sky in heavy sheets, creating a massive vortex of fire and heat as they exploded atop the bunkers and what remained of the surrounding city. Despite the urging of his subordinates that he should head inside, Gottberg remained atop the spire, holding his binoculars pressed against his eyes.

If this mission fails, I go down with it, he thought as he stared through the magnifying lenses.

Suddenly, Gottberg spotted a dim and distant flickering light on the road leading into the bunker from the northeast. A few seconds later, more lights appeared, and he realized that it was three trucks driving full speed in his direction.

"Where are the platoons?" Gottberg fired at Theodor. "They should be out there by now."

As if summoned by his anger, the two platoons he'd ordered appeared in his view. The one hundred soldiers sprinted to the west and took fortified positions inside a destroyed brick outpost, firing hopelessly into the air at their assailants over seven thousand feet above them. The flyboys took the bait, and a long row of bombers changed course and dropped their ordnance right over the German soldiers below. The sight was gruesome and nightmarish. The entire mass of soldiers vanished in a bright, loud fiery haze of flames and screams.

Theodor collapsed to the ground and pressed his hands to his ears, unable to control his emotions as the two platoons were blown away. Gottberg didn't flinch or turn his head in the slightest. He kept his vision trained on the three trucks and gave a sigh of relief as they drove through the massive metal gates and entered into Keroman III. His plan had worked.

Turning around, Gottberg flicked what remained of his cigar and stormed right past Theodor. Entering the bunker, he moved swiftly down the concrete stairs and met with the trucks at ground level. The soldiers inside the bunker didn't seem to notice the bombs exploding directly overhead. The bunker had a double-reinforced concrete roof over seven meters thick, and they knew that nothing the Allied bombers had was capable of making so much as a dent in it. From the ground level, the explosions were little more than distant thunder.

Gottberg moved straight for the officer in charge of the transport.

"We need this loaded up right away," he said, surprising the ensign who'd just spent over forty-eight hours driving over damaged and dangerous roads. "Pen six is just that way. The boat is crewed and ready to depart."

It took just thirty minutes for the soldiers to move the weapon from the trucks and into the forward torpedo room of the U-boat.

Lieutenant Otto Dietrich, the commanding officer of the boat, had been up since three in the morning, working alongside his sailors to make sure that their boat was ready to get underway. The engines were not a hundred percent, and they were having issues with the navigation equipment, but Dietrich would not let that stop them. His boat was the most advanced in the history of undersea warfare, but its construction had been rushed and off-the-books, naturally resulting in glitches here and there. Everything about the boat was secret. Even the hull number was known only to her sailors.

After verifying that their newly acquired cargo was secured, Dietrich did one final walk-through of the boat before meeting Gottberg up on the gangway.

"The tide is low," Dietrich said, glancing over his shoulder at the calm waters of Lorient Harbor, where the Blavet River met the Bay of Biscay. "And she draws more of a draft than other boats. She will not be able to fully submerge until she's clear of the bunker."

Gottberg realized what the lieutenant was getting at and looked back at him with a stern gaze. "The orders are to leave immediately, Lieutenant."

Dietrich nodded. He didn't understand or like the idea of cruising on the surface with packs of B-17s soaring overhead, but orders were orders. It wasn't for fear of his life. No, he'd accepted the fact that the odds of his surviving the war were slim to none. It was the mission that he cared about.

"Aye, sir," he said.

An abnormally loud rumble resonated from the world above them as a bomb exploded nearby. The bunker shook slightly, the metal gangway creaking against the hull of the U-boat.

Gottberg pulled Dietrich in close and stared into his eyes. "This mission cannot fail, Otto."

The younger officer nodded. "It shall not." Then, turning to a few of his men standing topside, he said, "Prepare to make way. We deploy now!"

Less than fifteen minutes later, every system was operating and the electric engines were running. Soldiers pierside cast the lines, and the U-boat cruised quietly out of the stall into the darkness beyond. Once in the deeper water of the harbor, air vented from the ballast tanks and water took its place, causing the boat to submerge.

Gottberg stood and watched as the boat quickly vanished into the night. Then, turning to a soldier behind him, he said, "Relay a message to Berlin. The Ghost is underway."

CHAPTER ONE

South of Islamorada, Florida Keys
November 2006

By the time Owen realized that he was being followed, it was already too late. Standing at the stern and facing aft over the transom of his fifty-eight-foot Grand Banks Eastbay, he focused his brown eyes on a distant white glow on the northern horizon. It was a large boat, and it was moving quickly towards him, cruising full throttle through the moonless Caribbean night.

Grabbing a high-powered monocular, he took a closer look at his pursuers and realized that it was an Interceptor Border Patrol boat, speeding towards them at close to sixty knots. Even with the upgraded pair of fourteen-hundred-horsepower engines, he knew that there was no way that they could outrun it.

"Shit," he said as he lowered the monocular.

His first mate, a young Jamaican man named Joseph, was standing at the helm up on the flybridge, his body twisted back to look at the light.

"Ow in da hell we nuh see dem on radar?" the young man asked, staring back in awe at the ever-approaching light.

There were a number of possible reasons why they'd missed the boat. Perhaps their equipment was faulty, or maybe it was their pursuers speed, or the design of their boat. But none of that mattered to Owen. No, there was no time to think about that. He needed a plan, and he needed one fast.

"Joseph, what's our depth?"

A moment later, the young man replied, "Fifty metas, Captain. We're right along di ledge."

Owen's heart raced. He knew that the patrol would be on top of them in less than a few minutes and that, given the high number of drug runs over the past year, they would do a full search of his boat. He had little doubt that they would find the fifty million dollars' worth of gold bars, cash, and diamonds stowed away in the main cabin.

"Ease back on the throttles," Owen said. "Then turn hard to starboard and face them."

The young man did as his captain instructed, slowing the twin Caterpillar engines and bringing the yacht to a stop with the bow facing directly towards the pursuing patrol boat.

Moving swiftly towards the sliding glass door leading into the salon, he looked up at Joseph and said, "Good. Now get down here and give me a hand."

Stepping inside, Owen walked over the immaculate lacquered teak flooring of the salon, which looked more like an expensive Paris boutique hotel than the inside of a yacht. He passed by a pair of barrel chairs on the port side flanking an entertainment center, and a settee on the starboard side beside an intricately designed table. A blue Stidd chair served the lower helm station, facing an array of electronics and the finely polished helm.

Moving down the five steps leading to the main passageway, Owen headed all the way forward and into the main cabin. He switched on the lights, knelt at the base of the walkaround queen island berth and rolled up a red Persian rug, revealing a hatch roughly five feet long and four feet wide. Sliding his index and middle fingers under the metal ring, he pulled it up, hinging it all the way open and letting it rest on the foot of the bed.

Inside the storage area was a large metal box, just a few inches smaller than the space it occupied. Kneeling on the port side, he reached for a metal handle and adjusted his fingers to get a good grip.

"Joe!" he yelled, and a second later he heard his mate's footsteps as he ran through the salon and down the passageway.

"It's nearly here, Captain," the young man exclaimed.

Owen ignored him and pointed at the other end of the metal box. In the blink of an eye, his mate dropped down, gripped the handle with his right hand and gave Owen a nod.

"Okay, on three. One… two… three!"

The box was heavier than either of them had expected, and they grunted, using all their strength to lift it out of place and set it on the teak floorboards beside them with a loud thud. The box had been filled with cocaine when they'd first installed it two weeks earlier. It was after their exchange in Miami that it had been filled with an assortment of diamonds, US dollars, and gold bars, making it much heavier.

Breathing heavily, Owen said, "Okay. Now all the way aft."

Joe's eyes went wide. "Wah wi a guh do?"

Owen knew that they had no choice but to get rid of it. Hiding the loot in the large metal box under the floorboards had worked for the routine customs inspection they'd undergone back in Miami. But this boat was chasing them down in the middle of the night. *These guys will search for hours*, he thought.

"Just lift," Owen said, bending down as if he were a weight lifter going for a record deadlift.

Gripping the handles tightly, he counted once more and they lifted the box, heaving it down the narrow passageway and up the small set of stairs into the lounge. Their fingers screamed and it felt like their shoulders were going to pop out of their sockets, but they both held on. Shuffling quickly through the sliding glass door, they took two more steps, then balanced it on the transom, letting the boat support its weight as they both caught their breath. At fifty-four years old, Owen surprised even himself with how much strength he had retained from his younger years.

After a moment, Joseph looked at Owen and shook his head. "Captain, wi cyaa just—"

"We can't let them find it," he fired back, motioning at the patrol boat. The engines were getting louder and louder with each passing second. Owen knew that the consequences of being caught would ruin their chances of taking down their targeted group of drug smugglers. If found, the loot could be linked to the transaction in Miami, which would mean a complete waste of their undercover operation. It was a risk he wasn't willing to take.

Checking the lock and making sure the box was sealed tight, he stepped over the transom and onto the small swim platform. Grabbing one side of the box, he looked up at Joseph expectantly. Reluctantly, the young man grabbed the box, whose contents were worth over fifty million dollars, and together they heaved it over the side and into the water with a big splash. Leaning over the edge, Joseph watched as the shining steel rocketed towards the seafloor, vanishing in just a few seconds.

Owen moved back through the salon and into the main cabin. Closing the hatch, he set the Persian rug on the hardwood and rolled it back to where it had been before. The patrol boat was close now, close enough for him to hear its powerful engines through the hull. He moved alongside Joseph back through the salon and into the main cabin.

"Stow your twelve-gauge in the hidden compartment on the port side," Owen said, his voice stern as he knelt down along the starboard side of the bed.

The yacht had a few secret hiding places, including one on either side of the queen-sized bed. Reaching beneath the mattress, Owen pulled a wide drawer out, then released a long piece of plywood that was completely hidden from view. Reaching towards his hip, he grabbed his MK23 SOCOM pistol, placed it inside the hiding place, then returned the plywood to its original place. Then, he shoved the drawer back in and rose to his feet.

Seeing Joseph standing beside him, he said, "That should be everything. You don't have any other weapons, right?"

His mate stared back at him for a moment, then reached into his pocket and pulled out a round metal object.

"Holy shit, Joseph," Owen said, stepping towards him. He grabbed the grenade from his mate's open hand. "What in the hell do you have this for?"

Joseph looked nervous as hell, and beads of sweat had appeared on his forehead.

"I'm sorry, Mr. Dodge," he said. "Mi broad it just inna case."

Owen shook his head, then knelt back down beside the starboard side of the bed.

"Just go back out and turn on all the outside lights," Owen said.

As Joseph ran through the door, Owen quickly stashed the grenade in the starboard hiding place, then followed him aft. Back in the salon, he moved over to the lower helm station and, staring into a flat-screen monitor, he pulled out a notepad from his pocket and scribbled down the coordinates of their current location. Once they were written, he opened a small compartment and pulled out a stack of papers, then moved out onto the deck through the sliding glass door.

"Let me do the talking," he said to his mate, who was standing nervously on the deck, looking out over the water at the approaching boat. Then, setting a hand on the young man's shoulder, he added, "It's gonna be okay."

They stood on the deck as the patrol boat slowed, then banked and eased up towards the port side of the yacht. It was a thirty-nine-foot Midnight Express, with a sleek, freshly painted white fiberglass hull with an orange stripe down the side next to the United States Customs and Border Patrol emblem. Owen had never seen a Border Patrol boat like it before, and its four Mercury Verado engines combined to give the boat over twelve hundred horsepower, which explained why it had been able to sneak up on them so quickly.

There were four guys standing on the deck of the patrol boat as it brushed up against the port side of the yacht. They were all dressed in full Border Patrol agent attire, including the tan short-sleeved shirt covered by a black bulletproof vest with CBP Federal Agent stenciled in white letters. One of the agents stayed at the helm, but the three others had moved over to the port side of their boat and were aiming their weapons at Owen and Joseph, yelling at them to put their hands in the air and drop to their knees slowly.

As the two of them knelt frozen on the deck with their hands raised, a large bald agent jumped over to the yacht and, holding an H&K P2000 pistol in his right hand, searched both of them with his left hand while the two other agents provided cover.

"Your boat has been suspected of drug trafficking," the agent said once he'd finished frisking both of them. His voice was low and powerful. Then he nodded to the other three agents and said, "They're clean." Looking down at Owen and Joseph, he added, "Alright, we have to do a thorough search of your boat now. Both of you sit up here on the transom, and don't make any sudden movements. A boat this size is going to take a while."

One of the agents hopped over and joined the big bald guy as he moved through the sliding glass door into the salon. Then a third agent hopped onto the yacht and walked over to Owen and Joseph. He was wearing a dark green CBP ball cap over brown hair that was trimmed neatly around his ears and had a black earpiece. He had a decent build, though he was much shorter than Owen's six feet, and had bronzed tan skin. It was clear by the way he carried himself that he was the guy in charge.

"Out for a pleasure cruise at zero dark thirty?" the agent said in a stern voice.

"I wish," Owen replied. "This is the best time to catch lobster. But, no, we're not out for a pleasure cruise. We're working."

That caused the man's eyebrows to rise as he stared earnestly into Owen's eyes. But before the man could speak, Owen continued, "We're delivering this yacht to its owner, Mr. Cartwright, in Barranquilla. We're scheduled to deliver it by Thursday afternoon but had to take care of some unexpected maintenance on one of her engines, so we stopped for the day in Miami. We just left four hours ago. We were hoping to still deliver it on schedule. There are a lot of captains out there looking for work and not a lot of yachts to deliver.

We'd hate to tarnish our reputation, so we're pulling an all-nighter."

The Border Patrol agent thought it over for a moment, then said, "I need to see both of your IDs, as well as the title and registration for this yacht."

Before he'd finished his sentence, Owen had everything the agent had asked for held out in front of him.

"That's both of our driver's licenses, as well as the documentation for the boat," Owen said. "As I said, the owner's name is Walter Cartwright, and I have a signed and dated document from him giving us explicit permission to move his yacht from its original location in Charleston, South Carolina, to Barranquilla, Colombia."

The agent went on to ask a series of questions regarding the trip and requested a day-by-day itinerary of where they'd gone, starting with the day they'd cruised out of Charleston a few days earlier. The search lasted over an hour as the guys inspected every inch of the boat, opening every hatch and storage compartment and shining their flashlights into every nook and cranny. When they were satisfied, they climbed back over to their boat, and the leader with the ball cap walked over to Joseph and Owen, who were still sitting at the stern. Joseph was on the deck with his back against the transom, his hands relaxed around his knees, and Owen was lying on the transom, staring up at the night sky, which had cleared slightly, revealing a few bright stars.

"I apologize for the trouble," the agent said, handing Owen back their IDs and the boat's documentation. "We received a tip about this yacht just a few hours after you guys left Miami."

Owen sat up, then glanced over at the agent. "I've been boating for years and all over the world," he said. "I think someone might've been trying to get your attention and draw you away."

The agent thought it over a moment. "The night's just getting started for us. If someone else is on the move, we'll find them. Alright, well, everything seems to be in order, Mr. Dodge. I apologize again for the inconvenience. As you might be aware, there's been an abnormal amount of drug runs through these waters over the past year. We can never be too careful."

"I understand."

"Well, thank you for your cooperation. You guys have a safe cruise to Barranquilla."

"Have a good night, Officer."

The agent stepped over the side and back onto his boat, joining the three others. In an instant, the four three-hundred-horsepower engines roared to life, and the thirty-nine-foot Midnight Express was accelerating through the calm water. In just a few seconds, they had the boat up on plane and cruising east at a lightning pace. With all the lights off, the patrol boat disappeared into the darkness, and even the sounds of its roaring engines soon went quiet.

Joseph stood and stretched his lean, muscular body for a few seconds before turning to his captain. "Gud ting wi tossed di haul."

Owen nodded and moved through the sliding glass door into the salon. Manning the lower helm station, he grabbed the notepad from his pocket and typed the coordinates he'd jotted down earlier into the GPS. Even on a calm evening like this, their yacht had drifted over two miles in the time it had taken the Border Patrol agents to conduct their search.

In less than five minutes, Owen had the fifty-eight-foot yacht idled over the spot where they'd dropped the metal box. Killing the engine, he yelled to Joseph, who was standing at the stern, "Dropping the anchor!"

His mate ran onto the bow and unclasped the safety strap securing the anchor to the boat just in case the windlass malfunctioned. He watched as Owen operated the windlass remotely, lowering slowly at first and then faster as the anchor splashed into the water. After the anchor hit the bottom, Owen let out a significant amount more slack before setting the anchor in place and switching off the remote operator.

Owen then grabbed a black mesh bag and carried it out of the salon. Setting it on the deck, he pulled out a pair of fins along with a waterproof flashlight, a dive knife, and a clear Cressi dive mask and snorkel. He was wearing swim trunks underneath his tan cargo shorts, so he slipped them off, pulled off his long-sleeved tee shirt, then sat on the swim platform and donned a three-millimeter wetsuit.

Joseph grabbed a BC from a nearby storage compartment, along with two scuba tanks. After clasping the two tanks to his BC, Owen strapped it over his body and secured the straps.

"Yuh wa mi to tie a rope to dis bag, Captain?" Joseph asked, holding the black mesh bag in the air. "Wi cya use it to bring everything up."

The young man was smart and knew all too well that there was no way in hell the two of them were going to bring up the entire metal box on their own. Not while it was full, anyway.

Owen nodded. "Yeah, go ahead and use that extra length of nylon. It should be plenty long enough. And hand me that crowbar while you're at it."

At 150 feet down, he knew that the pressure would make it difficult to open the box, even with the lock removed. The pressure would undoubtedly create a vacuum, and Owen didn't want to risk having to make an unnecessary trip if he couldn't get it open with his hands.

Owen looked down at the dark tropical water. He was no stranger to diving deep or at night. A diver in the United States Navy for thirty years, he'd retired as a master diver and had spent a large portion of his life beneath the waves. Though beyond the physical prime of his life, he was still in great shape, especially for a man in his fifties.

Sliding the mask over his face, he donned his fins and bit down on the mouthpiece. Turning on his flashlight, he took in a breath and dropped back into the water with a small splash. The warm water felt good, and he floated for a few seconds before receiving the mesh bag tied to the rope from Joseph. Then he gave his mate a thumbs-up and vented air from his BC. Once he'd dropped beneath the surface, he turned his body around and smoothly finned towards the seafloor.

He kept his body calm and moved at a leisurely pace, not wanting the pressure change to occur too quickly. He stopped kicking only twice as he equalized the pressure by pinching his nose and trying to force air out of his ears. The visibility was good, and it wasn't long before he could clearly make out the reef line by the bright beam from his high-powered LED flashlight.

There was a steep drop-off about twenty feet high and covered in numerous varieties and sizes of colorful coral. He finned his way along the edge, and it wasn't long before he spotted a glimmer of shiny metal and realized instantly that it was the box. As he swam closer, he saw that it was on its side and jammed between the rocky ledge and a massive boulder that was covered in coral and barnacles.

Shit, he thought as his hand grazed against the side of the steel box about five feet from the top of the ledge. From its position on its side against the ledge and boulder, there was no way Owen could open it to retrieve its contents. Digging his fingers under the heavy box, he pushed his feet into the rock below and pulled up, trying to dislodge it. But the heavy box didn't even budge.

He tried again, this time inserting the crowbar between the box and the rock, trying to lever it out. But again the box didn't move. *Maybe with Joseph*, he thought as he stared up into the inky water surrounding him. Realizing that there was no way he could get the box out and opened by himself, he left the crowbar on top of the bag to keep it from drifting away and finned back towards the surface.

After waiting at fifteen feet down for roughly three minutes, he swam up and broke into the night air above. Once on the surface, he swam over to the yacht and called out to Joseph, who was standing against the gunwale, surprised to see him back up so soon. Owen explained the situation to his mate, and within minutes, Joseph donned a full set of scuba gear and jumped into the water with him. Though not even twenty, Joseph was already a good professional diver and had worked as a dive master for various dive operations in Jamaica and Curacao.

As they slowly descended, Owen shined his flashlight in the direction of their destination below them. He knew as well as anyone else the potential dangers of doing two back-to-back dives to such a depth without waiting for the nitrogen to burn off. But he took the risk, not wanting to delay them any more than they already were. As he examined the area around the box, he realized that this portion of the ledge appeared different than the rest. There was a large section that was wider than the rest, and he could only assume that it was due to a geological anomaly of some kind.

When they reached the box, Owen instructed his mate to lean against the ledge and grab one side while he dug the prybar under the other side. When Joseph was in position, Owen gripped the heavy iron bar tightly and jammed the pointed end between the bottom of the box and the barnacle-covered rock face beneath it.

When the prybar was secure, Owen rested it against the large boulder, using it as a fulcrum. He motioned towards Joseph, making sure the young man was ready, then moved to the end of the prybar. Gripping the end tightly, he let all the air out of his BCD and pushed down on the crowbar as hard as he could, trying to lever the box out of place. Bubbles burst out of his regulator and danced up towards the surface as he yelled, summoning all of his strength.

In an instant, the crowbar slipped out of place, and since Owen was still forcing all of his weight on top of it, it slammed down against the large boulder with a loud and powerful clank.

Owen's eyes grew wide at the sound. It hadn't been the sound of metal against rock, but metal against metal. Confused, Owen examined the portion of the large boulder where the crowbar had struck. It was covered in barnacles and sediment, but Owen could tell that something was odd about it. Grabbing his dive knife from the sheath strapped to his leg, he scraped off a few of the barnacles, revealing a flat metal surface. He gasped and his heart raced as he realized that what he was looking at wasn't a rock at all, but part of a sunken ship.

CHAPTER TWO

There was no mistaking it. After gazing upon the abnormal wider section of the ledge with new, enlightened eyes, Owen was certain that he was staring at a lost German U-boat. He tried his best to suppress his excitement, but it wasn't easy. Over the course of his life, he'd dropped down beneath the waves countless times, and never had he experienced a feeling quite like the one that was overtaking him at that moment.

Resting the crowbar up against the metal box, he glanced over at Joseph, who was still floating beside it, staring at his captain incredulously. Owen pointed two fingers at his eyes, then turned and pressed his right hand against the wrecked U-boats conning tower. Making a fist, he knocked his knuckles against the metal, sounding out a melody of tings that made his mate realize what Owen was trying to tell him. Astonished, the young man let go of the metal box and finned over towards Owen.

Even through his mask and regulator, Owen could tell that he was smiling from ear to ear.

Owen transferred some air from his tank into his BCD, increasing his buoyancy slightly, then finned down the sail and along the topside of the wreck. He felt like he was in a dream as he swam over the submarine that, in all likelihood, hadn't been seen by man in over sixty years.

The U-boats were Germany's attack submarines, which had seen action in both world wars but had been most prominent during World War II. Owen hadn't studied the vessels extensively, but he had dived U-352, which had been sunk just off the coast of North Carolina. Staring at his newly discovered wreck, he noticed the similarities between it and the U-boat wreck he'd explored before, though it was difficult to make out any details given the fact that it was barely even visible.

Every inch of its dark hull was covered in rock, sediment, coral, barnacles, anemones, and an assortment of other various sea life. It explained why the wreck had never been noticed before. Even while diving inches away from it, Owen hadn't given the site more than a second glance.

After spending half an hour exploring the visible portions of the wreck, Owen was just about to head for the surface when something caught his eye just ahead of the forward tip of the U-boat. Moving towards it, he realized that it was a rounded oblong object about fifty feet from the U-boat and sticking halfway into the ledge and patches of coral. When he was close enough, he reached out and touched what appeared to be a metal tube about three feet wide with a worn old propeller stuck to the back of it. It was barely distinguishable after the years of saltwater corrosion and shifting tides, but Owen knew that it had to be a torpedo.

His first thought was why in the hell would the Nazis have fired off a torpedo after being sunk? And why hadn't it detonated and blown the ledge to smithereens?

Both questions festered in his brain as he ran his hands along its side, searching for any possible clues. In the back of his mind, he couldn't help hoping that the old deadly projectile wouldn't decide to flip the script and explode after all those years lying dormant. He knew the chances of that were slim to none, that time and saltwater deteriorated everything, especially intricate firing mechanisms. But regardless, there was no denying that on the other side of the metal casing was, in all likelihood, a payload capable of blowing Owen and everything within a hundred-foot radius sky-high.

As his hands grazed over the side of the torpedo, he spotted something unusual in the beam of his flashlight. It looked like a marking of some kind, but it was covered by grime and a cluster of barnacles and sea urchins. Grabbing his dive knife, he slid the sharpened steel blade carefully, scraping off decades of growth and muck and revealing a black symbol etched into the side of the torpedo. He gasped and his eyes grew wide. It looked like a skull and crossbones, and directly underneath the symbol were letters spelling out TOXISCH.

Instinctively, he moved a few inches back from the torpedo. His German wasn't great, but it didn't take a linguist to realize what the word meant. After taking a few moments to search the torpedo and finding nothing else, he glanced at his pressure gauge. He had just north of four hundred PSI in his second tank, meaning that it was time to head back up.

He rose slowly, breathing out the entire time to ensure that no air expanded dangerously in his lungs. During the entire ascent, he could think about nothing but the U-boat, and especially the mysterious torpedo.

After he surfaced, climbed aboard the yacht and removed all his gear, he told Joseph to start up the engines. His mate had surfaced twenty minutes earlier in order to watch over the yacht and was sitting with one leg over the side and one planted on the deck.

"We're nuh a guh bring up di loot?" he asked.

"We have no choice," Owen replied, shrugging. "Damn thing's stuck there."

"Wah bout dat ship? I've neva seen nuhting like dat before."

Owen patted himself down with a clean towel, then slid back into his tee shirt. "Let's keep that between us." He'd been thinking over a plan for the past half hour and had a pretty good idea of how he wanted to play it. "All we gotta do is get a boat with a crane. Doesn't have to be a big one— just enough to get that box up. Once we have it, we'll deliver it as planned, take down these drug runners, and then we'll deal with the U-boat."

The young man thought it over a moment, then said, "U-boat, Captain?"

As the two prepared to make way, pulling up the anchor, starting the engines and charting their course, Owen explained everything he knew about the Kriegsmarine and their impressive fleet of submarines. When everything was ready to go, they eased up on plane and cruised due southwest. Owen had an old Navy buddy in Varadero, Cuba, who owned a salvage business, making it the best option for getting a necessary rig quickly and without the usual hurdles of going through a bigger company. But before he headed there, Owen had a quick stop to make.

Both he and his mate were up on the bridge, with Joseph manning the helm and Owen seated beside him, writing diligently on a half sheet of paper.

"Wah dat, Captain?"

"It's a riddle."

"A riddle? Fi what?"

Owen thought it over for a moment, then replied, "Insurance. Just in case."

Less than an hour later, they arrived at the location Owen had instructed him to head towards, roughly a quarter of a mile south of the *Thunderbolt* wreck. Once the engines were off and they'd dropped anchor, Owen folded the paper and enclosed it in a plastic waterproof box. He then donned his full scuba gear, slid the plastic box into a pouch in his BCD and secured the Velcro around it.

"Isn't dis a popular site?" Joseph asked as Owen stepped over the transom, sat on the swim platform and donned his fins.

Owen smiled, "Not where I'm going." Then, just before he dropped down, he added, "Keep a watchful eye. This will take a little while. If you see anything suspicious, let me know with the communicator." He pointed to his forearm, where he had a small device strapped to his wetsuit. It had two buttons, one red and one yellow. Joseph had the same device, and if either of them pressed the red button, it meant that they needed help. The yellow meant "look at me"; either look up at the boat, or don a mask and look below, depending on who pressed it. It also required three rhythmic presses to work, so occasional accidental presses weren't an issue. It was a device Owen had invented himself and had used for years while diving.

Just under an hour later, Owen returned. He climbed aboard, and before he'd even slipped out of his BCD, he told Joseph to make waves for Varadero. Within a few minutes, he had the yacht up on plane and at her cruising speed of twenty-seven knots, heading south. Since it was three in the morning and neither of them had slept yet, Owen decided that they would take turns manning the helm so the other could get some shut-eye.

He took the first watch and told Joseph he'd wake him up in two hours. It wouldn't be a full night's sleep, by any means, but it would be better than nothing. In four hours, they would reach Varadero, and Owen wanted them both awake and ready to meet his friend.

As Joseph slept, Owen grabbed his backpack from the main cabin and headed up to the flybridge. He plopped down on the cushioned seat and kept a watchful eye on the horizon. Since most of the clouds had passed, he had a nice view of the moon and the stars above.

Once he was sure that Joseph was passed out, he reached into his backpack and pulled out a brand-new Suunto Core digital dive watch. It was the same watch his son Logan always used, and he'd given it to Owen as a birthday present earlier that year. Owen was old-school and preferred analog. His son had tried to convince him of the benefits the watch had built in, but Owen could never part ways with his old watch.

Holding the Suunto watch in his hands for a moment, he flipped it over, revealing a silver backing. He grabbed his dive knife, used the fine pointed tip to carve a few words into it, and then exchanged it with the silver Omega he was wearing.

"He'll figure it out," he said to himself as he placed his analog dive watch in his backpack. "He's smart."

He was confident that things would work out smoothly but knew from years of experience that it was always best to plan for the worst. The U-boat they'd found was remarkable, and Owen spent the rest of the two hours thinking about it and wondering what its story was. He also thought about the torpedo and wondered what kind of toxic contents the Nazis had loaded it up with.

Two hours went by quickly and, after a brief discussion with his mate, Owen went down into the main cabin, fell onto the queen-sized bed and closed his eyes. What felt like only seconds later, he woke up to the sound of a high-pitched rhythmic ringing coming from his front pocket. Reaching into his pocket, he glanced at the front screen of his cell phone, realizing it had been an hour and a half since he'd collapsed, then answered it.

"Hello?"

"Captain," Joseph said, "wi get anotha boat approaching. Yuh might wa come up here."

He told his mate he'd be right up, then rolled out of bed and moved down the passageway, through the salon, and out the sliding glass door. Wondering who in the hell was bothering them now, he heard the loud roar of multiple large outboard engines approaching their position quickly. Stepping over to the port side, he saw two large Cigarette go-fast boats cruising through the water at over eighty knots.

It was five in the morning, and the first hints of red sunlight were just starting to rise over the eastern horizon, sending a faint glow over the entire sky. Grabbing his monocular, Owen focused on the approaching boats and saw that they each had at least five men aboard, and a few of them had rifles in their hands.

Without a word, Owen headed swiftly through the salon and into the main cabin. Kneeling on the starboard side of the bed, he pulled out the drawer, reached under the plywood and pulled out his MK23. After sliding it into the back of his waistband, he headed back up for the cockpit.

The boats had cruised much closer, and Owen recognized one of the guys standing on the bow of the leading yacht. At six and a half feet tall and 250 pounds of muscle, the massive Hispanic body of Pedro Campos was unmistakable. But it was his short black Mohawk that differentiated him from his twin brother, Hector, who stood on the bow of the second boat and had a similar Goliath-like build. They were the two drug-running pirates Owen was working for in order to take down their entire operation from the inside. The plan had worked relatively smoothly—that was, until they'd had to wait in Miami longer than planned, then dump their haul into the ocean.

The first boat pulled up along the starboard side of the yacht, and Pedro vaulted over both gunwales, causing the yacht to rock slightly as his massive frame hit the deck. He was followed instantly by two other thugs. Walking his massive frame over towards Owen, who was standing on the port side and staring at the men, he glared and pointed a large finger into Owen's face.

"What the fuck is going on?" he said, his face fuming with rage. He was wearing a skintight black tee shirt with jagged white edges radiating from the word Tapout in the center, a remnant from the days when he and his brother had been professional MMA fighters. He also wore a pair of faded blue jeans and black tactical boots, making him look even taller than he already was.

"Get your finger out of my damn face," Owen fired back. He'd dealt with asshole hotheads hundreds of times in his life and had never been one to back down easily.

The giant of a man gritted his teeth and then dropped his hand. "You were supposed to have delivered the haul yesterday morning."

"He's running," Hector said as the second boat pulled alongside the port side. He snarled as he towered behind Owen, then spat a fat dip into the ocean. He looked almost identical to his twin brother except for his hair, which he kept short all over the top of his head, and a tattoo that ran all around his body, revealing itself up the sides of his neck. He was wearing a gray cutoff tee shirt and jeans.

"Shut up," Pedro said, eyeing his brother. Then, turning back to Owen, he said, "Are you running?"

That struck a chord with Owen, and he stepped towards Pedro with his chest raised. "Look, I don't know who you think I am, but I agreed to make this run and that's what I'm gonna do. As far as the schedule goes, that all went to hell when your dumbass buyers in Miami let me idle for two days before bothering to make the exchange. You guys are lucky I stayed. If I'd wanted to run, I could have sold the coke myself and been lounging on an island on the other side of the world by now."

Pedro shook his head, then waved a hand in the air. "Whatever. I don't give a shit. All I care about is the loot, and we're here now, so just hand it over and we'll be straight."

After a brief moment of silence, Owen said, "It's not here." Pedro's eyes grew massive and his mouth dropped open, revealing two gold teeth. But before the massive pirate could speak, Owen added, "We were tracked down and searched by Border Patrol and had no choice but to get rid of it all. If we hadn't, they would have found everything."

"Hid it where?" Pedro asked, he was breathing heavily but trying to control his anger.

"It's safe," Owen assured him. "We were heading to Cuba to get a salvage ship because it's stuck at the bottom of the ocean."

"Where is it? What are the coordinates?"

"Listen to me. We can get the cash, gold, and the diamonds to you, all of it, and we can get it to you by late this evening. We just ne—"

"Tell me the fucking coordinates!" he barked, getting into Owen's face. The three other guys gripped their weapons tighter. "You had your chance, Mr. Dodge. And you took too long."

Part of him wanted to just tell them, but he could see in their eyes that they would probably put a bullet in his head anyway. And what about the German U-boat? If he told them where the loot was, they would find it for sure. And then what? Maybe they would find a way to use the biological weapon that the Nazis had tried so hard to use. No, he wouldn't tell them anything.

"Look, you hired us to do a job and we're going to do it," Owen said calmly.

Pedro was visibly agitated. He thought over Owen's words for a few seconds, then shook his head and said, "Show us the hiding place." Then, turning to Joseph, he added, "Both of you."

Owen turned and moved confidently past the massive thug. As he opened the sliding glass door, Hector jumped aboard alongside his twin brother and the two followed him and Joseph inside. When they reached the main cabin, Owen bent down, moved the rug and opened the compartment. Joseph moved to the port side of the queen-sized bed, observing his captain.

Pedro had to walk sideways to fit through the cabin door. He glanced down at the empty storage space, his brother moving along the starboard side and searching the cabin ahead of Owen. Two more thugs entered and stood between Pedro and Owen. The cabin was suddenly very crowded, and Owen could feel the tension building.

When Pedro glanced back at Owen from the empty compartment, he had an uncharacteristic smile plastered over his face.

"You know, you fooled us, Mr. Dodge." Then sighing and shaking his head he added, "We thought you were the real deal." Owen didn't like where the conversation was going. Pedro took in a deep breath, then let it out. "And we hate to be made fools of. I have unfortunate news for you. You see, we met a few friends of yours yesterday. Mr. Briggs and Mr. Porter."

Owen's blood began to boil at the mention of the two detectives whom he'd been working with from the beginning of the operation.

"What did you do to them?"

Pedro smiled. "Only what they deserved." Owen's mind raced. They had been his two points of contact, and he'd relied on them when making decisions. He also counted on them to vouch for his being undercover when the time came. "And now, it's time to do the same to you."

In an instant, the two thugs standing beside Owen raised their weapons and forced him back. Pedro snatched the classic silver Colt revolver from his hip and aimed it at Owen.

Owen felt a rush of adrenaline overtake him as the barrel stared him in the eyes. He would only have a split second to react, he thought as he felt the cold steel of his MK23 SOCOM pistol lodged in the back of his shorts, pressed against his back.

"If we kill them, how will we find the money?" Hector asked, his powerful voice filled with worry.

"Never mind that," Pedro snarled. "We can use the GPS built into the yacht to see where they've been."

Pedro shot Owen an evil smile and thumbed back the hammer of his Colt. Owen felt time slow as the massive man narrowed his gaze.

"Captain Dodge!" Joseph shouted, just as Pedro was starting to squeeze the trigger. In an instant, the young mate grabbed the shotgun from behind the port side of the bed and trained it at Pedro. But before he could take aim, Pedro shot him two times straight through the chest.

As the shots were fired, Owen snatched his pistol, aimed it forward and fired off rounds into the thugs in a fraction of a second. Two of the guys went down, but as he moved his aim towards Pedro, he felt a sharp, powerful pain radiate from his back. The explosion of lead through his skin launched him forward and knocked the wind out of him, but he still managed to pull the trigger of his pistol one final time, sending a bullet streaking into Pedro's side.

As the massive man lurched sideways, Owen felt more sharp pains travel up his spine and heard the sound of automatic gunfire rattling inside the main cabin. Owen's body collapsed forward, slamming hard onto the polished teak floorboards. The pain was consuming. Own couldn't breathe or think. All he could do was watch, weak and helpless, as Hector walked around him and stood with an Uzi in his left hand.

He grabbed Owen's MK23, which had fallen to the deck, then helped his brother. As the room around him started to fade, he watched as Pedro and Hector stared down at his dying body. A moment later, they said something Owen couldn't understand, then turned around and walked towards the salon. Glancing to his right, Owen saw Joseph lying motionless in a pool of blood. Dead.

And he would be dead soon too, he thought. It was all over. He could feel the blood flowing out of him, could feel the bullets lodged in a trail up his back.

But as he lay in a storm of unbearable pain, holding on desperately to his last few seconds of life, he felt a sudden surge of resolution. Opening his eyes and focusing them as best as he could, he crawled on his hands and knees back along the starboard side of the bed. It was a slow and painful endeavor, and after what felt like an eternity, his arms gave out and his body collapsed against the teak floorboards.

Rolling over onto his side, he pulled out the drawer and dislodged the piece of plywood. Then, he extended his left hand as far as he could and wrapped his fingers tightly around the grenade. Glancing back towards the door, he saw that they'd left it open about six inches.

Summoning all the strength he had left, he turned around and inched his way towards the door. Every movement was painful, but he tried his best to keep his groans and breathing quiet. The last thing he needed was for the assholes to return and finish the job by putting a bullet in his head.

When he reached the door, he brought the grenade to his chest, gritted his teeth and pulled the pin. With every ounce of strength he had left in his body, he shot-putted the grenade through the open doorway, causing it to rattle and roll down the passageway.

Closing his eyes, he felt the last remnants of his life slip away as his head hit the deck. The sound of faint yelling followed by a loud, deck-shaking explosion were the last things that he heard.

CHAPTER THREE

Key West, Florida
October 2008

"Logan, what happened?" Charles asked as I moved swiftly back towards my dinner table.

I could barely hear him, though, as my mind raced, blocking out the world around me. All I could think about was the news I'd just received from a detective in Curacao: my dad's gravesite had been desecrated. My blood boiled, but I kept myself calm as I walked along the side aisle of the main dining area of Latitudes Restaurant, weaving around a few formally dressed waiters and waitresses carrying trays of food.

Angelina Fox, a blond bombshell whom I'd worked alongside as a mercenary for the past five years, was sitting at our table, right beside a window that overlooked the dark ocean. She wore a blue dress with diamond earrings, and her pretty blue eyes stared into mine as I approached her.

"I know that look," she said in her sexy Swedish accent. Then, sighing, she added, "I guess we won't be having dessert."

"I'm sorry, Ange," I said as I grabbed my wallet out of my back pocket, slid out two crisp hundred-dollar bills and set them on the table.

Ange was sharper than my dive knife and knew me well enough that she slid out of her chair and stood up without hesitation, and together we headed for the front door. We walked past Charles Wilkes, the sheriff of the Key West Police Department, who was wearing a Hawaiian-style button-up shirt and jeans as opposed to his usual uniform. He shrugged as we passed by and eyed us skeptically.

As the three of us moved through the glass double doors and into the warm evening air, Charles cut us off.

"You've got to tell me what's going on," he said in his low and powerful voice. He was maybe an inch shorter than my six foot two inches and had a strong, lean build with dark black skin. Though he was in his late forties, he looked and moved like a man much younger. "You can't just keep me out of it."

We walked along a crimson cobblestone pathway lined with gumbo-limbo and short lignum vitae trees, heading towards my boat, which was moored at a small private dock just a few hundred feet from the restaurant.

"It's personal," I said as our soles made contact with the treated-pine dock. "It doesn't pertain to anything in the Keys." When we reached my boat, a forty-eight-foot Baia Flash named *Dodging Bullets*, I helped Ange step aboard in her high heels, then turned back to Charles. "Look, I'll call you with my satellite phone with updates, but for now, I'm heading to Curacao, and that's all you need to know."

He seemed unsatisfied with my answer but nodded professionally and then helped me untie the mooring lines wrapped around the cleats. As I climbed aboard, he gave my boat an easy push away from the dock.

"Godspeed, Logan," he said.

I waved, then thanked him for delivering me the message and started up the twin six-hundred-horsepower engines.

As I eased the boat away from the dock, Ange stood beside me. "Curacao, huh?"

"Yeah, about that. Any chance you could let me borrow your plane?"

"To Curacao from Key West in a Cessna? That's over a thousand miles. Even with the upgraded engine and more efficient wings, it'll still take us over seven hours to get there. And we'll have to stop halfway to refuel."

"Still faster than trying to catch a last-minute commercial flight."

She thought it over a moment as I eased forward, picking up speed.

"Alright, I'll fly you there. But you gotta tell me what the hell's going on. And when whatever this is all about is over, you gotta take me out to dinner again."

"Ange, I can—"

"I'm not letting that baby out of my sight. Plus, I've seen you fly one too many times." She laughed, but when she saw the serious expression on my face go unchanged, she knew that something important was going on. As I cruised the Baia across from Sunset Key and into Conch Harbor Marina, a distance of less than a mile, I told Ange about the phone call. I pulled up alongside the dock at slip twenty-four, then killed the engines and tied her off.

Before disembarking, I moved into the main cabin and grabbed a black CamelBak that contained various items I deemed essential. Inside was my Sig Sauer P226 pistol with two fully loaded magazines, a night vision monocular, a satellite phone and a few other items. Ever since I'd had to fight off Black Venom, the notorious Mexican drug cartel, for the precious contents of a sunken Spanish galleon, I'd rarely gone anywhere without having it close by.

Throwing it over my shoulder, I met Ange at the stern and we climbed over the transom, then headed down the dock towards the parking lot. Glancing at my dive watch, I saw that it was just after nine and, being a Wednesday night in October, there wasn't a whole lot of activity in the marina. Just a few liveaboards hanging out on their decks, cooking on their barbeques and chilling out in the relatively cool evening air.

We soon reached the large paved lot, and I unlocked my black Toyota Tacoma 4x4, which was parked against a railroad tie in the first row. Once we were seated, I rolled the windows down and pulled onto Caroline Street, heading for my house over near the center of the island.

"I just don't get it," Ange said as the evening air blew softly into her face through her rolled-down window. "Why would anyone desecrate your father's grave?"

I shook my head. I'd been thinking the same damned thing ever since the detective had told me what had happened. My dad had been a career Navy man and had retired after thirty years of service as a master chief, the highest enlisted rank in the military. He'd been a diver, and since he'd always loved the ocean, he'd spent his retired years either on his sailboat in the Bahamas, at his condo on the California Coast, or at his other condo on the island of Curacao in the Southern Caribbean. Curacao was where he'd spent most of his time, and it was also where he'd died just under two years ago. Since he'd loved the island so much, he'd put it in his will that he wanted to be buried in a small cemetery on a hillside overlooking the western shore of the island.

"I don't know," I finally said as I turned onto my brick driveway lined with palm trees on both sides. "But I'm going to find out."

My neighbor's golden Labrador, Atticus, was hanging out in my yard and jumped around as I pulled up. Parking under my stilted house, I left the engine running as we stepped out, and I petted Atticus, grabbed the tennis ball from his mouth and chucked it over the palm tree-lined fence into my neighbor's yard. In a flash, he took off in a happy sprint around the backside of my property. I swore he had been an owl in a previous life, because he was always hanging out in my driveway whenever I pulled in late at night.

Ange and I headed up the side stairs leading up to the wraparound porch. On the deck by the side door, resting on a dark blue welcome mat with the image of a white conch shell woven into it, was a small FedEx package. I bent over, grabbed the package, then unlocked the door and shouldered my way inside.

Moving into the master bedroom, I changed into a pair of cargo shorts, a gray tee shirt and a pair of black Converse low-top sneakers. Ange changed beside me, slipping out of her blue dress and into a pair of jean shorts, a black tank top, and white Adidas sneakers. Since neither of us knew how long we'd be in Curacao, we each packed a bag of things we might need, including a few changes of clothes.

Moving into my bedroom closet, I pushed aside a few hanging shirts and opened my biometric safe, using my right thumbprint and entering my code into the keypad. Inside my safe, I kept an assortment of weapons of various types and calibers, ammunition for each of them, and a few stacks of various currencies. I grabbed a stack of Netherlands Antillean guilder, the official currency of Curacao, along with a stack of Jamaican dollars and US dollars. I always preferred to pay with cash if I could, a habit I'd formed after years of working as a mercenary around the world.

Once, the cash was loaded into my backpack, I set the FedEx package on top of it and zipped up the main pocket. Then I locked my safe back up, and Ange and I headed for the side door. When the door was locked, I turned on my security system, an advanced array of cameras and motion sensors I'd installed myself, and we climbed inside my Tacoma. Ange had told me that her seaplane was moored at Tarpon Cove Marina, a small marina that was only about a mile northeast of my house.

Within five minutes, we were parked and climbing aboard her white-and-blue Cessna 182

Skylane, which was tied off on the end of a narrow dock that was almost completely empty aside from a few smaller boats. The four-seat seaplane was twenty-nine-feet long, had a wingspan of thirty-six feet, and was powered by a single 230-horsepower engine that could propel the small aircraft at a max speed of 150 knots.

Once she'd completed all of her preflight checks, I untied the lines, then gave the port float a shove as I jumped aboard. Ange then made a quick request to the air traffic control tower at Key West International Airport. The ATC gave a rundown of the weather and wind and requested our destination, then gave us the okay.

It was a calm evening with just a few tiny whitecaps in the open ocean, but the water in the cove was as flat as glass. This made for a smooth ride as Ange raised the throttles and turned to port once we'd past the tip of the dock, facing us into the wind. With the small cove clear of all boats, she hit the gas and lifted us off the water and into the air with a smooth, professional takeoff.

I reached back, unzipped my backpack and pulled out the FedEx package.

"Finally arrived, huh?" Ange said, eyeing it as I cut off the plastic wrap.

I nodded, then opened the box, revealing my new cell phone. I'd finally gotten a replacement for the one I'd lost on Loggerhead Key. It was a second-generation iPhone, a nice upgrade from the first generation one I'd ruined. I had it out of the box and set up within a few minutes.

Within thirty minutes, Ange had us cruising at twelve thousand feet, an altitude we maintained for most of the trip. We landed near Port Royal on the southern coast of Jamaica to refuel and refill our coffee supplies. Then we were right back in the air, switching back and forth in the pilot's seat so that we could get a few hours of sleep.

Ange and I had first taken flying lessons together three years ago and had both received our private licenses. She had taken more of a liking to it than I, however, and spent a great deal of her free time flying all sorts of aircraft around the world. I was a little rusty at my takeoffs and landings, but cruising thousands of feet in the air and heading straight was no problem.

By zero six thirty, we saw the beautiful island of Curacao by the light of the rising sun, its brilliant beaches and crashing white surf shining like a beacon. Curacao is a Dutch Caribbean island located forty miles off the coast of Venezuela and nestled right between the islands of Bonaire and Aruba. It's a tropical island paradise with clear, warm waters that attract divers from all over the world. It was the place where my dad had spent most of his time after retiring from the Navy, and I'd visited him there a few times every year before he died.

Ange touched the Cessna down on the calm turquoise waters of Santa Martha Bay on the northwest side of the island. She eased back on the throttles, then turned around and brought the starboard float against the long dock in front of the Pearl Beach Resort.

After tying off the lines, we grabbed what we needed from the plane, then locked her up and headed down the dock toward the white sand. I had my black CamelBak strapped over my shoulders, and Ange carried only her small blue backpack and a decent-sized plastic hard case.

Ange was never one to take chances, and during the flight across the Caribbean, she'd questioned everything about what we were doing. The whole thing had seemed suspicious to her from the beginning, and after checking the Curacao Police Department website, she'd tried to get ahold of Dan Millis, the detective who'd called me, but she'd gotten no answer. Then, after calling Charles and getting the detective's cell number, she'd reached him, and he'd told us that he wanted to meet us at the cemetery that morning.

"Just seems wrong," Ange had said while we flew south. "I think there's more going on here than simple vandalism."

She'd had a good point. Why would a detective want me to fly all the way from Key West if it wasn't serious?

We both had a lot of questions regarding the situation, and she'd been suspicious enough to grab her collapsible Remington .338 Lapua Magnum sniper rifle. It was almost identical to mine, which I'd left back on my boat. Ange rarely traveled anywhere without the weapon. The truth was she could be as seemingly reckless at times as anyone who ever lived, but she rarely was so without first thinking everything through thoroughly.

We moved up a stone pathway leading through Pearl Beach, past a patch of coconut and palm trees growing out of green grass, then up towards the front desk of the Pearl Beach Resort and Condo Association. Meeting with the front desk attendant, we paid the moorage fee, then headed for the parking lot. In one of the covered parking spaces beside my dad's old unit, I lifted a plastic cover, revealing a classic Café Racer motorcycle with black paint and a brown leather seat.

It looked well taken care of, and I had a local boy named Jethro, who always brought the fish I caught to his father's kitchen to be cooked, to thank for it. He enjoyed working on engines and was happy to do it in exchange for taking her for a ride now and then.

Hopping on the leather seat, I started up the 750cc engine, then drove out of the parking lot with Ange's arms wrapped around my chest. Cruising right along the bay, heading inland, we breathed in the fresh island air. Curacao is not exactly what you usually picture when imagining a Caribbean paradise. Though it has some of the best beaches and diving in the world, its landscape is an arid desert, littered with cacti and with hills covering the western side.

After just a few minutes of driving, I turned onto the road to the West Point, heading southeast. I usually soaked in the tropical air and relished the feel of it blowing against my face, but I couldn't get the thoughts of my dad out of my head. My mind was consumed by countless memories, and I kept quiet for most of the trip.

CHAPTER FOUR

The road heading towards Willemstad, the capital of Curacao, wasn't too busy for a Thursday morning. The majority of Curacao's one hundred and forty thousand residents live on the eastern side, giving the western side more of a quiet and peaceful atmosphere. After just a few minutes on the main road, I turned south, cruising past the small town of Sint Willibrordus. We looked out at the flocks of pink flamingos that covered the shallow waters in front of the town, then cruised down along the coast.

Our destination was the Saint John Cemetery, a small, humble plot of land littered with less than a hundred tombstones. It was located just south of Harmonie, nestled into the side of a large hill overlooking the ocean on the south-central part of the island.

It was only about twenty-five minutes from when we left the Pearl Beach Resort until we turned onto Saint John Street, a winding paved road that led to a few houses along the hill, past the cemetery and up to a massive cell phone tower.

After cruising along a few switchbacks, we soon reached the entrance into Saint John Cemetery, marked by old concrete pillars, a statue of the apostle John, and a carved stone sign indicating the cemetery's name. As I slowed to pull in, Ange tapped me on the shoulder.

"Let me off here," she said, and before I could reply, her butt had already slid off the seat and her shoes hit the pavement.

I slowed to a stop and turned back to face her. "What's going on?"

Staring at me with her fiery blue eyes, she said, "I'm gonna take a little hike up to the top. I wanna check out the view." Then, handing me what looked like an ordinary ballpoint pen, she added, "Keep this in your pocket, and leave it on."

I could only nod as she turned and headed up the road, carrying her backpack over her shoulder and holding the hard case in her right hand. She disappeared around the corner in a matter of seconds. I'd learned over the years that Ange had a pretty good sense about things, and even though we both knew it was unlikely we'd run into trouble, she always planned for the worst.

I continued through the entrance and towards a small parking lot that was surrounded by cacti, jujube trees and brown grass littered with tombstones. The cemetery wasn't well taken care of, with shrubs growing as they pleased, rocks on the pathways and faded worn walls, but it was one of the most picturesque locations for a cemetery in the world. The steady slopes of green overlooked the white sandy beaches and the turquoise waters beyond. To the south, you could see the beautiful beach of Kokomo, the inspiration for the Beach Boys' classic tune. Looking beyond along the coast, you could see Willemstad five miles away, with its colorful Dutch architecture. To the north, the hilly desert landscape of the western side of the island provided a feast for your eyes, especially in the evenings, when the dying sun lit up the tropical sky.

It was still early, and there was only one vehicle in the small gravel lot: a silver SUV with tinted windows. As I pulled up alongside it, three men wearing gray suits and sunglasses stepped out. Two of them were big black guys, and the third was smaller and had olive skin. They moved confidently towards me as I shut off the engine and rested the motorcycle against its kickstand.

"You must be Mr. Dodge," the smaller man said. He had what sounded like a Venezuelan accent and I pegged him to be in his early thirties. "I'm Detective Millis, and these are Detectives Bosch and Hicks."

I nodded and introduced myself, surprised that there were three of them. It only solidified my thinking that this was no ordinary grave desecration, that there was something more going on.

Glancing at the handgun holstered to Millis's hip, I said, "I thought law enforcement here used standard-issue Glocks."

He hesitated a moment, which I thought was odd, then looked down at his Smith and Wesson M&P 9mm. Glancing back up at me, he said,

"Detectives can choose their own. Now, please, Mr. Dodge. If you'd just follow us."

The three of them led me along an old dirt path leading away from the parking lot. I'd been there many times since my dad had died, so I knew the grounds well enough. We stopped beside a small bench that was shaded by a divi-divi, a unique tree that bows southwesterly from the swift warm trade winds. A small gecko scurried off into a patch of green as I looked towards a newer-looking tombstone with my dad's name written on it.

"We had it taken care of," Millis said, reading my mind, as I saw nothing wrong with the plot except some recently shifted dirt. "I'm sorry, Mr. Dodge."

I shook my head. "You urged me to fly all the way here just to apologize?"

He thought for a moment, then took in a deep breath, let it out, and said, "No. The truth is, we believe that your father's death may not have been an accident."

My heart nearly stopped at that. Not an accident? I tried to remain calm but could feel the anger swelling deep inside me. I thought back to the detectives and coroners I'd spoken to years ago, who'd assured me that he'd died of heart complications while scuba diving.

"What do you mean?" I asked, my voice growing stern. "You mean somebody killed him?"

The man stared into my eyes and nodded softly. "Someone dug up your father's corpse." He took in a deep breath and added, "Look, we're trying to piece everything together, but we've hit a roadblock," the detective said. "It appears as though your father knew he was in trouble and left a clue in order to let someone know what happened to him. But none of us can figure it out."

I couldn't believe what I was hearing. I felt as though I'd stepped into a nightmare that just kept getting worse.

"What's the clue?"

He dug into the front pocket of his dress pants, pulled out an all-black wristwatch and set it on the bench beside me. I recognized it instantly as a Suunto Core military watch. It had been my favorite watch for years and had a built-in altimeter, barometer and depth meter display up to one hundred feet. It was also incredibly durable and rugged; I'd used it in some of the most dangerous environments on Earth without ever having a glitch. It only took me a second to realize that it was the exact same model and color as the watch I'd given my dad for his last birthday present.

"We found that strapped to the wrist of your father's dead body."

I shook my head, wondering what in the hell was going on. "But if that was with my dad, why did whoever desecrated the gravesite leave it there?"

He shrugged. "We don't know. Maybe they were looking for something in particular. But look on the back," he said, turning the watch over. "There's a few words carved into the metal backing."

Grabbing the watch, I flipped it over and examined the inscription he was referring to. "NEVER LOSE TIME" it said, and it looked like it had been carved using the tip of a knife.

I went quiet for a moment, lost in thought. None of it made sense, and I was starting to grow more and more suspicious of these guys. Who in the hell would dig up a dead body and leave a valuable watch? No, the story had more holes than a fucking cheese grater. Also, the main reason I'd come to Curacao was to see what had happened and to try and find the deadbeats who had done it, but the more time I spent talking to the detectives, the more I felt that they had their own agenda.

"I want to see the body," I said, my tone shifting from calm to stern in an instant.

I strode towards my dad's gravesite, but as I did, Detective Millis reached for the 9mm holstered to his waist. In my peripherals, I noticed the two other guys reaching for their weapons as well, and in the blink of an eye, I gripped my Sig, pulled it out from the back of my waistline and aimed it straight at Millis.

We stayed like that for a few seconds, my barrel locked onto his contorted face while three barrels stared back at me.

"Drop your fucking piece, now!" Millis shouted.

I spent a few seconds thinking over all the possible outcomes. I took a quick glance at the top of the hillside and the radio tower high above our position, then decided to do as he said and loosened my grip on my Sig.

As it hit the brown grass at my feet, Millis said, "And that knife you got as well."

I reached slowly for my dive knife, which was sheathed and strapped horizontally to the back of my black leather belt. Pulling it out, I dropped it onto the grass as well.

"Good boy," he said, lowering his pistol. "Now, we can do this the easy way or the hard way. But I promise you this, you'll be a whole lot happier if we do it the easy way. Got it?" I didn't reply, but he continued anyway. "Now, about this watch."

He pointed to my dad's wristwatch, which was still resting on the table.

I looked over the inscription one more time, then gritted my teeth and said with a cocky tone, "I think I'd prefer the hard way."

Without a word, the two muscle heads holstered their weapons and moved in on me. Clearly, these were the guys whose job it was to beat information out of people, and they looked like they enjoyed their work. But before they swung at me, Millis stopped them by raising his hand. Then, as the two guys froze in place, he stepped closer to me, bent down and grabbed my Sig from the grass.

Staring at me with an evil smile, Millis said, "You wanna know how your dad died, punk? The truth? Well, I was there that night. I saw the whole damn thing, and you know what? He was shot. That's right. He was murdered in cold blood. Riddled with hot lead and left to squirm. His body was entombed in a yacht a thousand miles northwest of here in over three hundred feet of water. It took us two years to find that damn wreck, and this watch was the only thing he had on him. Now, unless you want to end up just like him you'll tell me what this inscription means."

My mind ran wild. I couldn't believe what I was hearing. For two years I thought I knew the truth about what happened to my dad, but it turned out it had all been a lie. All of the hours I'd spent at that cemetery I'd been standing over nothing but dirt.

After a moment, I looked up at him with a fierce gaze and said, "What are you looking for that's so important?"

"None of your fucking business. Just tell us what it means!" he barked. He was starting to get really frustrated and was breathing heavily.

I didn't reply. Instead, I just stared down at the watch for a moment, then looked off into the distance.

Millis grunted. "Grab him and throw him in the car. We have plenty of methods we can use to make him talk."

As the two henchmen moved in and grabbed me with gorilla-tight grips, I said, "Wait!" Then I took a few quick breaths, trying to appear flustered. "I'll tell you."

Millis smiled, then told his men to release me. Staring up at him, I said, "But first, I think you should say goodbye to these two assholes, because they're gonna be dead in a few seconds."

The three men laughed, and Millis shook his head. "What in the hell are you talking about? How do you plan to kill them unarmed?"

Staring into his dark eyes, I started counting down. "Three... two... one..."

A split second after I said the word *one*, blood exploded out from the two guys' heads, one right after the other, and they both collapsed to the ground.

Millis's eyes grew wide, and his mouth dropped open. His two men appeared to have been killed by a ghost, as no rifle reports could be heard in the morning air. Before he could level his Smith and Wesson at me, I lunged at him, knocked the weapon out of his hand and forced him to the ground. He tried to fight back, but I blocked his attacks and kicked my right heel into his left knee, breaking his leg and causing him to yell out violently in pain.

Squeezing my hands into fists, I punched him across the face a few times, my knuckles cracking his cheekbones and jaw. Blood splattered out from his mouth as he grunted. All I could think about was my dad. How all this time, I'd been led to believe that he'd died naturally. And now—now I'd come to realize that the truth was much more sinister.

When I stopped, he lay on the grass with blood covering his face, his left leg bent sideways at a ninety-degree angle and a large portion of his facial bones broken. His breathing was loud and labored as I grabbed him by his fancy shirt and slammed his body up against the trunk of the nearest divi-divi tree.

"Now," I said, staring into his weary, beaten eyes, "you're gonna tell me who you really are, and who else is responsible for my dad's murder."

He coughed spatters of blood over his white dress shirt, then lifted his head slowly. "Your father fucked up," he said, the words struggling out of his mouth. "That's why they killed him. And now, they're gonna do the same to you."

"I don't think so," I shot back at him. Then, gripping my hands tighter around his shirt, I pulled him back and slammed him into the tree trunk a few times. "Who do you work for?"

His response was to reach for a small knife strapped to his ankle and slice it through the air towards my thigh. I stopped it by grabbing his wrist, bending his elbow and using a combination of his momentum and my body weight to redirect its course and stab it forcefully into his chest. He yelled out in pain as the sharpened steel penetrated his heart. I wrapped my left hand around his back and pulled, forcing the blade as deep as it would go. Then his eyes shut, his breathing stopped, and as I slid the blade out from his body, he collapsed onto the grass.

CHAPTER FIVE

The three men lay dead at my feet, their blood soaking the dirt and grass. I took a quick look around the area, just to make sure that no one had seen what had just happened. The place was empty, and the dead guys' silver SUV was still the only other vehicle parked in the cemetery.

I knelt down and searched Millis's pockets, finding a cell phone in the front left and a brown leather wallet in the back. Sitting on the old bench, I emptied the wallet, creating a pile of Visa credit cards, business cards, Netherlands Antillean guilders, and his driver's license.

"Enrique Colon," I said, reading his name aloud. Then I grabbed his cell phone and navigated through the contacts and glanced over the recent messages. After a few minutes, I pocketed his phone, then grabbed my dad's watch, which was still resting on the table in front of me, and examined it closely, reading the inscription on the back a few more times.

As I stood to move towards the motorcycle, I saw Ange walking about twenty feet away from me, her footsteps quieter than a ninja in the night. Her blond hair was tied back, and she wore a pair of aviator sunglasses and carried the plastic hard case in her right hand. She looked like an action hero as she approached me and stared at the watch in my hands.

"Can I see that?" she said, reaching out with her free hand. I handed it to her, and she examined it for a few seconds. "Never lose time," she read, then shrugged. "That's the clue that they wanted you to help them with? What does it mean?"

"It's not just about the inscription," I replied. "It's about the watch itself." She looked at me, confused, and I added, "I'll explain later. We should get out of here."

We hopped onto the Café Racer and I started up the engine, then accelerated us out of the cemetery gravel parking lot and back onto the main two-lane road leading around and down the hill. Glancing at my watch, I saw that it was almost zero seven thirty. We hadn't even been on the island for an hour yet, and we'd already killed three bad guys and found out a secret that changed everything I'd thought I knew about how my dad had died.

I had a lot of questions swirling around in my mind, and I knew that I needed answers. As much as I usually hated dealing with law enforcement, I knew that my best option was to talk to the real Curacao police and find out everything I could about my new enemies.

As we were cruising east towards Willemstad at over sixty miles per hour, with the sun beating on our faces and the warm air blowing past us, Ange tapped me on the shoulder.

"Your pocket's ringing," she said, loud enough for me to hear over the roar of the engine.

I slowed and pulled over into a dirt driveway that was shaded on both sides with coconut trees and had a great view of Kokomo Beach. Reaching into my pocket, I pulled out the dead guy's phone I'd grabbed back at the cemetery, hit the green button and pressed it up to my ear.

"Hello?" I said.

There was a brief moment's pause, and then a low, rough voice said, "Who is this? Where is Enrique?"

"I hate to be the bearer of bad news, but Enrique and those two other assholes are dead."

The man sighed. "Mr. Dodge?"

"That's right. And you can tell whoever your boss is that I'm coming for you guys, and I'm going to make you pay for what you did to my dad."

"You're a fucking dead ma—"

I hung up the phone before he could finish his sentence. Sliding the phone back into my pocket, I fired up the engine and accelerated back onto the main road, my heart pounding in my chest. Ten minutes later, I took the exit heading to downtown Willemstad, the capital city of Curacao. Willemstad is one of the most unique tropical destinations on Earth, known for its beautiful and colorful buildings that make it resemble a candy-coated version of Amsterdam. Cruising over the Queen Emma Pontoon Bridge, we entered the

Punda District along Saint Anne Bay and passed by rows of bright pink, teal, and yellow buildings.

Just across the street from the ocean, we pulled into a small parking lot in front of a large tan building with white trim. Above the main door, *Politie* was written in small silver letters, the Dutch word for *police*. It was the same place I'd gone two years earlier, when I'd met with officers and a coroner who had assured me that my dad had died of natural causes and had already been buried.

I backed my motorcycle into a small spot right beside the door and killed the engine, and we both headed inside. For obvious reasons, Ange left her sniper rifle locked up to the bike, but we both carried our concealed pistols as we entered through the door. Inside, we met with a receptionist, and after we told her we wanted to speak with Detective Millis, she dialed a number on her phone, said a few words, then led us past a row of cubicles to an office on the far side wall.

Through the glass, I saw a guy sitting behind a computer, and after the receptionist knocked, she opened the door and ushered us inside. The guy stood up and held out his hand.

"It's good to meet you, Mr. Dodge. My name is Dan Millis." He was a chubby, light-skinned, balding man in his mid-forties, bearing no resemblance to his criminal counterpart.

"Just call me Logan," I said as I shook his hand. "And this is Angelina Fox."

After shaking her hand as well, he offered us a seat in the two padded chairs across from him.

"What can I do for you?"

I leaned back in the chair. "It's about my dad."

His gaze narrowed and he looked off into the corner. "Your father's been dead for what, two years now?"

"Yes. He has." I was a little surprised that he knew about my dad. It almost seemed like he was expecting us, and that made me feel uncomfortable.

The man tilted his head and took in a deep breath. "Well, I think it's time to move on, don't you agree?"

This guy was already pissing me off and I'd only known him for about a minute. "I was moving on. That is, until I got a phone call telling me that his gravesite had been desecrated. Then I flew here from Key West this morning, met the guy who called me, and he told me that my father had been murdered. Then he threatened to kill me too."

His eyes grew wide, and he leaned back in his chair, looking at me with confusion. "Wait, rewind just a little bit. Who was it that contacted you?"

I stared back at him. "A man pretending to be you."

He shook his head at that. "Then what happened next? After they threatened to kill you."

I grinned. "I took care of it."

He looked at me like I was in the principal's office after getting in trouble. "You took care of it?"

I nodded.

"Alright. And why exactly did the guy who was pretending to be me threaten to kill you?"

I explained to him about the watch, the engraving on the back, and how they were looking for something that only my dad had known the whereabouts of.

After listening to my story he leaned back, paused a moment and said, "I see. Look, Logan, I really hate to be the one to tell you this. Truthfully, we never wanted you to find out about any of this. It's just unfortunate, it really is."

"What in the hell are you talking about?"

"Were you ever aware of any illegal activity that your father was involved in?"

My blood boiled as the words came out of his mouth. "No. And I don't know what it is you think you might know about him, but he was no criminal. He served thirty years in the Navy and retired as a master diver. He was straight as an arrow. Never got so much as a speeding ticket. He was an honorable man."

"Look, please calm down. I'm just the messenger here. And good men get sucked into that kind of life all of the time. We see it often. We have strong evidence that your dad was involved in the drug trade. I know it must be hard to accept, but your father was a—"

"Call my dad a criminal one more fucking time and—"

He cut me off by placing a large manila folder on the table in front of me. I grabbed it and, reaching inside, I pulled out a small stack of pictures. They were a little blurry, but in each one, I could see my dad as he worked alongside a few other guys on a yacht moored beside what looked like a warehouse of some kind.

"I'm a detective, Logan. I deal with evidence. That is all."

I shook my head. "Why are you just now telling me about all this?"

He paused a moment, then sighed. "Look, from what I've read about the case, they didn't want to tarnish an honorable man's reputation by implying that he was a drug runner. But regardless of what he was involved in, I assure you, your father died of natural causes. There's a copy of the coroner's notes there."

"Well, then, the coroner was paid off, because my dad was murdered."

He sighed. "I'm sorry, Logan. I really am. It must be hard to hear this. Hard to take it all in. But evidence is evidence, and that's what we deal with."

My blood boiled just looking at him. I didn't know what his deal was, but I was willing to bet that he was making something extra under the table by working with whoever had murdered my dad. It would explain why every time we'd called the station asking for him, the phone had gone to the damn imposter's phone that was resting in my pocket.

"Is there anything else I can do for you, Logan? I have a lot of work to do."

I'd originally wanted to ask about the guy Enrique, but I knew that I wouldn't get anywhere with this clown. "Yeah," I said, standing and grabbing a pencil from his desk. "When you get a chance, go ahead and shove this up your ass." I dropped it on the desk and Ange and I walked out of his office. After she'd walked through, I slammed the glass door so hard that it almost shattered the glass. Without saying a word, we moved across the main room and out the front door.

"You're just making all sorts of friends today," Ange said as we climbed onto the bike.

"At least I didn't shoot him," I said, starting up the engine and feeling like that entire visit was a complete waste of time. I hadn't learned anything about my new enemy. "God knows I wanted to."

As I slid the kickstand up, the front door opened behind us. Turning around, I saw a young dark-skinned woman shut the door behind her and run down the stairs towards us. *What the hell now?* I thought.

"Mr. Dodge!" she said. Her voice was soft and as calm as you'd expect, considering she'd probably just run across the entire building to get to us. "I would like to talk with you."

"I think I've had enough talk with detectives for one day," I said.

"I'm not a detective," she said. "I'm in charge of the records, and I have some information that I think you'd like to hear regarding your dad."

Glancing back at the police building, I decided that I didn't want to discuss anything in there. "Meet me for brunch at the Green Iguana in twenty minutes." I didn't wait for a reply. I just started up the engine and hit the gas, cruising out of the parking lot and back along the waterfront.

Her name was Alice Pierce, and twenty minutes later, Ange and I were sitting beside her in cushioned bamboo chairs under the shade of a green umbrella. The Green Iguana had always been one of my favorite places to eat in Curacao. Our table was right on the boardwalk, nestled between the blue waters of Saint Anne Bay on one side and the colorful Dutch-style buildings on the other. We hadn't realized just how hungry we were from the long night of traveling until we glanced at the menu. Ange ordered a Colombian steak with mashed potatoes and broccoli. I got the catch of the day, which was red snapper with Spanish rice and asparagus.

As we waited for our food and I sipped on ice-cold lemonade, I stared over at Alice, giving her the floor.

"First of all," she said, her voice calm, with a hint of worry, "I'm sorry for everything that's happened. And I'm sorry about Millis. He can be a real jackass. But I wanted to talk with you because, well, part of what he told you is true." I felt the anger deep inside me start to return but wanted to hear her out. "There is evidence to suggest that your dad was working with drug runners. I've been trying to piece some of it together, but it's a hard trail to follow. Just the day before your father passed away, two Dutch Caribbean Coast Guard special agents were killed. And I believe those two agents were your father's points of contact."

"Points of contact?" I said, shaking my head. Then my eyes grew wide.

"You think he was working undercover?" Ange said, thinking the same thing I was.

Alice nodded. "I think he was trying to help bring them down from the inside. Then things went south, everyone involved was killed, and the whole thing was covered up."

We sat in silence for a moment, and I thought everything through. Though my dad had been many things, an undercover agent? The thought had never crossed my mind until that moment. The waitress brought over our food then, and we spent a few minutes enjoying the delicious food and taking in the view.

When we were about halfway through our meals, I slipped my hand into my pocket and pulled out the driver's license I'd pulled off Enrique's dead body. Setting it on the table in front of Alice, I said, "What can you tell me about these guys?"

She glanced at the name momentarily, then said, "They're a group of drug smugglers that run drugs all over the Caribbean. And over the past few years, they've grown larger and larger."

"Who runs the show?" I said. "Who murdered my dad?"

She sighed. "I don't know who pulled the trigger. But they're led by two brothers: Pedro and Hector Campos."

I tilted my head and narrowed my gaze. Both of their names sounded familiar.

"Wait," Ange said. "Are you talking about *the* Pedro and Hector Campos? The former MMA fighters from Bolivia?"

Alice nodded. "That's right."

Ange's words snapped the memory from deep within my mind in an instant. I'd read about them years ago in the news, when they had both been booted from professional MMA for fighting dirty and for beating people outside the ring. I knew that they had disappeared from the limelight but had no idea they'd gotten into the drug trade.

"So you're telling me that these two former fighters are running this whole thing?" Ange said.

"Yes," Alice said. "And, in all likelihood, one of them murdered your father, Logan."

When we finished eating, I dug into my wallet to pay the bill using the cash I'd brought. I was glad to have met Alice and finally thought that I was getting some of my questions answered. After I set the bills on the table, Alice pulled a ballpoint pen out of her purse and wrote her phone number on a napkin.

Handing it to me, she said, "That's my private number. If you need anything else, just call."

I nodded, folded the napkin and slid it into my black leather wallet. As we sat for a moment, I noticed that a new waiter I hadn't seen before was approaching us. He had dark skin and giant muscles oozing out of his Green Iguana tee shirt, and he was well over six feet tall. He smiled as he approached and reached for the bills with his left hand. But in his right, I saw something that made my eyes grow massive. Under a folded white napkin, I saw what looked like a Taser high-voltage stun gun.

CHAPTER SIX

Just as my eyes zeroed in on the weapon, the big guy glared at me, energized the two metal prongs with eighteen million volts and stabbed them straight towards my chest. In an instant, I jerked my body backward, balancing momentarily on the two rear legs of my chair and narrowly avoiding the Taser as I grabbed his wrist with my left hand and slammed it into the table. It shattered the ceramic plate in front of me and rattled the glasses as I planted my feet on the ground and kicked my chair behind me.

Forcing his hand free, he yelled and tried to hit me with the Taser again, this time aiming for my face. Narrowing my gaze, I bent my knees, twisted my body, then grabbed hold of his arm and forced the Taser to pass by just over my right shoulder. I forcefully hyperextended his elbow with a loud crack, then hurled his body over mine and slammed it hard into the rust-colored cobblestone.

The incident had lasted less than a couple of seconds, and as I turned back to look at the table, I saw Alice standing nervously, her body shaking as she stared at the guy writhing in pain on the ground. Ange, however, was focusing her trained eyes on the group of people around us. People eating their meals or just passing by, many of them frozen and staring in our direction.

"We need to leave," Ange said, her voice stern. "We need to leave now!"

She motioned towards where I'd parked the motorcycle in the narrow alley alongside the restaurant. But before we could head in that direction, two more guys appeared, moving in on either side of us. One of them was slightly taller than me and held a metal baseball bat in his hands. The other was shorter but looked more muscular than a gorilla.

The guy with the bat reached us first and swung at me like a major leaguer trying to catch up to a ninety-mile-per-hour fastball. I jumped back, then moved side to side a few times, avoiding the bat as it flew through the air just inches from my body. As he lifted the bat high above his head, gearing up to slam it into me, I hit him with a powerful side kick straight into his neck. His body flew backward, and he crashed to the ground with a grunt and a loud thud.

Lunging towards him, I ripped the baseball bat from his hands and whacked him across the head, knocking him unconscious. A long-haired guy wearing a wife beater grabbed Ange from behind. Bending her knees, she dug her heels into the ground and hurled him over her shoulder, slamming his body to the ground. As I turned to look at the short muscular guy, I saw that he was sprinting straight for me. Still holding the bat in my hands, I moved to hit him with it, but before I could, he tackled me hard onto our table. The combination of both of our body weights caused the table to give, cracking and colliding with the cobblestone beneath us.

Reaching for my neck, he strangled me with a viselike grip and yelled at me like a wild animal as we struggled. Feeling the world around me start to fade, I reached for anything I could and grabbed one of the tall glasses. Shattering the rim against the broken table, I gritted my teeth, then stabbed the sharp broken edges into his chest. He yelled violently as the glass penetrated, causing blood to gush out. I punched him square in the face, then gripped his waist and threw him off me.

Just as I rose to my feet, I saw two more guys running at me. Before the first one could reach me, Ange grabbed one of the bamboo chairs, twirled it around and crashed it into his back. His body jerked forward and he tripped, landing hard on his face. As Ange hit him a few more times to finish the job, the second guy continued straight for me. I took a few steps back and realized that I was standing right on the edge of the promenade. I waited until my attacker was just a few feet away, then jumped to the side, grabbed his white tee shirt tightly, and flung him over the edge. A second later, I heard a loud splash as the guy made contact with the water ten feet below.

I did a quick scan of the area, then ran over to Ange and Alice. Ange was standing over three big wannabe tough guys who wouldn't be getting up on their own anytime soon. All in all, there were seven guys on the ground, writhing in pain, as I placed a hand on Alice's shoulder.

"We have to move," Ange said, weaving through the tables and running across the street towards where we'd left the motorcycle parked in a narrow alley beside the restaurant.

Staring deep into Alice's eyes, I said, "They're after us. Just lie low and get out of here. We'll be in touch."

As the last word came out of my mouth, the air was filled with the loud rattle of automatic gunfire. Instinctively, I dropped to the ground in an instant. Screams filled the air as crowds of people ran chaotically as fast as they could away from the area. Looking around, I saw a guy wearing a backward hat and holding an Uzi about two hundred feet away from me in the middle of the street. My eyes grew wide as I watched him take aim at Ange, who was hopping onto the motorcycle in the adjacent alley.

I grabbed my Sig from the back of my waistband, then sprinted towards the guy. When it looked like he was about to fire, I took aim and fired off three rounds into the side of his chest. His body jerked sideways and his hands flew wildly into the air before he crashed to the pavement. I continued running towards Ange, and in the corner of my eye, I spotted a few more guys closing in around us.

As I turned to take aim, Ange started the engine, burned rubber and drove right beside me.

"Get on!" she yelled, her blue eyes focused.

Without hesitating I hopped onto the leather seat with my back against hers, facing backward. Just as I hit the seat, she fired the throttles and turned sharply to the left, accelerating us back down the alley alongside the Green Iguana.

I took aim as we bounced up and down on the uneven backstreets, firing off a few rounds at the guys chasing us and forcing them to take cover. I held on tight as Ange weaved between large dumpsters and passed by a few guys sitting out back for a smoke break. When we reached the end of the alley, Ange turned hard to the right, skidding for about five feet between a taxi and a brown van before changing course, heading down along the oceanfront.

We passed by street markets, cafes and crowds of people as we cruised along the ocean, dodging traffic and heading back over the Queen Emma Pontoon Bridge at over sixty miles per hour. When I didn't see anyone following us, I turned my body around and looked forward, the fresh sea air whipping against my face. Holding on tight, I kept a sharp lookout for hostiles as we cruised west, heading towards the Pearl Beach Resort. Ange was smart to avoid heading back to the police station. I was sure they wouldn't be of much help to us and knew that if I took one more look at that fat jerk, it would take all my self-control to stop me from punching his face in.

Instead, we kept cruising along the waterfront, weaving around cars. After a few seconds of no activity around us, I spotted a new blacked-out Chevy truck driving on the wrong side of the double yellow lines, heading straight for us.

"Logan!" Ange shouted, her eyes trained forward.

"I see them," I said, raising my Sig over her shoulder. There was a guy leaning out the passenger-side window, aiming what looked like an AK-47 straight at us. Squeezing the trigger on my Sig, I fired off round after round, shattering the windshield. I hit the guy in the passenger seat twice, and he jerked back into the seat, shooting a spray of bullets high into the air. When the truck was roughly a hundred feet in front of us, I put a bullet through the driver's neck, causing blood to gush out and his body to whip sideways. The truck turned with him, smashing through the concrete barrier just in front of us and crashing into the ocean.

Ange took a sharp right, almost knocking me out of my seat, then stomped on the gas, accelerating down a small side road. As she cruised past a neighborhood of houses and a large hotel, I heard the loud roar of an engine coming from behind us. Just as I turned around, I saw that a guy on a motorcycle was gaining on us and that he held an Uzi high in the air with his extended right hand. He aimed it at us and held the trigger, sending a stream of bullets in our direction. Ange turned sharply as lead flew past us, sending bright sparks flying into the air as the bullets made contact with the pavement.

She drove us onto a small footpath that wedged itself between houses, trying to put distance between us and our pursuer. As I twisted my body and took aim at him, Ange yelled at me to hold on as she hit a large bump that sent us flying ten feet into the air. She stuck the landing well, our tires barely bouncing more than an inch off the concrete as she maintained our speed. Just as I was turning to look back at our pursuer, I spotted a landscaper's truck parked on the side of the road, right next to a concrete wall just a few hundred feet in front of us.

"Pull sharply along the other side of that wall, Ange!" I yelled over the roar of the engine as I holstered my Sig.

When we reached the wall, Ange squeezed the life out of the brakes and turned on a dime. We disappeared from view just as the guy behind us hit the jump. I hopped off the bike, grabbed a metal rake from the landscaper's truck and pushed myself right up against the edge of the wall.

I heard the roar of his engine grow louder and louder. Just as he was about to appear around the corner, I gripped the rake tightly with both hands and swung it as hard as I could. The metal prongs at the end stabbed right into his chest just as he appeared, launching his body backward off his motorcycle.

His bike kept going without him, balancing itself for a few seconds before crashing into a similar wall on the other side of the road. Pulling the prongs free, I stepped around his thrashing body, grabbed his Uzi and hopped back onto the Café Racer behind Ange. He probably wouldn't die from his wounds, but he sure as hell wouldn't be chasing anyone anytime soon.

Ange hit the gas and brought us back onto the main road, heading west. Within a few minutes, the road turned inland, converging with the road to the West Point. She hit the gas even harder, sending us screaming across the pavement at over a hundred miles per hour. She drove like a professional racer, causing the wind to roar against our faces as the midmorning sun warmed our backs.

We both kept our eyes peeled, looking for anything or anyone suspicious. After about twenty minutes, we turned onto Santa Martha Avenue, the road that hugs the eastern shore of Santa Martha Bay and passes right by Pearl Beach. When we were within a mile of the resort, I saw something unusual in the sky ahead of us.

"That doesn't look good," Ange said, staring up ahead at what I now realized was a black pillar of smoke coming from the Pearl Beach Resort.

Holy shit, I thought as I stared at the blackness rising up like a warning into the tropical air. Reaching for my holster, I grabbed my extra magazine and exchanged it with the partially empty one in my Sig. I had a combined twenty-three rounds left. Fifteen in my fresh mag and eight in the other. It probably wouldn't be enough to combat the force we were about to encounter, but I also had the guy's Uzi and Ange for cover.

As we approached the resort, I tried to think of a plan as fast as I could. Up ahead, we both spotted two vehicles, a green truck and a silver SUV, blocking the gate at the main entrance into the resort. As if she'd read my mind, Ange turned us down a dirt footpath that led through a thick growth of palm and coconut trees and ended at the white sandy beach. Slowing down slightly, Ange turned sharply, spitting up a sheet of sand high into the air as she drove along the crashing waves towards the resort.

"Okay," I said, having gotten an idea. "Cruise along the beach, then head in for the palm trees and drop me off. Once I'm gone, head for the higher units and provide cover as best as you can."

Fortunately, the beach appeared to be empty of hostiles, making it the best place to attack from. Ange didn't reply, and when we reached the patch of palm trees I was talking about, instead of dropping me off, she turned to the right and drove the motorcycle right up onto the dock that extended far out over the turquoise water.

As she drove over plank after plank, putting more and more distance between us and our enemies, I shook my head. "What the hell, Ange? What are you doing?"

Her only reply was to hit the gas even harder, sending us flying towards her seaplane moored at the end of the dock at upwards of sixty miles per hour. As we neared the end, she slowed, then slammed on the brakes, skidding us to a sideways stop right next to her plane.

"Ange, what the—"

"Use your head, Logan!" she said, killing the engine and stepping onto the dock. "There's gotta be at least twenty of them, and they have the entire place surrounded."

As I climbed off the leather seat, she flipped down the kickstand and planted it on the dock. Then she turned and stared at me with her intense blue eyes.

"You know me, Ange," I said, glancing back at the smoke rising up from my dad's condo. "I don't back down from a fight. I don't run away."

She shook her head, "Yeah, well, one of these days, it's gonna get your ass killed."

I gripped my Sig, scanned the condo's grounds and walked towards the beach. "Just cover me," I said sternly.

As I glanced back over my shoulder to look at Ange, she hit me with a strong roundhouse kick, her foot striking me right in the cheek and slamming me hard to the dock. Then she stepped towards me, forced her heel into my right hand and ripped my Sig away. Ange was a fourth-degree black belt in tae kwon do, and it always amazed me how fast she could throw a punch, land a kick or put someone in an unbreakable hold.

"Crawling right into an ambush won't solve anything," she said, staring me in the eyes.

I took a few calming breaths, slowing my heart rate and turning my brain back on. What was happening to me? I was usually the calm one. The collected one who always thought things through. Even back on Loggerhead Key, when a small army had surrounded me and killed three Coast Guardsmen in cold blood, I hadn't let go and completely given into my anger. I'd still used my head and hadn't been so reckless. I guess it was the thought of my dad being murdered that had switched my psyche into the highest gear imaginable.

Seeing that I'd calmed down, Ange jumped onto the starboard float of her Cessna, unlocked the door and threw her backpack and the hard case containing her sniper rifle behind the two front seats.

Stepping back onto the dock, she turned to me and pointed towards the resort. "Attacking them now is just plain stupid, and you know it too. No, if we fight these guys, we do it more prepared, and hopefully with greater numbers."

She was right, of course. She usually was. Taking all of them on right now would be stupid.

But those guys had murdered my dad, and every part of me wanted to run over there, guns blazing, and avenge his death.

"Besides," she added, untying the mooring lines, "you have what they want. You're the only one who can help them find whatever it is they're looking for." She opened the door, turned back to me and added, "Let's make these assholes come to us."

I took one more look back at the resort. Even from the end of the dock, I could see the massive flames pouring out of my dad's old condo. Scanning around the rest of the grounds, I spotted a handful of guys carrying guns, searching vigorously. Turning back to Ange, I gave the float a push off the dock, then jumped aboard. Ange had already started up the engine by the time I slammed the door shut.

I looked back through the glass as she eased the throttles, accelerating us over the calm water of Santa Martha Bay. I noticed a few guys running down the dock towards us, but they were too far away to make an attack. Then, just as we were picking up enough speed to take off, a truck drove down the dock, stopping right at the end. It was far away, but I saw a massive guy step out and stare at us as we took off and gained elevation. Less than a minute later, he vanished from view, and the island of Curacao soon became just a beautiful speck on the horizon behind us.

A few minutes after taking off and before we'd reached five thousand feet, the phone I'd grabbed from Enrique at the cemetery started to ring. Digging into my pocket, I pulled out the phone, pressed the answer button and held it up to my ear.

I didn't say anything, only listened, waiting for the person on the other end to speak first.

"You've got my attention, Logan. I'll give you that," a low and powerful voice said. He spoke in a Bolivian Spanish accent, and I knew instantly that it was one of the Campos brothers.

"What the hell do you want?" I said sternly, loud enough for him to hear me over the howling of the engine.

After a moment's pause, he said, "I would like to offer you one final chance to live. If you turn back now and tell me everything I want to know, I'll let you walk. I offered the same deal to your dad. I suggest that you be smarter than he was and accept the offer."

My blood began to boil and I gritted my teeth. "There won't be any deals. I'm gonna make you pay for what you did."

"Fine by me. I prefer doing things the hard way. There's nowhere you can go where I won't find you. I'll be seeing you again very soon, Logan."

"Yes," I said sternly. "You will, Campos."

I hung up the phone abruptly and dropped it on the dashboard. After a brief moment of silence, I turned to Ange. "Thanks for getting us out of there." Then, taking in a deep breath, I sighed and added, "That place was crawling with bad guys, and they were expecting us to go there."

She smiled. "Don't mention it. I know how it feels to lose parents. I'm sure I would have done the same thing if I were in your position, but we have to be smart about this. You'll have your chance to get revenge, I'm certain of that. Let's just try to do it on our terms." I thought over her words and nodded. A second later, she glanced at my cargo shorts pocket and said, "Now, about that watch.

CHAPTER SEVEN

Just as we were reaching our cruising altitude of ten thousand feet, I reached into the front pocket of my shorts and pulled out the wristwatch that the drug runners had found on my dad's dead body. The digital display still worked and was even giving a reading of our altitude and the barometric pressure inside the aircraft.

Holding it out in front of Ange, I said, "Does this watch look familiar to you?"

"Yeah. It looks just like yours."

"Right," I said, holding it right beside the one strapped to my wrist. They were practically the same make and model, just a few years apart, and while mine was black with silver lining, my dad's was black with blue lining. "I bought this watch for my dad for his birthday the year that he died."

Ange shrugged. "I don't get what any of that has to do with the location of whatever it is these guys are after."

I nodded, understanding her completely. To anyone other than myself, the watch and the words engraved on the back would have absolutely no meaning at all. I was the only person alive who could figure out the clue, and that was exactly what my dad had wanted.

"You see," I said, "my dad was old-school. He'd been using an analog dive watch his entire life and never had a desire to switch over to digital. So when I bought him this watch, it was more of a joke between us than anything else. I honestly never thought he would actually wear it."

Ange glanced at me with raised eyebrows, letting me know that I still wasn't making any sense.

I continued, "About four years ago, my dad and I were diving near *Thunderbolt* when we discovered a narrow opening in the rock at about 150 feet down. Since we both still had a good supply of air left in our tanks, we decided to check it out. We shined our flashlights ahead of us and slowly finned into what we soon realized was an underwater cave. It appeared to go on into the darkness forever. After about ten minutes of swimming, the cave began to angle upwards. A few moments after that, we were staring up at a cavity of air, our exhalation bubbles disappearing as they broke through the surface overhead. We finned up through the vertical slug of water."

I paused for a moment, and when Ange looked at me with intrigued eyes, I continued, "After breaking the surface, we climbed out of the water, took off our BCDs and explored the area with all the excitement of a kid on Christmas morning, hoping to stumble upon something rare or valuable.

The cave wasn't very big, maybe the size of the inside of a school bus, so it didn't take us long to search every inch of the place and realize that there was nothing but rocks. As we moved back towards our scuba gear, I noticed a smaller cave jutting through the rock and mostly hidden in the corner. As I struggled over slippery rocks, trying to squeeze my way inside, my dive watch slipped off my wrist and fell into a narrow crevice. We spotted it far below but knew that there was no way to reach it. So we left it and headed back up for the surface."

We sat in silence for a few seconds, listening to the engines and the propeller as we flew through the air. I looked over at Ange and could tell she was trying to work all of it out in her mind. Then she reached for my dad's watch, turned it over, and read the inscription one more time.

"NEVER LOSE TIME," she said, reading the words aloud. "Your watch. The word time is underlined, referring to your lost timepiece."

I nodded. "Exactly."

Then she handed it back to me and said, "So, whatever it is these guys are after, your dad must have hidden inside that cave."

"It looks that way."

"Do you remember where it is?"

"Yeah. Believe it or not, it's actually close to the *Thunderbolt* wreck. You and I have cruised past it many times. It's just south of it, actually, and like I said, it's pretty deep at one hundred and fifty feet down. Not a lot of people are comfortable diving that deep."

She smiled and shook her head. "Leave it to your dad to outsmart people even from the grave."

"The best thing is, they could've been trying to understand that clue for years and they never would've gotten it. No one would have."

A few hours later, we landed in Jamaica to refuel, this time pulling into a different, smaller marina about fifty miles west of Port Royal. After paying the attendant with a small stack of Jamaican bills, we climbed aboard and took off for Key West. It was a long trip, and we took turns piloting, giving each other time to rest and enjoy some of the delicious Jamaican barbeque we bought back at the marina.

It was a beautiful day in the Caribbean. Blue, cloudless skies as far as the eye could see and a calm ocean below. I'd always enjoyed flying over the Caribbean, especially in a Cessna, where the cruising altitude of usually just over ten thousand feet offered a much better view than that of a commercial aircraft. Looking down through the window, I watched as we flew over Jamaica and Cuba, as well as the shining white sand and turquoise waters of all the hundreds of smaller islands and shoals that littered the deep blue ocean below.

It was just after five in the afternoon when we touched down back in Tarpon Cove in Key West. Easing alongside the dock, Ange turned us around, then killed the engine just as the starboard float made contact with the fenders. Opening the door, I jumped out and tied her off, and then we grabbed our stuff and headed down the dock towards the parking lot. She'd already paid to moor the plane there for the entire month, so she only smiled and waved at the dock attendant as we headed for my

Tacoma, which was still parked right along the water.

Tossing our gear on the backseat, we hopped inside, and I drove us over to my house just a few minutes away. I kept my eyes alert as I turned off Palmetto Street and onto the gravel driveway of my house. I knew that it was incredibly unlikely that any of the Campos brothers' drug runners had already reached Key West, but I always preferred to err on the side of caution. It wouldn't take a genius to figure out that I lived here, and I knew that it was only a matter of time before they showed up.

I parked underneath my light-gray, white-trimmed house that was propped up on stilts and, after disengaging the security system, we walked up the stairs and in through the side door. After grabbing a quick shower, we dressed in fresh clothes and headed over to Conch Harbor Marina. I'd called Jack Rubio, one of my oldest and best friends, while in the air using my satellite phone, and we'd agreed to meet on his boat, the *Calypso*. Jack had been running Rubio Charters, a fishing and diving charter, ever since his father had passed away.

Pulling into the marina, I parked right along the railroad ties, then we both got out and headed down the dock. Jack had the *Calypso* moored at slip forty-seven, just down the dock from my boat, and when we approached his white forty-five-foot Sea Ray, we saw that the deck hatch leading down to the engine room was propped open.

I stepped onto the swim platform, straddled the transom and peeked my head down into the engine room. Jack's messy blond hair, tanned skin and lean frame were unmistakable. He was wearing nothing but a pair of board shorts, and his body was awkwardly positioned behind the generator.

"Need a hand?" I said, sliding over the transom and stepping down the small metal ladder that extended down to the engine room.

He froze and peeked his blue eyes over the back of the massive machine. "Just about got it."

A second later, he crawled out from behind the machine, pressed a few buttons on its front panel, and started it right up. When it purred like a cat, he turned to me, grinning from ear to ear. "Just needed a little love."

Jack had always been good with engines, generators, radios, and pretty much anything else that had electrical and mechanical components. He'd learned to be after years of running charters all around the Lower Keys.

I climbed out of the engine room, followed closely by Jack. He was covered from head to toe in sweat and oil, so he grabbed a nearby towel before giving Ange a hug. After closing and locking the hatch, we headed up to the bridge and sat on cushioned white seats surrounding a small table. The view was great up there, and Jack opened a nearby cooler and handed out coconut waters and bottles of Keys Disease beer. Keys Disease was a local brewery that both Jack and I loved and had both invested in, mainly to encourage them to bring back our favorite brew they called *Paradise Sunset*.

"So," Jack said, leaning back into the cushioned seat. "What have you two been up to? You know you gave Wilkes quite the scare when you ran off on him last night."

It was hard for me to believe that it was only last night that Ange and I had been eating at Latitudes. It felt like a week had passed by, we'd done so much. I started at the beginning, telling Jack first about the phone call and about how Ange and I had flown down to Curacao to figure out what was going on. Then I told him about the drug runners who'd impersonated detectives and how we had gone to Willemstad, met with a real detective, and then been chased off the island by a swarm of bad guys while eating brunch.

"Damn, sorry to hear about your dad, bro," he said, shaking his head. "He was a great guy and should never have gone out that way. Truth is, I've always been a little bit suspicious about his death."

I nodded. If I was being honest with myself, I had been too. I mean, sure, my dad wasn't the healthiest eater around. He enjoyed his bacon and greasy cheeseburgers as much as most men do. But a heart attack while scuba diving? It had always struck me as odd, considering he was one of the calmest people I'd ever seen underwater. I'd even argued with the coroners and detectives about it two years ago when they'd told me, but they'd assured me over and over that it was the truth. I wasn't sure how it had all gone down behind the scenes, but I thought more than one guy had gotten an unexpected payday for that one.

Running his hand through his long blond hair, Jack looked out over the horizon at the soon-to-be-dying sun and said, "So, what happens now? Sounds like these assholes are gunning for you."

I took a drink of beer and said, "Now we find whatever it is they're looking for, and we use it as bait."

Ange and I had talked for a few hours on the plane ride north and had gone over different possible plans of action. It was similar to the way operations went both in the Navy and in the civilian sector. We tried to think like our enemies, putting ourselves in their shoes and trying to figure out how they would act in order to develop a counterattack. It had worked for me hundreds of times before, and I knew that it would work here.

It was just like in the old pirate tales I used to read. If an English pirate hunter wanted to catch a notorious buccaneer, he first had to think like a pirate. That's how the best pirate hunters succeeded, and that's how famous pirates like Bannister, Teach, and Kidd had met their ends.

We discussed our plan of action with Jack and told him about the watch. Grabbing it from my pocket, I set it on the table in front of him and told him the same backstory I'd told Ange. "It's the Lost Grotto, Jack. I'm sure of it. And we're gonna dive down there tomorrow and find out what it is my dad went to such lengths to keep hidden."

Jack examined the watch and smiled. "I'm with you, Logan. But as you know, that cave's right by *Thunderbolt*, and it's popular this time of year."

"Which is why we need to go early and just try and blend in as best as we can."

"You think any of those guys you two ran into in Curacao will be following us?"

"I have no doubt about that. Which is why all three of us will be packing."

We agreed to set out early the following morning and spent the rest of the evening enjoying a few more cold ones and watching the sunset over the water, painting the sky with reds, oranges, and purples in a sight that never got old. Jack fired up his grill and cooked up a feast of hogfish, lobster, and stone crab claws. He used a combination of various seasonings, including Swamp Sauce, a local favorite of ours, then cut open a few lemons, plated the food and set it all in front of us. I hadn't realized just how hungry I was until I started to dig in, savoring every bite of the fresh and flavorful seafood and washing it all down with a few Paradise Sunsets, my favorite Keys Disease brew.

When our plates were empty and our bellies full, Ange and I thanked Jack for everything and told him we'd see him bright and early in the morning. I stumbled my way down from the pilothouse and over the transom. As I stepped from the swim platform onto the dock, Ange gripped my left arm.

"I think you might have had one too many, Dodge," she said, laughing as we walked with our arms intertwined down the dock.

She was right. Usually I was pretty good at controlling myself. I mean, sure, I had my nights just like most men do, but for the most part, I practiced the art of self-control. I guess it was the culmination of everything that had happened in the past twenty-four hours that had made me reach the bottom of the bottle faster than usual.

Seeing no reason to drive back to my place, we walked just a few hundred feet down the dock to where I had the Baia moored at slip twenty-four. We paused before boarding, watching for the slightest ripple around the hull to signal that someone might be aboard. Once we were confident that there was no one inside, we headed into the main cabin and crashed onto the queen-sized bed. We were both tired from the long day, but watching Ange undress and kissing her soft cherry-red lips easily convinced me to put off going to sleep for a few more hours.

CHAPTER EIGHT

I woke up the following morning to the sound of my radio turning on and playing Kenny Chesney's "Beer in Mexico" on Island Vibes. Without cracking open my eyes, I dropped a hand on the OFF button and crawled out of bed before it woke up Ange. I took a moment to admire her beauty as she lay halfway beneath my white comforter. Her blond hair was sprawled out over her head, leaving only a small glimpse of her tanned face, and her long, toned legs stuck out slightly, allowing me to see her sexy feet and white-painted toenails.

Forcing my eyes to look away from her, I took in a deep breath, cleared my head, and headed for the salon. We had a busy day ahead of us, and I knew that I would have to be focused and alert at all times, ready for anything. I scooped some medium roast into my coffeemaker, then poured the water and started it up. Breakfast would be light. It was already five in the morning, and the sun would be waking up within the next hour. I cut into a few mangos, then sliced up some bananas. Ange woke up a few minutes later to the smell of the coffee, and after making quick work of our breakfast, we hopped into the shower together.

After toweling off, I put on a pair of swim trunks and a tee shirt. Ange put on a white bikini, then covered it with a pair of short jean shorts and one of my cutoff shirts. Moving out into the cockpit, I saw a faint glow in the distance as the sun was just starting to rise over the eastern horizon. We'd agreed that it was imperative that we leave early, given the popularity of the nearby dive and snorkel sites.

I took a few minutes to check over all my gear, making sure I had full scuba tanks and checking the integrity of every strap, flap, and clip of my BCD. At zero five thirty I saw Jack walking down the dock, carrying his gear bag over his shoulder. Jack was one of the best divers I'd ever met, and he knew the Keys as good as anyone alive, so I was glad that he'd agreed to tag along. After making sure all our gear was properly stowed, we untied the mooring lines and disconnected both the shore power cable and freshwater hose. After Jack gave me the thumbs-up, I started up the twin six-hundred-horsepower engines and eased us away from the dock.

The weather forecast called for partly cloudy skies with less than a ten percent chance of rain, but Jack knew that it was wrong. He'd always told me that he had that islander instinct that can't be taught. And after living in the Keys for almost half a year, I'd grown to rely on his forecast more than any other.

"We'll have until one o'clock before the rains come," he said, staring up at the sky, which was barely covered with scattered gray clouds.

Along the equator, seasons don't exist in the usual sense. Instead of the normal four seasons, there exists a rainy and a dry season. The dry season lasts from November to April, and the rainy season from May to October. Since it was mid-October, we were still barely in the rainy season, which meant downpours came and went with little notice at times.

The waters leading out into the open ocean were calm. There wasn't much wind as I cruised us out between Sunset Key and the familiar waterfront attractions of Mallory Square and the Key West Aquarium. It was always cool to see Mallory in the early morning with very few people around, and then marvel at how it became a different animal entirely by midafternoon, filled with live music, quaint shops with doors propped open, street vendors and an assortment of interesting characters showing off their talents for anyone who wanted to watch. The laid-back lifestyle of the Keys combined with the wild and crazy nightlife to make Key West one of my favorite places on Earth.

I picked up speed as we headed south around Fort Zachary Taylor. Turning to port, I put us on a direct course for the *Thunderbolt* due northeast of us, then brought us up to the Baia's cruising speed of forty knots. All three of us kept a sharp eye out on the horizon, the threat of the Campos brothers and their drug-smuggling posse ever lingering in our minds.

Ange kept a pair of binoculars glued to her eyes for practically the entire trip, scanning the area around us in all directions. It wouldn't be easy to spot someone following us, given the fact that there were already a handful of boats on the water. The reef running along the eastern side of the Keys is one of the most popular destinations for diving and snorkeling in the world. And even though it was still technically the rainy season, the tourists were beginning to flock south.

After an hour and a half, we reached our destination and dropped anchor about a quarter of a mile away from the *Thunderbolt* wreck. The *Thunderbolt* started out life as the USAMP *Major General Wallace F. Randolph*, a 188-foot-long mine planter. She'd spent years changing hands, being used as an oilfield exploration vessel and a lightning research vessel. Years of being hit by lighting were what had earned her the name the *Thunderbolt*. She was eventually scuttled in 1986 as part of the Florida Keys Artificial Reef Program and now rested in 120 feet of water.

There was one boat already anchored just south of the wreck, about a thousand feet north of us. There were seven people gathered on deck, and six of them were donning scuba gear. After reading its name, Jack recognized it as a charter based out of Marathon. There were two other boats cruising the turquoise water surrounding us, which only had a few small whitecaps, but neither of them looked suspicious.

I bent down, opened a storage compartment hatch at the back of the console, and pulled out my BCD, fins, mask, and snorkel. I didn't usually wear a wetsuit while diving in the Keys, but since we'd be going so deep, I grabbed my three-millimeter from inside the guest cabin closet and pulled it snug over my body. Jack did the same with his wetsuit, and then we strapped our nitrox-filled tanks onto the backs of our BCDs. Nitrox has a higher concentration of oxygen than normal air, which would allow us to stay down longer and be less susceptible to decompression sickness. It would also be essential, considering that it was over a 150 feet down just to the opening of the cave. At that depth, a normal tank would offer only a few minutes of bottom time due to the increased density of the air.

Once the tank was secure, I grabbed my titanium dive knife from a nearby compartment and strapped it to the inside of my right calf. There it would be easily accessible with my right hand and less likely to get stuck on something than if it was on the outside. I also grabbed a high-powered Prolight dive flashlight, securing it in the front pocket of my BCD, and my Cressi dive computer, which I strapped around my left wrist.

Once our gear was good to go, Jack and I slid our BCDs onto our backs and tightened them snug. Ange did a buddy check, making sure we didn't have any loose-hanging straps or tangled hoses, then gave us a thumbs-up. I used eight pounds of sandbag weights and velcroed them into the side pockets of my BCD to help my body sink, then grabbed my mask and fins and moved onto the massive swim platform.

I sat on the transom next to Jack, and as I slid my feet into my fins, I turned back to Ange and stared into her blue eyes. "Look," I said, "we don't know for sure that we weren't followed. Just be careful and—"

As if reading my mind, she lifted my gray cutoff shirt that she was wearing, revealing one of my spare Sig Sauer P226 pistols strapped around her waist. Then she motioned towards her hard case resting on the half-moon cushioned seat beside the dinette.

"If any of those thugs come near this boat, it will be the last thing they ever do," she said confidently.

I couldn't help but smile as I turned my head forward and donned my dive mask. Jack and I gave each other a fist bump, then he said, "Time to solve us a mystery," before standing and stepping out into the ocean.

As his wave splashed over the swim platform onto my fins, I stood up as well. *Alright, Dad*, I thought as I stared down at the blue ocean beneath me. *Time to figure out what you were trying to hide.*

I took a big step out, splashing through the surface and gazing at the clear water around me. The warm Caribbean seawater felt good as it seeped into my wetsuit, and I bobbed for a few seconds before letting some air out of my BCD and sinking rapidly alongside Jack.

Looking around through the glasslike water, we saw long trails of bubbles dancing towards the surface over by the *Thunderbolt*. The six divers had jumped in a few minutes before us and the leader had almost reached the top of the wreck. The visibility was roughly ninety feet, so we could only see the outline of the front end of the shipwreck as we descended towards our own seemingly insignificant destination.

From afar, the opening into the cave was impossible to distinguish. It sat nestled beneath an overhanging ledge, which meant that you had to swim almost all the way to the seafloor beside it in order to see it. It had only been by a matter of dumb luck that my dad and I had stumbled upon it.

We'd been diving the *Thunderbolt*, of course, and after exploring the wreck, we'd spotted an enormous leatherback sea turtle swimming south, heading along the ledge. It was swimming slowly so we decided to follow it as best as we could while my dad used his underwater camera to snap a few photos. Due to the lighting, the pictures hadn't turned out well, but just as we were about to head up towards the surface, my dad had spotted a dark opening in the ledge. Upon further examination, we'd realized that it was the opening of a cave. Our hearts had both raced with excitement, but the gauges on our dive tanks had forced us to surface and spend over an hour letting the nitrogen bleed off before diving down to explore it.

Jack and I finned with calm strokes past the top of the brightly colored ledge that was covered with coral and teeming with sea life. It rose up from the ocean floor about forty feet and marked the point where the coastal waters off the southeastern shores of the Keys transitioned from shallow turquoise waters to the deep blue open ocean. A fine layer of sediment clouded up as we reached the bottom. Glancing at my dive computer, I saw that we were 154 feet down.

Looking ahead, Jack and I saw the opening of the cave just ten feet ahead of us. The opening was menacing, dark and about half the size of a common doorway. Only one of us could fit at a time, so I pointed a finger at myself, then pointed forward and then pointed a finger at Jack and pointed two fingers forward, indicating that I wanted myself to lead and him to follow. He gave the universal okay signal, pressing his index finger to his thumb. Looking back at the cave, I grabbed my flashlight, switched it on and then finned slowly through the opening.

The cave was extraordinary. It was filled with sea urchins and the antennas of hundreds of spiny-tailed lobster peeking out from their hiding places below. As we moved deeper, it started to open up a little, allowing Jack and me to swim side by side. It was pitch black aside from the bright beams of our flashlights, which scanned over the unique rock formations.

Fortunately, the cave didn't branch out like many caves do, so we didn't have to worry about getting lost. But we still had to successfully navigate through the ups and downs, twists and turns and widening and narrowing of the cave.

Cave diving presents many dangers, and I had read my share of stories involving experienced divers who'd ended up trapped beneath a fallen boulder or forced to make a last-ditch effort for the surface due to faulty equipment. Those stories rarely ended happily, and usually resulted in the terrifying and lonely deaths of those involved. Because of the dangers, Jack and I moved slowly and made little to no contact with the rocks around us. We also routinely checked both our gauges and our dive computers, making sure that everything was functioning properly.

After five minutes of swimming through the cave, it started to angle upwards. The cave narrowed around us like a massive mouth closing in as we angled so much that we were now swimming straight up. Roughly thirty feet above us, the cave opened and, shining our flashlights, we could see the glassy reflection of the rippling surface as our bubbles rose up and broke free.

We kicked for the surface, breathing out continuously to prevent the dense air from expanding and damaging our lungs. When we were only about fifteen feet from the surface, I noticed something in my peripheral vision. Keeping my flashlight pointed up, I glanced down into the dark water beneath my fins and saw a small speck of light. It was faint, and it was coming from far below us in the cave, but there it was.

Tilting my head upward, I saw that Jack had moved about five feet above me and was just about to break the surface. I kicked my fins through the water with two powerful strokes, catching up to him. We broke through the surface together, then removed our mouthpieces and breathed in the damp cavern air. Keeping my flashlight trained up into the small dry space, I looked back down at the faint light below.

"What is it?" Jack said, eyeing me skeptically.

"Someone's following us," I said, looking around at the main portion of the cave, which was about twelve feet tall, twenty feet wide, and made up of large pointy rocks. "We need to get out of the water."

I slid my mask down to hang around my neck, then slipped out of my fins and held them by their rubber straps in my left hand. Grabbing hold of the black jagged rocks, we pulled ourselves out of the water, unclipped our straps and slid out of our dripping BCDs. Setting our gear behind one of the larger rocks so it wouldn't be visible from the water, we climbed around to the other side and leaned over a small ledge, staring down as our pursuer's lights grew brighter in the dark clear water below. It looked like there were two of them, and as they ascended, we switched off our flashlights and kept covered behind the ledge. We were only a couple of feet above the surface, but we could remain out of sight if we kept our bodies low, pressed against the cool rock face.

We watched as their bubbles floated up, and less than a minute later, one of the guys broke through the surface. He held a bright flashlight in one hand, which illuminated the cave across from us, and a Glock 26 subcompact pistol in the other. He was well within my reach, so as he slid down his mask, I grabbed my dive knife, leaned over him and stabbed its sharp tip through his right hand, causing it to open and let go of his weapon.

Blood gushed out from his hand, and he yelled through his mouthpiece. As his pistol sank into the deep abyss below, I sliced his breathing hose in half, causing air to hiss out violently from his tank. Then I stabbed a giant hole in his BCD, causing air to explode out and throwing off his buoyancy. Digging my right foot into his body, I kicked him down as hard as I could, and with the air bubbling away from his BCD, he sank like a rock into the darkness below.

As the first thug sank, his body on a fast and direct course for the rocks below, thug number two reached the surface. Seeing what had happened to his buddy, he looked frantic and paranoid as he appeared out of the water, holding his Glock out in front of him and firing it in our general direction before the barrel had even cleared the water. The loud booms of gunpowder were deafening in the tight confines of the cave. His bullets rattled and ricocheted off the black rocks, shooting up bright sparks.

I kept my body low and out of sight behind the ledge and felt Jack's presence beside me. When the thug stopped firing momentarily, I glanced over the edge. Seeing that he was looking towards the other side of the cave through the dark lenses of his mask, I sprang into action. Still gripping my dive knife tightly in my right hand, I jumped off the ledge and splashed down behind the thug, the force of my body landing on top of him causing us both to sink a few feet beneath the water.

I wrapped my legs firmly around his waist and stabbed my knife through the center of his chest before he realized what was happening. He yelled underwater, sending a stream of bubbles towards the surface a few feet above us as blood flowed out from his chest. His body struggling in my arms, he tried to aim his pistol at me, but it was no use. I had his body in a full nelson, and no matter how hard he wailed, kicked and flailed his arms, he couldn't get himself free.

Grabbing hold of his right hand, which gripped his pistol firmly, I forced it into his abdomen and pulled the trigger a few times, sending two nine-millimeter bullets exploding into his dying body and putting him out of his misery. We bobbed on the surface, and within a second, his body went limp in my arms. I relieved him of his weapon, then deflated his BCD, sending his corpse sinking to the bottom of the vertical slug of water to join his friend below in a watery grave.

I swam through the bloody water, grabbed the corners of a black slippery rock on the edge and pulled myself out. Fishing my flashlight out of the small pocket in my wetsuit, I turned it on and climbed over the space where we'd left our gear.

"Damn, Logan," Jack said, meeting me by our gear. Then, glancing down into the water he added, "Those guys the drug smugglers?"

I nodded. "Some of them."

We both shined our flashlights towards the far western corner of the cave. Though it was short and narrow, the cave extended a long way into the darkness. Jack and I climbed over large rocks and steep crevices as we navigated a hundred feet or so into the darkness. Soon the cave became so narrow that we had to practically crawl to fit and, remembering the time my dad and I had explored the cave together, I knew that I was close to the spot where I'd lost my watch.

It had happened while I was trying to jump from one rock to another. I'd slid on its flat surface, and when I'd grabbed onto a sharp corner to stop my downward momentum, my watch strap had made contact with the rock, unclasped and slid right off my wrist. It fell through a tiny crevice and completely disappeared from view. As I shined my flashlight around me, I looked down and realized that I'd found the spot.

Kneeling down and holding on to the corners of a large rock, I turned to Jack. "This is it."

He nodded, and just as I looked up he said, "What's that?"

I noticed it too. There was a small groove only about half a foot wide, and there was something foreign sticking partway out of it. Keeping myself steady on the rock, I straightened my body, reached out my hand and grabbed a yellow plastic container. As I brought it close and examined it by the light of my flashlight, I realized that it was one of those small waterproof cases used to store valuables you don't want to get wet while out on the water.

I felt both excitement and confusion at the same time. This was what my dad was trying to keep out of the drug runners' hands? This was the secret he had taken with him to his grave?

Sitting on the rock across from Jack, I unclasped the two plastic locking devices and hinged open the lid. Inside, there was nothing but a small folded-up piece of paper, which I grabbed with two fingers and unfolded. Flattening it out in front of both of our lights, I saw that the paper had lines of text written in my father's handwriting.

Written in blue ink on the first line were the words "A Lone Wolf. A Toxic payload." The lines that followed contained a series of various questions, all with answers that corresponded to a certain number. *He's giving me coordinates*, I thought as I read over the questions that no one on Earth would be able to answer but me.

I read the first line aloud and then handed the piece of paper to Jack, running the words over and over again in my mind. I knew I could figure out the coordinates, but the first line left me puzzled. One thing was certain, whatever my dad was trying to keep hidden wasn't inside the cave.

Jack handed it back to me, then shrugged, "Any idea what it all means?"

I nodded. "It's coordinates." Then, looking back over towards the main section of the cave, I thought about Ange and how those two guys I'd taken out probably weren't the only bad guys nearby. I folded the paper, closed it back into the container I'd found it in and stowed it in the pocket of my wetsuit. "Come on. Let's get out of here."

CHAPTER NINE

The trip back was slower since we had to perform a safety stop at fifteen feet beneath the surface. Safety stops are vital to prevent depressurization sickness, a condition which can lead to severe headaches, numbness, dizziness and even death. We'd made quick work of the cave, though, navigating down past the two dead guys and weaving our way through narrow rocks and coral before reaching the open ocean. After three minutes of neutral buoyancy, Jack and I nodded at each other, then finned eagerly towards the blue sky above.

My boat was still anchored in the same place, just ahead of the forward section of the *Thunderbolt* wreck, and rocked leisurely in the calm morning water. We surfaced slowly, peeking through the water and doing a quick survey of the boat before rising all the way out. Ange had slipped out of her jean shorts and my old tee shirt and was wearing only her white-and-blue bikini as she lay on her back on the sunbed. Her toned and tanned skin sparkled under the Caribbean sunshine as she eyed us through a pair of dark aviator sunglasses.

I kicked over towards the swim platform, then slid my mask down. "Ange, everything alright?"

As Jack and I approached, she stood up and watched us from the other side of the transom. "Yeah, everything's fine. Those two divers dropped down over there about a hundred meters away. I watched them but thought they were just locals. That is, until the boat came over this way."

I slipped out of my fins and climbed up the small ladder onto the swim platform. After lending a hand to help Jack up behind me, I slid out of my gear and dried off with a fresh towel Ange handed me.

"What did they do?" Jack asked as we climbed over the transom.

She grinned. "What did they try to do is the better question. There were two of them, and they cruised up along the port side, yelling at me to put my hands on my head." I smiled, already knowing where the story was going. "Instead I put my hands on something else and fired a few rounds in their direction. When they tried to fire back, I took out the first guy and wounded the second. He managed to cruise full throttle into the horizon like the little chicken that he was."

Jack and I both laughed. I wished I could've seen the look on their faces when they'd realized just how much more there was to Ange than met the eye. At first glance, she looked like a Victoria's Secret model. But she was just as deadly as she was attractive, and her enemies usually learned that the hard way.

"What kind of boat were they on?" Jack asked.

"A damn fast one. Looked like a Cigarette."

Jack and I made eye contact and shook our heads. A Cigarette is a specialty go-fast boat designed from the ground up for speed. Used as racing boats by many people around the world, they can typically accelerate up over eighty knots, making them look more like a blur than a boat when they cruise past. As fast as the Baia was, I knew she'd be no match against a Cigarette in a boat chase.

"So, what did you find?" she said, her eyes glancing back and forth between us. "I don't hear any treasure clanking in your pockets."

I grabbed the waterproof container from my wetsuit pocket and handed it to her. "There's a message in there written to me from my dad."

Ange held the container out in front of her for a moment, then looked up at me. "Mind if I read it? If it's personal, I understand."

I waved her off, telling her that I wanted her to. I appreciated the fact that she'd asked, though.

Grabbing a pair of binoculars, I climbed up onto the bow and took a look around. A few more boats had shown up and were anchored near the wreck buoys, along with a few sailboats far out in the distance and a pair of Jet Skis racing a few miles away from us, closer to the shore. None of them looked suspicious, but it was hard to tell. I thought it was doubtful that they would only send one boat. Surely they would have learned their lesson after what had happened in Curacao.

After seeing that the coast was relatively clear, I climbed back down into the cockpit and helped Jack unstrap and stow all of our gear. Ange was sitting at the dinette, staring intently into the unfolded piece of paper.

"It's gotta be latitude and longitudes," she said, glancing over at us. "I sure hope you remember all of these seemingly obscure numbers." I grinned at Jack as I unzipped my wetsuit and pulled it off. "But this part: 'A Lone Wolf. A toxic payload.' What do you think that means?"

I shrugged. "I don't know. But we all know that there's someone in the Keys who probably does."

"That old sea dog will love this," Jack said. "You know how crazy he gets when he hears a good mystery."

We were referring to Pete Jameson, the owner of Salty Pete's Bar and Grill in Key West. He'd spent his entire life living on that island and he knew more about the ocean, and the Florida Keys in particular, than anyone I'd ever met. He'd been helpful in our search for the lost Aztec treasure, and if anyone knew what those words meant, there was a good chance that it was him.

Ange grabbed a few coconut waters from the nearby Yeti, then opened them and handed one to each of us. Looking out over the endless blue surrounding us, I cracked it open and took a few long swigs. The cool drink felt good, and before I knew it I'd chugged the entire thing, not realizing just how thirsty the long dive had made me.

Once all our gear was properly stowed, I pulled up the anchor using the windlass, coiled up the chain, then pulled out the dive flag. Sitting in the cockpit, I started up the engines and we cruised back towards Key West, taking in the beauty of the islands as the warm wind blew through our hair.

I gave Jack the controls, grabbed the plastic container with the folded message inside, and headed into the salon. Shutting the hatch behind me and sitting at the dinette, I grabbed a small notepad and pencil, then opened the folded piece of paper. I assumed that the questions would give the coordinates in order, so I drew twelve small horizontal lines on the notepad paper, one for each number in a set of twelve latitude and longitude coordinates.

Each of the questions caused a smile to appear on my face as they brought back different memories with my dad. Some of them were pretty simple. For example, on one line, he had written, "My Favorite baseball player?" And as I read the words, the image of Joltin' Joe DiMaggio wearing the pinstripes and rounding the bases at Yankee Stadium appeared in my mind. And I wrote down the number five on the corresponding blank line.

Others required a little more thought. For example: "What was your mother's favorite condiment?" It was difficult, since I barely remembered my mom, but my dad had brought up her unhealthy obsession with Jack Daniel's barbeque sauce a few times. I wrote the number seven over the corresponding line.

I read and answered all six questions, some numbers being double digits and some repeat numbers, and by the time I was finished, I had a full set of coordinates.

I read the coordinates and said each number aloud a few times in order to lock them into my memory. Once I had them memorized, I tore the notepad paper to shreds, then folded up my dad's note, put it back in the container and slid it into my pocket. I threw the tiny remains of the torn-up paper into my trash can beneath the sink and headed out into the cockpit.

By the time we eased into the marina, it was just past noon and a cluster of light gray clouds had blown in from the east. After pulling up against the dock and tying off the lines, I changed into my cargo shorts and a pair of tan Converse low-tops. From my black CamelBak, I grabbed my Sig and holstered it to the side of my belt, where it was concealed behind my shorts and tee shirt.

Ten minutes after pulling into the marina, we were off the Baia and heading down the dock towards the parking lot. The three of us kept our heads on a swivel, knowing full well that if the drug runners were following us out on the water, then they were probably doing the same on land. We hopped into Jack's blue Jeep Wrangler and headed over to Pete's place with the top down.

His restaurant was located on Mangrove Street, just close enough to the bustling streets of downtown to attract tourists and just far enough to stay relatively quiet. That is, unless it was a night when Pete had a band playing. On those nights, Salty Pete's was as loud and wild as anywhere in Key West.

Just a few minutes later, we pulled into the small gravel lot in front of a structure that looked more like a house than a restaurant. It was two stories, had a large porch out front and looked a hell of a lot better since Pete had used some of the Aztec gold money to give it a proper restoration.

After we found the Aztec treasure under an underwater formation known as Neptune's Table just south of the Marquesas Keys, most of the thousands of gold bars had been sold off. The artifacts had been sent to various museums, and most of the money had been donated to the poorest regions of Mexico. Along with a few of my friends, however, I had been given a handsome finder's fee, which allowed me to help fix up the old restaurant, buy a house, and live a comfortable lifestyle in the tropical paradise I'd fallen in love with as a kid.

Walking under a white-lettered sign bearing the name of the restaurant, we moved through the wooden door, causing a bell to ring out inside. Even given the time of year, the place was nearly half-full, the mouthwatering smell radiating from their kitchen summoning every tourist and local within a mile radius.

Before the door had shut behind us, Mia, the lead waitress, called out to us from across the room.

"Well, if it isn't three of my favorite people," she said, smiling as she approached us. She held a stack of menus in one hand and a pitcher of iced tea in the other. As usual, she had her light brown hair tied back and was wearing a salmon-colored Salty Pete's tee shirt, which she'd tied into a knot behind her back to make it fit her petite frame. She was pretty, and though she'd been working there for six years, she was only twenty-two years old.

I returned her smile and said, "It's good to see you, Mia. Nice to see the place is getting a lot of business."

She filled up a few tall glasses with her pitcher as she approached us. After hugging Ange and kissing her cheek, she sighed and said, "Sometimes I miss the old days, when unsuspecting tourists would walk in only to be scared off moments later by the run-down appearance or one of Pete's antics."

"Is that old sea devil here?" Jack asked.

"Should be here any minute, and he better be. We're running low on fish, and if he doesn't get here soon, I'll have to send someone over to the market."

We headed up a set of wooden stairs in the center of the room. The second story was covered with rows of clear glass cases and various artifacts from all over the Keys, including an entire section dedicated to the Aztec treasure. Most of what we'd salvaged had been sent to major museums in Mexico and Washington, D.C., but we'd been able to keep a few items in Key West, which also attracted tourists to the restaurant.

Opening a sliding glass door, we found a nice table on the patio that was shaded by a large umbrella and cooled by a fan and mister. The patio boasted 180-degree views of the ocean, which were obstructed only by a few tall coconut trees.

Less than a minute after we sat down, Mia arrived and took our drink and appetizer orders. We enjoyed a few orders of conch fritters, a specialty in the Keys, and washed them down with delicious and refreshing Key limeade. After we ordered our entrees, the sliding glass door opened and Pete walked out onto the patio, his lips contorted into a smile that spread from ear to ear.

"Just the scallywags I wanted to see," he said in his rough voice, laughing and patting each of us on the back as he removed an old-style camera that was slung around his neck and handed it to Jack. "I caught the biggest Mutton Snapper in history today, mark my words."

Pete was in his sixties, with a few straggling gray hairs growing out of his tanned bald head and a good-sized gut that made him appear almost as wide as he was tall. But his most distinguishing feature was a metal hook he had in lieu of a right hand, which he'd lost in an epic sea story that changed more frequently than the tides.

We took turns looking into the small LCD screen as Pete hovered over us. "She put up a hell of a fight. A worthy opponent."

"She's a beauty," Ange said, admiring the large red-and-silver fish.

"Ah, she is," Pete said, nodding. After a few seconds, he added, "You all enjoy, now. I'm gonna head down and help Oz with the filets. We're gonna have snapper for weeks."

"Hey, Pete," I said as he turned to head for the door. He glanced over his shoulder and looked at me. "You mind joining us for a few minutes? We could use your help with something."

Intrigued, he sauntered back over and sat across from us in the fourth cedar chair situated around the round table. Staring at me with his deep brown eyes, he smiled and said, "What have you guys stumbled onto this time?"

Without a word, I reached into my pocket and pulled out the small plastic container. Unhooking the clasp, I pulled out the folded paper, unfolded it and handed it to Pete. His eyes lit up like a kid unwrapping his first birthday present. He read over the words twice as I sipped on my limeade and threw a few more fritters down the hatch, relishing the flavor.

"Who wrote this?" he finally said, his face filled with excitement.

I took a quick look around. Fortunately, there were no other parties braving the heat out on the patio. I wanted to keep this conversation between us.

"My dad," I said. "And he left it hidden in a secret cave over by the *Thunderbolt*."

His eyes lit up, and when he asked how we'd found out about it, Ange and I told him the story, starting with the phone call I'd made at Latitudes Restaurant.

"Damned shame," he said when I told him the part about my dad being murdered. "I'm sorry to hear that, Logan."

"Not as sorry as these guys are gonna be," I said, then continued with the story.

By the time we finished, our food had arrived and we couldn't help but dig into the freshly cooked seafood as Pete thought it over. I was happy to see that Isaac, Jack's fifteen-year-old nephew, was helping out around the place. He had a broom and was sweeping up the patio around us. He was homeschooled but was so smart and ahead for his age that he took a few classes at the local college. But aside from pedaling his bike to and from the campus a few days a week, he rarely left the house. Jack decided it would be a good idea for him to get a part-time job so he could earn a little spending money and get out of his shell at the same time. When Jack's brother had died in a car accident years ago, Isaac's mom couldn't take care of him, so Jack had been raising him ever since. He'd lived in Chicago much of his life and had had a hard time adjusting to life in the tropics.

"It's the first line I'm hoping you can help us with," I said, pointing at the top of the paper.

Clearing his throat, Pete read the words aloud. "A Lone Wolf. A toxic payload."

I stared expectantly into his eyes behind his wrinkled tan skin. He read the words a few more times, then leaned back in his chair.

"Well?" I said. "Any ideas?"

He sighed and said, "Nothing comes to mind. But perhaps—"

"I think it's referring to a submarine," a voice said from the other side of the patio, cutting Pete off and causing our entire table to go silent. I dropped a forkful of fish, leaned back and looked in Isaac's direction. He was standing beside the railing, holding his broom in one hand and looking off into nowhere, lost in thought. "Yeah," he continued. "That's gotta be what it's talking about."

I shook my head. "A submarine? What makes you think that?"

Seeing that all eyes were on him, he walked quickly over to the table and looked down at the piece of paper. He was lean and lanky, built like Jack except with darker hair and pale skin. He was wearing a green Salty Pete's tee shirt and a round straw hat, and he looked like he had about a gallon of sunscreen on his legs, arms, and face.

"Right here," he said, pointing at the first words. "A Lone Wolf. And it's even capitalized. It has to be a submarine." The four of us stared at him, eagerly awaiting an explanation. Glancing up from the paper, he grinned when he saw our expressions. "While learning about World War II at the college, we read about German U-boats. A group of U-boats cruising in formation was referred to as a Wolf Pack."

I gave a blank stare as I thought over his words. I'd read about the German submarines before, but it had been a long time ago. I knew that there were a few that had been found in recent times, but the idea of my dad finding one left me speechless. Looking over at Jack, I saw a proud grin materialize on his face.

Pete nodded. "The boy's right."

Jack patted the young man on the back. "You become more islander every day."

Isaac's lips contorted into a smile. He stood proudly beside us, and I was amazed that none of us had been able to figure it out.

"Wait a minute," Ange said, staring at me. "So you're saying that your dad found a German U-boat?"

I shrugged. "Maybe. I have no idea what else it could be referring to."

"Amazing," Jack said, shaking his head. "If it's true, it could change history. We're talking about a lost German submarine!"

"But how could a submarine stay hidden for so many years?" Ange asked.

"It happens. It's a big ocean," Pete said. "There was that U-boat up north off the coast of New Jersey that wasn't discovered until 1984. U-

869, I believe. There's a lot of ways a wreck can stay hidden. Hell, after all these years, that thing's gotta be covered in sediment and sea life. It would be difficult to identify."

The table went quiet for a moment. Grabbing the paper, I said, "The real question is, if he did find a lost U-boat, what does that have to do with these drug smugglers? Why are they after it, and why would my dad go to such great lengths to keep it hidden from them? I mean, it has historical significance, but what use could these thugs possibly have for it?"

The five of us went silent. There were a lot of questions, a lot of pieces to the puzzle that didn't seem to fit anywhere.

Pete leaned forward, his elbows propped against the oak tabletop. With a stern voice, he said, "A toxic payload." As the words came out of his mouth, I could tell that we all had the same thought. The Nazis had planned to attack the continental United States with a biological weapon of some kind. "So what's the endgame here, Logan?"

Without hesitating, I said, "We find this sub before these thugs do, secure its contents and rain justice upon their doorstep." After a moment's pause, I added, "These guys murdered my dad. One way or another, I'm taking them down. It's gotta be that way."

CHAPTER TEN

As we finished up our food, I asked Pete question after question about U-boats and the Nazis' experiments with biological warfare.

After about the third one, Pete said, "I think you should talk to a friend of mine who knows a hell of a lot more about the Third Reich than I do. Professor Murchison teaches over at Florida Keys Community College, and the man's a history buff. A real genius. The guy used to teach at Harvard before he got fed up with the cold and migrated south. He comes in here every now and then, but your best bet would be his office over at the campus."

I thanked them for all their help, then pushed back my chair and stood up. "Pete, this young man deserves a raise," I said, ruffling Isaac's long curly hair.

The three others stood up as well, and I patted Pete on the back. "The food was delicious as usual.

You know, if you're not careful, this place might actually make a profit for once."

He laughed. "Been in the green for two months now. I think it's the Aztec treasure exhibit. Tourists flock from all over the country to see it."

As we headed for the screen door, I glanced at Ange and said, "Well, I think it's time we learned some more about this Lone Wolf."

Jack drove us back to the marina and, having a scheduled dive charter for the midafternoon, headed down the dock as Ange and I hopped into my Tacoma.

Florida Keys Community College is located right across from the Lower Keys Medical Center on College Road. The campus has a location befitting a fancy resort, nestled between forests of mangroves right along the clear tropical water. With white concrete buildings, crisp green lawns, well-manicured landscaping, an Olympic-sized swimming pool and impressive dive training programs, I decided that if I'd ever had a dream college, it probably would have been this place.

I parked in a visitor spot right in front of a cluster of buildings and palm trees behind a sign that had the word Information stenciled across it in white lettering. Ange and I headed inside and asked one of the college receptionists where we could find Professor Murchison. She told us he was giving a presentation.

"Which classroom is he lecturing in?" I asked.

The pretty black woman in her mid-forties smiled behind a pair of brown-rimmed glasses. "You don't know very much about Dr. Murchison, do you?" She went on to explain that his presentations attracted visitors from across the state, sometimes even from abroad. "He's speaking over in Tennessee Williams Theater. It's the only space we have that's big enough, and sometimes even it gets filled up." Glancing at an analog clock that said it was almost one in the afternoon, she added, "But he should be finishing up soon."

After asking where we could find the theater, we headed back out the automatic door, walked about three hundred feet along a nice paved walkway, then entered through the large semicircular entrance of the Tennessee Williams Fine Arts Center. The woman hadn't been kidding about the crowd. I estimated that the two-story theater had at least five hundred seats, and almost all of them were taken. But moving upstairs, we claimed a few empty padded seats in the back row of the mezzanine and watched the end of his presentation.

Dr. Murchison looked like he was in his fifties, with a tanned complexion, thinning dark hair and a long wiry frame. He wore brown slacks and a blue dress shirt with rolled-up sleeves. The first thing I noticed about him, however, was his excitement and enthusiasm for what he was talking about. He had a passion in the way that he spoke and carried himself on the stage that impressed me from the beginning. It was clear that he loved what he did and that he was very good at it. It also helped that he had a smooth and articulate English accent that you could listen to for hours.

His presentation was about the Vicksburg Naval Campaign during the Civil War. He spoke especially about the Battle of Island Number Ten, a little-known sea battle that had resulted in the first

Confederate position lost along the Mississippi River.

When he finished, the entire crowd rose to their feet and gave a loud and resounding round of applause. He bowed cordially with a big smile on his face, then stepped off the stage and met with a small cluster of students looking to ask him questions and thank him for giving such an interesting talk.

Ange and I waited until the last of the group left, then headed downstairs, catching him just as he was packing a stack of books and notepads into an old leather shoulder bag.

"Dr. Murchison," I said as we moved over to him along the side of the stage. He looked up as he slid his bag over his shoulder. "My name is Logan Dodge, and this is Angelina Fox." He smiled earnestly as he shook both of our hands.

"I've heard of you, Mr. Dodge," he said. "You helped find the Aztec treasure, right?"

I nodded. "But if it weren't for Angelina, it would be in the hands of Mexican cartel members right now."

He smiled and bowed to her, and I saw her blush a little bit, which was pretty rare for her. "Of course," he said. "Well, it's an honor to meet both of you. What can I do for you?"

I paused for a moment and took a quick look around the theater to make sure that we were alone, an action which sparked his curiosity.

When I saw that it was just the three of us, I said, "How much do you know about German U-boats?"

His eyes lit up as I said the last few words. "Did Pete tell you to talk to me?" he said, smiling.

When I nodded, he continued, "Best seafood in the Keys over there at his place. Maybe even in the world." He glanced towards the door. "Would you two mind walking with me to my office?"

We followed him out of the theater, down a long linoleum hallway and through a side door leading out into the warm tropical air. I was amazed as he moved with the light and purposeful gait of a man much younger than his years.

Walking beside him made me feel like I was the most popular kid in school. Every single person we passed as we strolled along a white walking path leading to an adjoining building across an amphitheater smiled and said hello. Though most of the greetings were directed at Dr. Murchison. It was easy to tell that he was well liked and respected by everyone on campus, both students and faculty.

He led us into a two-story rectangular building with the words Lockwood School of Diving plastered in black paint across the white backdrop. Up on the second story, he unlocked a metal door with a small glass window and ushered us into his office in the upper corner of the building.

"Most of the offices are located back in the administration building," he explained. "But I like the view here better, and this room wasn't being used for anything at the time."

He wasn't kidding about the view. His office had a pair of large windows that took up most of the far wall and overlooked the endless blue horizon. I don't know how else to explain it, but his office looked like it belonged to Indiana Jones, with shelves covered with artifacts, old texts, and leather-bound books, and an old wooden desk with worn coins and a model of a Civil War ironclad resting on its faded surface.

An adjoining room was filled with shelves, books, and artifacts as well, and it had a small desk with a large magnifying glass resting on top of it. All told, his office made it clear that this was a man who had seen, learned and experienced things very few people do.

"Please have a seat," he said, motioning towards a pair of antique black leather chairs beside his desk.

Despite the amount of stuff everywhere, the office was still roomy. I estimated that both rooms combined to give over a thousand square feet of space. As I sat down, I noticed a model of a submarine in the corner, sitting on a shelf beside an old mirror.

Dr. Murchison followed my gaze, then smiled. "To answer your question, I know a great deal about German U-boats. Anything in particular you two would like to discuss about them?"

I glanced over at Ange, who gave me a slight nod, letting me know that she was getting the same trustworthy vibes from him. I reached into my pocket and pulled the folded paper out of the plastic container. Unfolding it, I handed it to the professor.

He looked intrigued as he grabbed it and narrowed his gaze as his eyes went back and forth on the page.

He examined the paper, reading it over a few times as he stroked his chin with his fingers. "Well, that's very interesting."

"Yes," Ange said. "We think he might be referring to a lost U-boat."

"He?" he asked, his eyes still glued to the page.

"My dad," I said. "He wrote this just before he died."

"I see. And this part down here? It looks like questions to get the coordinates."

I smiled. "We figured that part out and we're pretty sure we know where it is. We just want to know what we're getting ourselves into. And... we were wanting to try and understand what he means by 'a toxic payload.'"

He read the words over a few more times as if unable to believe what he was seeing, then set the paper on the table and whispered something under his breath that sounded like incredible.

Leaning back in his chair, he looked up at the two of us and said, "You know, during World War II, the German U-boat was one of the most dominant Navy vessels in the sea. Pound for pound, they were arguably the most effective warships in the history of mankind, and from 1939 to 1944 alone, U-boats sank over three thousand Allied ships." He leaned forward, his chocolate-colored eyes lighting up. "They hunted in groups called Wolf Packs." He grabbed a handful of pencils from a nearby Conch Festival cup and laid them out on his desk, simulating an Allied convoy. "They'd roam the seas, sometimes in packs as large as twenty, cruising six miles apart and scanning for targets. When a target was spotted, they'd swoop in, diving beneath the surface just long enough to sneak up, fire their torpedoes and make their stealthy escape. In their heyday, a Wolf Pack could take down an entire Allied convoy, complete with frigate escorts, without so much as taking a single hit. They were masters of their tactics and terrors of the Atlantic, striking fear in the hearts of every Allied sailor from the Gulf of Mexico to the western coast of Africa and all the way north to the Arctic. Oftentimes, U-boats cruised close enough to American soil to see the headlights of driving vehicles through their periscopes and tune in to local news stations."

He paused for a moment to clear his throat, then continued, "But near the end of World War II, as advances in radar and antisubmarine aircraft were utilized by the Allies, the Wolf Packs were broken apart and hunted down one by one using depth charges. By 1944, the average lifespan for a Nazi submariner was three months, and seventy-five percent of all those who volunteered never made it home.

"But Karl Dönitz, the commander of the Kriegsmarine, had been working hard on a solution. The best German engineers, some of the greatest minds in the world, put their heads together, their pens to paper and their builders to work day and night. Relentlessly they worked until they had achieved the unimaginable. In less than a year, they designed and created a prototype of their new warship, U-boat model XXI. It was without question the most advanced submarine in the history of mankind. This boat took the bar of what was possible at the time, raised it about five feet above the competition and then raised it a couple more times. While the best subs at the time could stay down maybe twelve hours, the model XXI could stay submerged for up to fourteen days and travel twice as fast underwater as any sub of its time. These were feats unheard of in undersea warfare.

"Had the XXI been rolled out a few years earlier, the war might have had a very different ending. But unfortunately for the Third Reich, only two of them were ever finished, and neither were ever deployed, or so the history books say."

"What do you mean by that?" I asked, curious as I hung on to each and every word he said in his smooth English accent.

He smiled. "Well, there's a story that one of these U-boats snuck out of Germany and was sent on a secret mission from a submarine base in what remained of German-occupied France. The story goes that, seeing that the twilight of the war was upon them, Dönitz sent a final attack run, one last attempt to strike their enemy in the heart. Supposedly, they loaded up an XXI with a biological weapon and ordered it to sail across the Atlantic and strike American soil."

"Do you think there could any truth to it?" Ange asked, listening as intently as I was.

He nodded. "Yes, I do. Look, I've been to the Keroman submarine bunkers in Lorient. Even at the end of the war, when the entire city was leveled to ruins, the bunkers remained." He grabbed a large book of maps and opened it up to a page near the middle. He pointed to map of Western France. "The Germans had a massive biological weapons facility here in Nantes, just eighty miles from Lorient. I've also read accounts from English pilots who spotted a German submarine as it submerged and escaped out of the Blavet River in July of 1944. I've also read entries in Dönitz private journal, as well all of the Führer's memoirs, mentioning a secret U-boat referred to only as the Ghost. Yes, it is entirely possible, and the fact of the matter is, the Germans had both the technology and the chemical weaponry to pull off such an attack."

Looking back at the paper still resting on his desk in front of him, he took in a deep breath and said, "Tell me, was your dad an avid scuba diver?"

"He was a retired master diver in the Navy, and he'd dove multiple U-boat wrecks before. The one off North Carolina and the one found off New Jersey, I believe."

His eyes grew wide, and he smiled. "Well, then, this has sure sparked my interest. I'm somewhat conflicted, however. I've always believed the story to be true, but if this wreck does exist, extreme care must be taken during its salvaging. If one small mistake were to be made handling a biological weapon that's been under the ocean for over sixty years, the effects could be catastrophic."

"We'll be careful," Ange said.

There was a moment of silence as I thought over his words. Glancing back up at him, I said, "Thank you for meeting with us, Dr. Murchison."

He waved me off. "Please, my friends call me Frank. And it's no problem at all. This is my life's work, after all."

Ange and I stood, then shook his hand one more time. We turned and headed for the door, but as I reached for the brass knob, he said, "Would you be willing to do me one favor?"

I turned. "What's that?"

"If by chance you do find her, and I have all the confidence in the world that you may—might I request the opportunity to help with the salvaging? I too have dived U-352 and U-869, and I have some experience in underwater salvage."

"Absolutely," I said. "Yours will be one of the first numbers we'll call."

We headed down the stairs, out through the main doors and back to my Tacoma. After climbing inside, I started up the engine and turned the air conditioning up full blast to cool the interior, which felt like a sauna when we entered.

We sat in silence for a moment, thinking about everything Frank had said.

"It's no wonder my dad died to keep its location a secret," I said after Ange asked what was on my mind. "If the sub is there and it does have a powerful biological weapon aboard, it could mean the death of thousands of innocent lives if it falls into the wrong hands. Maybe millions."

CHAPTER ELEVEN

We spent the rest of the afternoon on the Baia, formulating a plan to dive down and explore the location given in the coordinates. At around four, a thick gray curtain of clouds spread over the islands, and it rained heavily for about forty-five minutes. We spent that time in the salon, sitting on the white couch and looking over charts, maps, pictures and doing a few internet searches.

After plugging the coordinates into the boat's GPS, we found that the location was about thirteen miles south of Islamorada. Using the depth charts, we were able to get a rough idea of how deep the water was.

"Jack was right," Ange said, staring down at the chart resting in front of her. "The water's over three hundred feet deep out there. It's five miles beyond the reef line."

Over three hundred feet? I glanced over to verify it myself. The deepest I'd ever dived was 250, and that was pushing it. I wasn't a deep wreck diver or a commercial diver by trade, just a former Navy SEAL who'd used diving as a means to stealthily approach unsuspecting enemies for years. I enjoyed diving the reefs, catching lobster, spearfishing and taking in the scenery, but I rarely dove below a hundred feet.

"Fortunately, I have this," I said, reaching for a plastic hard case stowed under the couch we were sitting on. Since the table was covered with charts, books and the laptop, I set it on my lap and unclasped the hefty plastic hinges. Inside was a commercial-grade underwater drone, the same one I'd used with Samantha Flores to explore and discover the lost Aztec gold, which had been swallowed by the ocean floor at a localized tectonic fault zone and was only accessible through a long and narrow cave.

Sam, my ex-girlfriend, had been on a research expedition for Florida State University, where she was a professor of marine geology. She'd brought the drone with her, and after we'd found the gold, she'd purchased a new one and given me her old one. I'd bought an extended leash for it, giving it a six-hundred-foot range, so if the U-boat proved to be too deep for diving, the drone would be a useful alternative.

The entire time we researched, I thought about the drug smugglers who'd murdered my dad and were now after us. Every morsel of my being wanted to track them down and take them out, but I knew that the best way to get revenge would be to take away the very thing they wanted most. My dad had died trying to protect something, and I knew I had to find it and protect it at all costs.

"It can't just be about the sub, though," I said, thinking everything over. "These pirates aren't after a U-boat. To them it's just a hunk of rusty old metal. No, these guys are looking for something else."

"Maybe they know about the biological weapon. I mean, why else would your dad give you these coordinates?"

I thought it over a moment. "I don't know. But tomorrow, we're gonna find some answers."

It was after nine when we decided to call it a night, stowed all of our research and locked up the Baia. As we moved down towards the foot of the dock, I marveled at how drastically the weather had shifted. A sky that only a few hours earlier had been littered with clouds was now as clear as glass, revealing a sparkly swarm of distant stars.

The air was still warm, and though there was a nice breeze coming off the ocean, the evening summer air was humid. We rolled down the windows and cruised along backstreets, making the five-minute drive back to my house. There weren't a lot of people walking around, just a few straggling tourists, so for the most part, the drive was quiet and the streets mostly empty.

I turned onto Palmetto Street, heading northwest. As I drove past my mailbox and was just about to turn right onto my driveway, I came to a sudden stop.

"Something's wrong," I said, my eyes scanning along Palmetto Street and down my gravel driveway. My neighbor's golden lab, Atticus, was nowhere in sight, and the lights on my porch were out. I switched off my headlights, turned off my air conditioning and listened to the eerily quiet night air, which was devoid of its usual symphony of Keys scaly crickets.

"Logan!" Ange gasped, staring and pointing towards my house. Following her gaze, I saw a dark shadowy figure moving slowly in my kitchen behind the front window, his body grazing against the ruffled half-opened curtain.

I put my Tacoma in reverse and slowly backed up into my neighbor's driveway, just enough to be out of the street. Killing the engine, I reached into my CamelBak resting on the backseat and grabbed an extra magazine. My Sig was already holstered to the inside of my cargo shorts, out of view behind my shirt. I slid the extra fully loaded fifteen-round magazine into the loop of fabric beside my weapon. Reaching back into the bag, I grabbed my night vision monocular and opened the door.

Most people would probably call the police, but the idea never crossed my mind as I moved with Ange along the blue fence and thick hedge that separated my property from my neighbor's. The tall palm trees lining both sides of my driveway provided extra cover as we moved north towards my backyard. Ange had grabbed her Glock and was holding it with both hands.

We posted up on the end of the fence, right beside the narrow channel about fifty feet away from where my Robalo center-console was stored. Though our eyes had adapted well and the half-moon overhead offered decent lighting, we still couldn't see the inside of the house very well. I switched on my night vision monocular and took a look around.

"Three in the living room," I said, seeing their dark figures as they tore apart my place, throwing furniture everywhere. The more I watched, the more my blood boiled within me. "Another in the bedroom."

"See the guys under the house?" she whispered.

I angled my monocular down and saw the two guys she mentioned, their bodies barely visible behind the stilts holding my place up. One of them was talking into a phone while smoking a cigarette, and the other stood aimlessly, throwing a few occasional punches at my hundred-pound Everlast heavy bag hanging from the support beams.

We spotted another guy walking around the wraparound porch, making seven in all. As I watched them move haughtily around my house, I grew more and more angry, and soon I developed a plan.

"These guys aren't gonna shoot at me," I whispered to Ange after lowering my scope. "At least not right away. They'll try and take me alive so I can help them find whatever it is they're looking for. If I die, the chances of them finding it will be slim to none, and they know it too. We can use that."

"Just promise to leave a few for me," she said, staring daggers at the intruders.

As I stood to leave, she wrapped her toned arms around my neck and pulled me close. Breathing out passionately, she pressed her soft lips against mine and kept them there for a few seconds before pulling away.

"For good luck?" I said, smiling back at her.

"No," she said softly, shaking her head. "Because you're sexy as hell when you go into SEAL mode."

I gave her another kiss, then turned around and moved swiftly back towards my Tacoma, keeping my body low and out of sight. Climbing into my truck, I quickly started up the engine, then took in a deep breath. *These guys want me to pull into my driveway and cruise up to my house. Well, they're about to get their damn wish.*

I put the truck in gear and rolled out of my neighbor's driveway, taking a sharp right onto Palmetto Street. Half a second later, I took another right, my off-road tires crunching over my gravel driveway.

There's a time to be stealthy and there's a time to break some skulls with reckless abandon. Since I knew that my truck would be a dead giveaway and that each of the seven thugs would instantly be aware of my presence, I decided on the second approach. When I was about thirty feet away from the two thugs standing under my house, I switched on my brights. As they shielded their eyes, I shoved my right foot down on the gas pedal, pressing it against the floor as hard as I could. My tires kicked back an avalanche of gravel before gaining traction and accelerating forward.

The two thugs barely had enough time to scream before the front end of my Tacoma slammed into their bodies, shattering their bones as they draped helplessly over my hood. I let go of the gas and hit the brakes just as my truck reached the back of the paved slab, sending their blood-splattered bodies hurtling into my backyard like rag dolls.

Without bothering to shut off the engine, I climbed out of my Tacoma, reached for my Sig and stepped over towards the two lifeless bodies. I'd hit them at over thirty miles per hour, so I knew that they were done for, but I put a bullet through each of their chests just to make sure. The two gunshots rattled the quiet night air, and I heard the others yelling from upstairs.

As I moved towards the stairs on the side of my house, I heard loud boots shuffling overhead. They were heading for the stairs right beside me. Keeping out of view, I aimed my Sig through one of the gaps in the handrail and put a bullet into a guy's chest just as he appeared. The force knocked him over the side headfirst, and he landed awkwardly on a dwarf lantana bush.

I moved around the corner, keeping my Sig raised as I took on the first few steps. As I reached the top of the stairs, the barrel of a .50-caliber Desert Eagle appeared around the front right corner of the house, followed quickly by a large black man with a lean, muscular build. His eyes grew big and he managed to fire off a single round right past me before I knocked the weapon out of his hands. As it tumbled onto the porch, I hit him with a powerful front kick that landed right in the center of his throat, causing him to gag as I crunched his trachea.

Grabbing his shirt, I pulled him down as hard as I could, then jammed my right knee up into his face. His body flew backward and slammed against the deck. He was out cold. I glanced up just in time to see the three other guys as they ran out the door on the other side of the house, squared up at me and raised their weapons.

I fired off three shots as I dove to my left, hitting at least one of them before disappearing around the corner of the house. I landed on my chest just fractions of a second before a stream of automatic gunfire cut through the air behind me.

Windows shattered above me and wood splintered out into tiny pieces as they held their triggers down. The sounds were ear-shattering, and they seemed to be moving closer. Gripping my pistol, I crawled towards the back side of the wraparound porch. It was hard to tell how many were still on their feet, but I knew that at most, I'd only taken down one of them. Climbing on top of my AC unit, which was surrounded by a pine wood lattice, I grabbed the ceramic tiling of the roof and pulled myself up. I moved swiftly towards my attackers, planning to strike them from above. The roof was mostly dry, but there were a few wet spots from the heavy rain earlier in the evening, so I watched my step.

When the gunfire finally ceased, one of them yelled at the other to move around to the front side of the porch. Glancing over the edge, I could tell that there were just two left standing. Holding tight to my Sig, I popped up to take them out. But before I could, Ange appeared out of nowhere from the darkness behind them. She must have climbed up the northern façade, and I watched as she caught the two unsuspecting thugs by surprise.

Swiftly and without hesitation, Ange wrapped her left arm around the thug closest to her. Pulling him tight and using his body as cover, she put a bullet through his chest, sending a spray of blood out from his abdomen. Before the other guy could do anything but gasp, Ange had her Glock trained on him and fired another shot, this one hitting him straight in his forehead. His head transformed into a messy gob of bloody bone and mutilated skin as he collapsed onto the deck.

With blood still dripping out of the first thug, Ange let go of him, letting his dying body fall face-first to the deck. I could feel the grit and determination oozing from her as she took a step towards the dying thug and slammed her heel into his head, ending his life.

Calmly and collectively, she took a look around, making sure there weren't any more stragglers. I did the same, and after a few seconds, we realized it was just the two of us. Our eyes locked on to each other, and as they did, I holstered my Sig, grabbed the ceramic edge of the roof and dropped down onto the porch.

A moment later, I looked at the two dead guys, then turned to her. "I had them, you know."

She smirked. "Really, now? Because I seem to remember seeing you run away like a little girl."

"I was getting a better angle." I grabbed the side door's doorknob, twisted it and pushed open the door.

I flipped on the living room and kitchen lights, revealing the mess that was the inside of my house. Every cabinet door was open, every shelf cleared, every couch cushion dislodged and every drawer emptied. After looking over the entire house, it was clear that they'd been there a while. In the living room, I looked at the bullet holes in the walls and the shattered window, knowing the man-hours it would take to bring the house back to its original self.

As I headed back for the side door, I reached into my pocket and smiled as I wrapped my hand around the only thing that would have been useful for them. Whatever they'd found in here, at least there was nothing that would give them the location of the U-boat.

Just as I stepped out onto the porch, I heard the sound of sirens piercing the night air. I wasn't at all surprised that someone had called the police after the symphony of gunfire that had shattered the peaceful air, so loud I was sure it had been heard for miles. The truth was, I was leaning towards calling them myself. I had put it off long enough, and it was time that law enforcement knew what was happening here.

I'd always dreaded dealing with law enforcement, and after spending eight years in the Navy, I knew firsthand how difficult and slow dealings with the government could be. But I also knew that the more eyes, ears and guns we had working against these drug smugglers, the better our chances were at taking them out and keeping them from getting their hands on a deadly weapon. I had also started to build trust with Key West's sheriff, Charles Wilkes. Though we'd only met maybe five times, we'd developed a mutual respect for one another, and I knew that he could help us.

A moment later, bright flashing red and blue lights appeared through the hedging and two police cars turned onto my gravel driveway, their sirens deafening as they pulled up to my house. I walked down the stairs beside Ange, and we both had our empty hands raised high in the air.

"So what's the plan here?" she said quietly as we reached the bottom step.

"We tell them everything."

She looked at me with a scrunched-up, confused face, then shook her head. "Why would we do that?"

Before I could reply, the police cars stopped and their doors opened in unison. A few of the officers had their sidearms raised and aimed towards the house as they took cover behind their doors. Fortunately, Charles was in the front and after seeing Ange and me standing calmly by the stairs, he told his men to stand down and holster their weapons.

Charles moved his tall, lean frame over towards our position with light steps. It always amazed me how he seemed to carry himself like a man in his twenties, rather than in his late forties. After working for the FBI for thirty years, Charles had "retired" and migrated south, where he could walk over white sandy beaches instead of snow in the wintertime.

He walked confidently over towards us with two other officers right on his heels. One of them I instantly recognized as Officer Benjamin Kincaid, a young and cocky deputy who was about my height and had short blond hair and blue eyes. Though we hadn't gotten along well at first, we'd grown to respect each other and I'd even gone shooting and jet skiing with him a few times.

"You know, this is exactly the sight I thought I'd see when we got the reports of gunfire coming from this address," Charles said in his low voice that managed to be calm and powerful at the same time. He glanced over our shoulders and his eyes scanned to the side, no doubt noticing the two dead guys lying in their own blood in front of my truck and the guy lying facefirst in the dwarf lantana bush beside my porch. "What's the situation?"

"As we were pulling into the driveway, we spotted a few guys standing under my house and holding firearms," I said without hesitating. "When we drove closer, they yelled and aimed their weapons at us. In self-defense, I plowed into them, and then we jumped out and engaged in a gunfight with the other five. There's six dead. The seventh probably won't be able to speak for a few days, but he should be fine." It was the truth, for the most part. If I'd told him about us doing reconnaissance before we'd attacked, he would have asked why we hadn't called the police first.

Charles listened intently and ordered a few of his officers to search the place. Less than a minute later, more sirens resounded over the night air, and the bright lights of two ambulances appeared, turning from Palmetto Street into my driveway. The officers went to work, doing a full investigation of the property, taking pictures of the bodies and asking both me and Ange for our full statements. It wasn't until after eleven at night that they had all the bodies loaded up and hauled away.

After cleaning up the place, Ange and I sat on my gray sectional couch while Charles sat across from us in a cushioned rattan chair.

When it was just the three of us inside, Charles turned to us and said, "I sent a squad car down to the Conch Harbor Marina. He checked out your boat and said it doesn't look like anyone's broken into it. I'm gonna keep a few guys in the parking lot there tonight, as I'm assuming you won't be staying here."

I was glad to be dealing with Charles. He was smart as hell, and he was a good, honest man to boot. He'd stood up for me and defended me while dealing with the aftermath of the incidents that had taken place on Loggerhead Key as Tropical Storm Fay had raged through Southern Florida, and afterward. A lot of bad guys had died, but they'd all been necessary and in defense of myself and an innocent young family, and Charles knew it. The situation would have been much more painful had it not been for him.

When I thanked him, he added, "Now, are you gonna tell me what's going on here, or are you gonna keep me in suspense?"

I told him the story for the most part and put special emphasis on the part about the lost German U-boat and how if these pirates found it, they could get their hands on a biological weapon. The truth was, I was going to go after these guys whether there was a weapon or not, but the prospect made urgency a key factor.

"So what's your big plan here?" he asked. "I mean, these guys know where you live and where you moor your boat. How do you plan on getting to this sub without them following you? And how do you plan to take them out on your own?"

In an instant, the pieces of a plan coalesced in my mind. I'd been mulling it over all day, but it came together just then. It wasn't perfect by any means, and it was risky, but it was the best I could come up with.

"I'm betting on them following me," I said. "In fact, I want them to." Charles and Ange both looked at me like I was crazy. I smiled and stood. "I've got an idea of how we can find this wreck and trap these guys at the same time, but we're gonna need a lot of bodies." I glanced at Charles. "We're gonna need the Coast Guard and Navy on this."

He thought it over a moment, then said, "I work closely with both branches. I could get their help. But the last thing I want is to put anybody in harm's way if we can avoid it."

"Oh, this won't," I assured him. "If it works, we should be able to get these guys to surrender. If not, we'll have them severely outnumbered." I grabbed my phone, punched in a few numbers I knew by heart, and held it up to the side of my face.

"Who are you calling?" Charles asked.

"The cavalry," I replied with a confident smile.

CHAPTER TWELVE

By the time we finished with the police at my house, drove over to the marina and got settled into the main cabin of the Baia, it was well after midnight. The night was calm and clear, with only a few clouds covering the bright stars above and an occasional ripple against the hull. Given the long, busy day, we both fell asleep as soon as our heads smooshed into my soft feather pillows.

After spending years in the Navy, performing primarily reconnaissance missions, I've developed the ability to sleep anywhere and to take advantage of downtime by falling asleep instantly. In the field, you never knew for sure when your next opportunity to sleep would be so you took it whenever you could.

At zero six hundred, I woke up to the sound of rain beating against the bow hatch overhead and the rumbles of distant thunder. It was still the rainy season in the Keys, and the weather often shifted from sunny to rainy to back to sunny again in less than an hour. I felt Ange's soft, warm body pressed against mine as I lay on my back with her draped over me. When I opened my eyes, the cabin was mainly dark, the only light radiating from the port and starboard portholes and the partly covered hatch just over our heads, displaying a grim, gray sky above.

Slowly, I slid out of bed and walked barefoot through the door and into the salon. After switching on my coffeemaker, I stepped out through the hatch and into the cockpit. The rain was heavy, but the wind wasn't too bad, allowing me to stand at the edge of the cockpit without getting wet. I took a look around the empty, lifeless marina. The only movement was the gentle rocking of moored boats, and as I drew my gaze up towards the parking lot, I saw the interceptor police vehicle still parked in the first spot beside the stairs leading down to the dock.

Seeing that the coast was clear, I climbed back into the salon, the smell of fresh coffee wafting into my nostrils as I entered and shut the hatch behind me. I didn't have a lot of food on the boat, but I always had fresh fruit so I proceeded to prepare my favorite breakfast: freshly sliced mango, banana and a warm cup of coffee.

When the coffeemaker finished its cycle, I grabbed my blue Rubio Charters mug and poured a cup. Just as the dark liquid reached the rim, Ange walked out from the bedroom wearing only a black bra and panties. I admired her incredible figure and must have looked like a schoolboy staring at his crush. She'd awoken and moved towards the salon with such light movements that I hadn't even noticed she was up until the door had swung open.

"Like what you see?" she said, catching me red-handed.

I smiled. "Always."

We sat on the soft white cushioned half-moon bench seat that wrapped around my dining table and ate the small but delicious breakfast. When we were finished, we cleaned up, took a hot shower together, then got dressed. After checking the news via our cell phones, we realized that the heavy rains were part of a small storm that had formed in the Gulf and was gliding along towards the panhandle. It wasn't strong enough to do any serious damage, but it meant that we'd have to postpone any time out on the ocean until it subsided, which was predicted to happen later this afternoon.

We spent the day inside, taking shelter from the storm and using the time to learn everything we could about the lost U-boat and the drug runners we were dealing with. Since Charles still had contacts in the FBI, he was able to obtain and send us the profile sheets for both Campos brothers and a few of the other known members of their operation.

I'd known about their somewhat celebrity status in the States when they'd had tremendous success competing as professional MMA fighters. Both of their careers had been cut short, however, when they were both banned from MMA for fighting dirty just a few months apart.

The older brother, Pedro, had been banned first for kicking a guy in the nuts, then tackling him onto the mat and putting him in a coma for two weeks. Three months later, his younger brother, Hector, had knocked out the ref, then jumped out of the ring, grabbed a sportscaster's microphone and knocked out his two front teeth with it. Both stories had made national headlines and had been the talk of the fighting community for over a year.

"Damn," Ange said, reading over their profile sheets. "These guys are real psychos."

We learned that after being banned from professional fighting in the United States, the brothers had traveled abroad, fighting everywhere from Mexico and Colombia to Russia and Ukraine, and even the Middle East. As they racked up their fight counts, their skills developed even more and their tempers grew worse, earning them worldwide reputations as guys who were too nuts to compete in organized fighting.

After a few years of traveling from country to country, the two brothers had vanished from records for five years. It wasn't until 2004 that their rap sheets noted that they'd both been suspected of drug trafficking in Brazil, their home country of Bolivia, and the United States.

We took a break before dinner to get a quick workout in, doing a circuit of different push-up variations, body weight squats and pull-ups using the hardtop above the cockpit. I always enjoyed working out with Ange because she was in incredible shape and I had to really push myself to keep up with her. She was into triathlons, and she'd even convinced me to do one with her one time. Even though it hurt like hell, I'd enjoyed every minute of it. There's something I've always enjoyed about pushing myself beyond my limits and finding out what I'm made of.

After showering and changing into a pair of tan cargo shorts, a tee shirt and Converse low-tops,

I enjoyed a big meal of grilled lobster tails doused in Swamp Sauce and freshly squeezed lemon juice. We ate out in the cockpit, enjoying every bite as we watched the dark red sun slip under the distant western horizon. When we finished, it was almost eight. Ange, being so absorbed in the research, decided to stay behind, so I kissed her passionately, then headed down the dock towards the parking lot.

The rain had died off around seven, leaving the ground soaking wet and littered with small puddles. I walked up the stairs, and after telling the officer still parked in the lot that everything was fine, I climbed into my Tacoma, started the engine and pulled onto Caroline Street.

Ten minutes later, I was pulling into a large roundabout that circled a parking garage. Key West International Airport is a small two-terminal airport, and there weren't very many vehicles. I pulled up to the curb and put the Tacoma in park along a row of glass windows and automatic sliding doors. Just beside the windows, behind a group of people standing with their roller bags, was a massive painting of a Conch Republic flag, its dark blue vibrant against the faded white backdrop of the airport building. In the middle of the flag was a conch shell with jagged yellow streaks bursting out from it.

I hadn't been idling for even a minute when a tall, lean man with light skin, short dark hair and a clean-shaven face walked out through the automatic doors. He was wearing jeans, a tee shirt, and dark-rimmed sunglasses, and he carried a classic-looking leather backpack strapped over his shoulders. His stride didn't change as he moved straight towards the passenger side of my Tacoma. Keeping his eyes forward, he opened the door, climbed inside and sat down beside me, placing his backpack at his feet. He shut the door and then patted my knee as I put the truck in gear and hit the gas.

Glancing over at him, I smiled. "It's good to see you, Scottie. Thanks for coming."

"You pulled the best friend card." He laughed. "I was about to hop on a flight to Paris, but you know me, I'm never one to pass up a little excitement. Now, what in the hell have you gotten yourself into?"

By way of an answer, I reached into my center console, grabbed one of my extra Sigs and handed it to him. Not only was Scott Cooper the smartest guy I had ever met, but he had also been my division officer when I'd first shown up to the SEAL team after completing the rigorous training to earn my gold trident. Before being commissioned in the Navy, he had been a Rhodes Scholar, and he was currently in the middle of a six-year term as a US senator representing Florida. As we cruised back to the marina, I gave him a brief overview of the situation and our plan for that evening.

"I'm sorry to hear about your dad, Logan," he said solemnly.

Scott had first met my dad in San Diego while we'd carried our gear off a Boeing C-17, walking beside each other. My dad had also always been there to greet us when we got back from deployment, wrapping his arms around us and telling us how proud he was. Scott's dad had left when he was young, and I knew those interactions meant a whole hell of a lot to him. The three of us had even taken a weeklong trip to the Galapagos back in '99. Scott had always admired my dad, and the two had remained close throughout the years.

"You say these guys attacked you at your house last night?" he asked. "Well, they're not popping out of thin air, so where are they at?"

"They're in the Keys somewhere," I said. "Hiding out. Waiting to make their move and find what they're looking for."

"And what exactly is that?"

I told him the story about the U-boat and what we'd learned while talking to Professor Murchison. Scott came to the same conclusion as me: that keeping the potential weapon out of their hands was the number one priority.

I pulled into one of the parking spots in the first row of the Conch Harbor Marina, just a few spaces down from the police car still staking out the place. We walked down the dock under a dark sky above that was full of bright distant stars. The marina was calm and quiet again, except for a small group gathered outside the Greasy Pelican, the marina's restaurant. When we were halfway to my boat, my phone vibrated. Grabbing it from my pocket, I checked my new message from Sheriff Wilkes: "Standing by," it said.

I slid my phone back into my front pocket, and when we reached slip twenty-four, we both stepped onto the swim platform, then over the transom into the cockpit. When I opened the door, I saw Ange and Jack seated around the table, drinking coffee and examining the research in front of them. After the two greeted Scott, we went into mission mode, going over every detail of the evening's plan. I grabbed a large map of the Keys, slid it into a hard plastic cover and rested it on the television stand across from the dining area. Using fine-tipped erasable markers, I sketched out our different routes, using different colors to correspond to each of us.

"Since the Baia is being tracked, Jack will take it out and head this way," I said, sketching a dotted line out of the marina, around the southern tip of Key West, and then wrapping around to head northeast along the Lower Keys. "Once you get to the Seven Mile Bridge, you'll cut across to Spanish Harbor and around Big Mangrove Key. Meanwhile, the three of us will take off in Ange's Cessna, fly north, then turn back around and land at the dive site. After dropping us off, Ange will fly back to Tarpon Cove, then pick us up two hours later."

"And what do I do once I've led them to Big Mangrove?" Jack asked.

"Charles has a team of Coast Guardsmen as well as Navy patrollers standing by. Hopefully we can have them so outnumbered that these guys lay down their weapons. If they don't—well, either way, they're going down."

"How deep is this wreck, supposedly?"

I glanced over at Jack, who nodded, then said, "It's ten miles off the coast of Layton. Based on our depth charts, it's over three hundred feet. But I did a diving charter earlier today and we took our patrons out that direction. Based on the coordinates Logan's dad gave him, we're looking at just over one hundred and thirty to one hundred and sixty feet down. The variation's probably caused by underwater chasms and ridges."

Once everyone was set with their roles, I moved into the guest cabin and came out with two sets of rebreather gear. I performed weekly and monthly maintenance on all of my equipment and was confident that both sets were functioning and ready to go, but Scott and I checked them both over anyway just to be sure. We did a full integrity check of all straps, hoses and valves, verifying that everything was snug and airtight. Then we checked the battery, verifying its ability to hold and maintain a charge.

Once those checks were complete, we checked the CO_2 scrubber and verified that it didn't need to be replaced. When we were satisfied that the gear was ready to go, we loaded them both up into a large black duffle bag and set it beside the door leading into the salon.

Out in the cockpit, I grabbed my black mesh bag and loaded it with two pairs of fins, masks, snorkels, a flare, flashlights and two large three-millimeter wetsuits. By the time all our gear was loaded up, it was just after eleven o'clock. We'd decided that the three of us would head over to Tarpon Cove at midnight, so I brewed another batch of coffee.

"I'll have you tracked via satellite," Scott said, motioning towards Jack. "So if these assholes try anything before you reach Spanish Harbor, the Navy and Coast Guard can close in on them. Also if any of them manage to escape, we'll track them and hopefully find out wherever it is these guys are congregating."

Jack nodded. "It would take more than a Cigarette to catch me in the Keys."

I smiled and made eye contact with Scott. "Do you really think your dad stumbled upon a lost U-boat?" he said, his eyes lighting up. "I mean, this is monumental if he did. A rewrite-history-books kind of thing."

"Yes," I said, confidently. "But one thing's certain: this is going to be one hell of a dive."

CHAPTER THIRTEEN

Just before midnight, we loaded up all of our gear into the back of my Tacoma. As we stepped off the Baia to head out, I handed Jack a small waterproof radio.

"Channel four, privacy code eighty-two," I said. Utilizing the privacy code with the two-way radio would make it so, even if someone were listening to channel four, they wouldn't hear anything without also having the correct corresponding code. "Ange and I will both have one as well." Then I handed him the keys. "There's a shotgun under the master bed in the port roll-out compartment. Are you armed?"

He lifted his tee shirt, revealing a compact Desert Eagle strapped to his waist. I had no doubt that even if he were chased by a faster boat, Jack could outrun it. I doubted there was anyone alive who knew the hundreds of islands, shoals, sandbars, reefs, and ledges in the Keys as well as he did.

Before stepping onto the dock, I threw an arm over Jack's shoulder. "Be careful," I said. "I doubt these guys will try anything until you stop. It's the location of the site they're after. But still…"

"You too," he said. "And watch out for the current. It gets pretty bad out there well beyond the reef line."

I nodded, hearing the wisdom in his words. "Thanks for doing this, Jack."

"Don't mention it, bro," he said, waving a hand at me. "I'd walk through traffic for you. We're family. You may not believe it, but I want satisfaction for what happened to your dad as well. And anyone who messes with these islands and the people here has to mess with me as well. And don't worry about me. The day some drug-running asshole chases me down in the Keys is the day hell freezes over."

I laughed. "I've got your word, then? Not a scratch on her?"

"Will you get going, you pirate?" he said, grinning as he finished the line of dialogue from one of our favorite movies.

I stepped onto the dock, joining Ange and Scott there, then the three of us moved down towards the parking lot. A soft breeze blew in from the east, causing a few small whitecaps to form out at the mouth of the bay between Wisteria and Sunset Key. It would make landing out on the open ocean in a seaplane difficult, but I knew that if there was anyone who was up to the challenge of something difficult, it was Ange.

The parking lot was less than a quarter full, and they were mostly vehicles that I recognized, owned by people who lived aboard their boats. The police vehicle was still parked near the front, and we walked right by an officer leaning back in his chair and watching a video on his phone. He had an empty box of Red Buoy Donuts resting on his dashboard, and he looked like he was about to pass out.

As we climbed into my Tacoma, I spotted a silver Kia that was parked in the back row, its sleek, short body mostly covered by an overhanging gumbo-limbo tree and flanked on both sides by palmetto bushes. It struck me as suspicious, since I hadn't seen it before and it was the only car parked that far away from the footpath down to the dock.

I thought I saw movement inside, but it was hard to tell since all of its windows were heavily tinted. Sure enough, as I started up my Tacoma, pulled out of the parking lot and headed down Caroline Street, I saw a pair of bright red brake lights illuminate to life far behind us through my rearview mirror.

A few turns and stops later, they were just a few hundred feet behind me. There were only a few other vehicles on the road. It would be easy to head down a quiet street, put my truck in reverse, then let them get close and plow my tailgate through their window. A car like that would crunch like an accordion and there'd barely be a scratch on my truck to show for it. But I decided on a quieter approach and turned down Duval Street.

"Where are we going?" Scott said. He was looking over his gear and hadn't been paying much attention to our surroundings.

Ange, however, had noticed everything. She turned around from the passenger seat, staring back at the Kia. "There's a car tailing us. What's the plan here, Logan?"

Since I was close, I decided to do the same thing Scott and I had done while being tailed by Black Venom seven months ago. Making sure the guys in the Kia saw me, I turned sharply into a small alleyway between the Green Parrot Bar and Pirate Scooter Rentals, then cut a hard left behind the building.

I killed the engine and told the others to follow my lead and cover me. They each grabbed their pistols and climbed out alongside me. We were surrounded on all sides by brick walls, and my Tacoma was blocked from view by two massive green-and-blue dumpsters.

Reaching through the open window into the backseat, I unclipped a large black carabiner from my CamelBak and walked over behind the back wall of Green Parrot alongside the others. All four fingers of my right hand slid comfortably into the carabiner and I squeezed tightly to the metal as the Kia pulled slowly around the corner, its bright lights illuminating the alley beside us.

When it rolled into view, I stepped towards the driver's side, reared my right arm back and slammed my fist into the window, shattering the glass as my fist continued through and made contact with the driver's face. He grunted loudly as his head jerked sideways, wrapping around the edge of the seat.

The guy in the passenger seat gasped and reached for a pistol at his side. But before he could aim it in my direction, Ange popped up behind me with a Sig leveled at his head.

"Move another inch," she said, her eyes intense and her breathing controlled. "See what happens."

Seeing that the driver was out cold, I looked at the other guy and said, "Drop the gun and unlock the door."

He looked pissed but saw that he was surrounded, so he relented, dropping the weapon to the mat at his feet and pressing the button to unlock the doors. Just as he did, the passenger door flung open and Scott reached inside, grabbed the guy by his shirt collar and hurled him out of the car. I heard a loud crack as he slammed into the pavement, which was followed by a few loud *fuck yous* and then silence.

Three minutes later, their unconscious bodies were zip-tied to a metal handrail behind the dumpsters. After searching them, we found a few knives, another handgun and a few wallets, but the most useful thing was a cell phone. After moving their Kia out of view and leaving a note on the dash, saying that these two assholes were criminals, we hopped back into the truck and drove towards Tarpon Cove Marina.

With Ange driving, I flipped open the cell phone and read a few of the recent text messages. Most of them were to phone sex girls, pleading for pictures without wanting to send money. But at the top of the message list was a long thread with texts sent every hour on the hour, informing someone of our positions. The most recent message was sent just before midnight and said "Targets on the move." Since the guy was an idiot and vague as hell, I knew I could use the message to our advantage when we took off.

The parking lot at Tarpon Cove Marina was almost entirely empty, the only vehicles belonging to the few boats parked along the two docks. Unlike Conch Harbor Marina, Tarpon Cove didn't allow liveaboards, so the only boats were temporary moorings. The three of us climbed out, grabbed our gear and headed down the dock towards Ange's Cessna. The marina was quiet as we dropped everything on the dock beside the float and loaded it all into the backseat.

Grabbing the radio, I made sure the channel and privacy code were set correctly, then called Jack and told him T-minus three minutes. Once everything was aboard, we untied the two lines, and then they settled in while I shoved us off, forcing my weight forward into the starboard float and jumping over from the dock.

Ange made quick work of her list of preflight checks, and when she was ready to start up the engine, I called Jack, letting him know that it was game time. Then, using the cell phone I'd taken, I sent a quick text informing the thug's contact that their target was on the move on their boat, heading out of the marina. Once the message was sent, I removed the phone's battery, then threw it out the window into the water below with a splash.

After we donned our headsets, Ange started up the loud engine and accelerated us away from the dock. The takeoff was more bumpy than usual, but fortunately the water inside the cove was sheltered from the wind by surrounding buildings as well as palm and coconut trees, making it less choppy than the open ocean. Once in the air, Ange turned north and quickly brought us up over two thousand feet. The sky was clear aside from a few sporadic patches of clouds, a dark abyss full of bright twinkling stars and the glow of a half-moon illuminating the islands and ocean below us.

Ange leveled the aircraft at three thousand feet and maintained a cruising speed of 150 knots as we flew over the Lower and Middle Keys. Leaning over and peeking down through the glass, I could make out the solid black outline of US-1 as it traversed from island to island, heading towards the mainland of Southern Florida. Forty-five minutes later, Ange eased on the joystick, making a long, sweeping turn and putting us on a course southeast, heading straight for the coordinates I'd entered into her top-of-the-line onboard GPS system.

"Ten minutes out," Ange said into the microphone connected to her headset.

Scott handed me my wetsuit and rebreather gear from the backseat. I did a quick calibration of the oxygen sensors, then did a final check of the battery, filter, and pressure to make sure everything was ready for the dive. Unlike scuba, rebreathers utilize a closed-circuit diving system, meaning that instead of exhalations exiting from your regulator into the water, they're filtered and scrubbed of CO_2, then returned to be inhaled as breathable oxygen.

Once I'd verified all of my gear was in order, I pulled my wetsuit up over my body, then zipped up the back. Grabbing my high-powered dive flashlight, I stowed it in the front flap of the rebreather along with an underwater video camera. I stowed my radio in a plastic waterproof case and slid it into the large pocket of my rebreather, then strapped my dive knife to my calf.

My heart raced as Ange brought us down in altitude, the silvery-tinted water below getting closer and closer in the cockpit windows. Part of me felt like I was back in the Navy, being dropped off in a part of the world we weren't supposed to be in and performing missions that only a small handful of men ever knew about. Glancing at the GPS, I saw that we were less than a mile away from our target.

Ange eased back on the throttles and brought us to just a few hundred feet above the open ocean. Far off in the distance, beyond the faintly glowing ocean's surface, I could see a few specks of light penetrating the darkness from the small towns in the Middle Keys.

"Hold on tight," Ange said as she slowed even more.

A few seconds later, the floats made contact with the ocean below. We bounced a few times over the chop, but as I'd expected, Ange handled it perfectly. As she slowed the Cessna over the water, I turned on my rebreather and strapped it onto my body. Grabbing my mask, I slipped it over my head, then opened the door and gave a thumbs-up to Ange.

"Two hours if no call," I said, reminding her of our previously discussed plan.

Just in case the radio malfunctioned, I didn't relish the idea of having to swim ten miles through open ocean to reach the nearest land. I'd strapped my flare into my BCD, and it would allow her to see us floating on the surface if she was anywhere within a mile or so.

She gave me a thumbs-up and yelled over the engine, "Be careful."

Holding my fins by their straps in my left hand, I turned, stepped down onto the starboard float and jumped into the water. We'd still been moving about five knots over the light chop, so my body splashed and swirled a few times in a white, bubbly haze before I gained control.

Scott had jumped over the other side and was treading water just ten feet away from me as Ange piloted the Cessna forward. I watched as she slowly picked up speed, controlling the plane into a smooth takeoff and rising high into the night air.

One by one I strapped my fins over my booties, then Scott and I took a quick look around. After seeing that there were no boats on the water, we nodded to each other, then let a controlled amount of air out of our BCDs, causing our bodies to sink into the warm, dark water. Once fully submerged, I grabbed my flashlight and turned it on, illuminating a wide beam of crystal-clear water around me. Scott did the same with his flashlight, and we both angled our bodies downward, heading for our destination 130 feet below us in the dark abyss.

We finned methodically, our bodies shooting down through the water quickly. Glancing at my dive computer, I saw that we were sixty feet down, and just a minute after that, the distant light of our flashlights reached a dark, rocky formation below. Jack had been right about the current. I hadn't noticed it during the descent, since there was no point of reference, but once we could see the seafloor below us, it was clear that we were drifting north at a speed of at least two knots.

As we swam closer, I realized that the rock formation was a massive, steep ledge that stretched as far as we could see in both directions Since water distorts the size of things, it was difficult to tell how tall it was, but I estimated that it dropped down at least thirty feet.

Placing my free left hand up to my nose, I pinched and tried to breathe out of my ears, equalizing the pressure in my body to the water around me as I'd done a few times on the way down. At 130 feet, the pressure underwater is approximately five bars, or five times atmospheric pressure at sea level, meaning we would feel around seventy pounds per square inch against our bodies, as opposed to the 14.7 pounds per square inch felt at the surface.

As we moved in closer, hovering just over the ledge, the intricate details took form. The ledge was sprawling with colorful life, from hordes of sea urchins, anemones, and sponges to assortments of coral that covered practically every surface in view. We saw a few parrotfish, an angelfish, a school of yellowtail snapper, and a large loggerhead sea turtle swimming blissfully past us, heading south along the ledge. The world was quiet, calm and dark, and as we panned our flashlights over each and every surface, we saw nothing that was foreign to the marine landscape.

We finned towards the corner of the ledge, then headed for the bottom, where large rocks covered in barnacles and sediment riddled the ocean floor. I swam along a portion of the ledge that jutted out slightly and, seeing something suspicious about the rock face, I grazed my hand against it as I swam, weaving between the thick stretches of coral.

Glancing ahead, I saw that a portion of the rock stuck upwards like a chimney. Blinking my eyes a few times, I saw the ledge with new eyes and realized that we were swimming just inches over a wreck. Forming my gloved hand into a fist, I pounded against the rock and gasped as I heard the higher-pitched sound of metal rather than the low thud of rock.

Grabbing the carabiner hooked to one of my straps, I tapped it against my metal oxygen cylinder a few times, getting Scott's attention. As he turned and glanced my direction, I shined the beam of my flashlight on the portion of the rock sticking up out of the ledge, realizing now that it was a conning tower. He eyed it skeptically for a moment, then swam in closer. After feeling it over with his hands for a few seconds, he froze, then turned to me with eyes wider than the open ocean. I smiled back at him behind my regulator, unable to contain my excitement.

After realizing what it was, I was able to see the large portion jutting out from the ledge with newly enlightened vision. The U-boat was incredibly difficult to see, even knowing that it was there. Years of fallen rocks, erosion, sediment, coral growths, barnacles and other sea life had caused its rounded metal hull to blend in perfectly with its surroundings.

I shined my flashlight from one end of the large cigar-shaped vessel to the other and estimated it at around 250 feet, which was a match to the dimensions given to us by Professor Murchison for the type XXI U-boat.

Before looking it over any more, I grabbed the advanced waterproof dive camera from my rebreather pocket, turned it on and pressed the record button. Holding the camera in my left hand and my flashlight in my right, I surveyed the entire wreck from one end to the other alongside Scott.

We moved from the two screws in the stern, which were barely visible under a shroud of thick coral, and forward along the topside of the wreck. The U-boat was wedged at a forty-five-degree angle against the ledge, with the cone facing southwest and the screws facing northeast. About a third of the way forward, there was a large crack in its hull that spread from the deck all the way down to the keel.

As we swam closer to the damaged hull, we saw that it was too small for us to fit through. But shining our lights inside, we saw a jungle of jagged metal, loose-hanging wires, broken pipes and rusted old valves, all covered in layers of grimy muck. I stared in awe at the inside of a German war vessel that no human had seen in over sixty years. A ship lost to the tides of time and forgotten by history. Whether the damage to the hull had been caused by an enemy torpedo or from when it had rammed into the ledge, it was difficult to tell. But one way or another, it was clear that the boat had lost control and hit the solid rock of a ledge at a very high speed.

We continued, finning our way past the conning tower and down along the forward cone section of the boat. The forward fifty feet or so was smooshed in like an accordion, with most of the hull bent and folded over in large ripples. Through a few cracks in the metal, we could see a swarm of mechanical and electrical equipment, hidden beyond layers of corrosion and sediment.

As I aimed my camera at the front of the boat and stared all the way down its side, Scott continued swimming without me even noticing him. A few seconds later, I heard two loud metal clinks, turned myself around and saw him hovering over a dark, foreign-looking object stuck halfway in the ledge. As I swam closer, I realized what it was. A torpedo.

As I moved alongside Scott, he paid particular attention to a portion of its side that was barely visible between the ledge and coral. Focusing my gaze closer, I looked at part of the torpedo that appeared to have less growth on it than the rest—as if someone had scraped some of it away in order to see something. Scott looked at me, then pointed at what appeared to be a marking on its side. I moved my mask within a foot of its round metal casing and saw a skull and crossbones symbol, along with the word TOXISCH carved deep into the metal.

This was it, I thought as I looked it over once more. This was what my dad had found and wanted to keep hidden from these drug runners. He had been keeping them from obtaining possibly one of the deadliest weapons in history.

After examining the torpedo thoroughly, we swam with the current back along the top of the wreck, this time focusing our attention on the starboard side of the vessel that was smashed up against the ledge. Leaning our bodies against the conning tower, we stopped for a moment and I checked my dive watch. We'd been down for an hour and a half and needed to allow time for safety stops on the way up.

Glancing at Scott, I motioned for us to head up and he gave the okay signal. Just as I reached to add some air into my BCD, I spotted a bright metallic flash reflecting back the light from my flashlight. Curious, I swam closer. It was a metal box, wedged right between the hull of the U-boat and the rocky ledge.

CHAPTER FOURTEEN

Less than a minute after we broke the surface, removed our mouthpieces and breathed in the fresh Caribbean air, we heard the sound of an engine cutting through the calm darkness like a knife. Looking up at the partly cloud-covered sky, we spotted Ange's Cessna cruising our direction from the north and dropping in altitude.

Reaching into my BCD, I pulled out the flare, removed it from its plastic housing and ignited the bright red flame to life. The blinding light radiated across the darkness, revealing a horizon that had become even more whitecapped since a few hours earlier.

Ange brought her small aircraft down easy, cruising into the wind, which blew in from the east and was getting stronger and stronger with every passing second. As if she'd done it a thousand times, Ange glided to less than thirty knots, then touched down, the two hollow metal floats making contact with the water's surface at the same time.

The Cessna bounced a few times as it slowed over the crests of the large open-ocean rollers.

As she pulled right alongside where Scott and I were treading water, I drowned my flare in the ocean and kicked towards the aircraft. It slowed to a stop and bobbed up and down in the waves as I made my way around to the starboard side.

Removing my fins, I reached up, wrapped my right hand around a metal handle and hoisted my body out of the water. I kept myself balanced on the shifting float as I unstrapped my rebreather and pulled it off my body, handing it to Ange through the open passenger door. A few seconds later, Scott and I were both inside, slamming the doors shut behind us and toweling off our dripping bodies as Ange executed a perfect takeoff.

Just as the Cessna transitioned from the rough, bouncy movements on the ocean's surface to the smooth, gentle cruising through the air, I noticed something below us. Leaning over and peering down through the glass, I spotted what looked like a dark speedboat, its sleek body being propelled through the water by a row of powerful outboard engines.

It was hard to tell in the darkness. The boat was far away, and it was moving at over seventy knots in the opposite direction that we were flying. But by the light of the moon, I thought I saw the massive dark frame of one of the Campos brothers.

"Shit!" I said, though not loud enough for anyone in the cockpit to hear me over the roar of the engine and the sound of the wind beating past us. I grabbed a headset hanging from a metal clip on the dash in front of me, donned it and spoke into the microphone.

"There's a boat down there," I said, motioning back through the starboard window.

Ange looked at me, surprised, then angled the joystick in her hands to turn right about ninety degrees, bringing the long silver streak of the boat's wake into view.

"Looks like a Cigarette," Scott said, peering through the glass in the backseat. "Thing's really moving!"

After getting a good look, Ange angled us back onto a western course, raising our altitude to two thousand feet.

"What's Jack's status?" I asked.

Ange manipulated a few buttons on her controls, then said, "Spoke to him thirty minutes ago. Said he was heading through Spanish Harbor Channel and just a few minutes out from Big Mangrove with two go-fast boats on his tail."

There was no use trying to communicate with Jack over the loud roar of the engines. Instead, I used the time to tell Ange what we'd found and discuss with Scott everything that we'd seen. Ange didn't circle around this time. There was no reason, since we were all certain that the Cigarette belonged to the Campos brothers and their fellow drug runners.

There was no doubt in our minds that they'd managed to find the site, or at least get pretty damn close. Though we didn't know if there was anyone left in their crew who could handle a dive that deep, we knew that they were resourceful and would probably reach the wreck in a day or two if not stopped.

Thirty minutes after takeoff, Ange brought us down easy and landed in the middle of Tarpon

Cove, easing the small aircraft around and pulling the floats right up against the dock. I opened the passenger door, jumped onto the dock and tied us off. Just as Ange killed the engine, I reached for the radio clipped to my belt.

"Jack," I said, holding the talk button. "What's your status?"

I released the button, and a few seconds later, Jack's voice came through the speaker. "We've got two in custody. One of the boats was captured, but the other managed to escape. No shots fired."

"Roger that."

"Did you find the Lone Wolf?"

"Affirmative. Along with her payload."

Scott and Ange unloaded our gear from the backseat, handing it to me so I could set it on the dock.

"What's your pos?" I asked Jack.

"En route to the marina with two Coasties."

I told Jack that we would meet him there, then clipped the radio back onto my belt. As we grabbed the gear bags and threw them over our shoulders, Scott dialed a number into his cell phone and talked to someone as we walked down the dock.

"I don't know how those guys followed me," Ange said, shaking her head.

"It's not your fault. Once they lost contact with the guys tailing us, I bet they sent every boat they have out scouring the ocean. Seeing the plane landing was inevitable, and having a boat that can push at over eighty knots helps a lot."

When we reached the parking lot, we loaded everything into the bed, then climbed inside and headed back towards Conch Harbor Marina. As I pulled us out of the driveway, Scott ended his phone call.

"That was my contact at Langley," he said. "He informed me he has something that we need to see."

A few minutes later, I turned into the parking lot of the marina and parked alongside three police vehicles in the front row. Through the windshield, I could see a group of police officers standing on the pathway leading down to the docks, huddled in a small circle and talking amongst themselves.

As I stepped out of my Tacoma, Charles emerged out of the group and walked towards us.

"I hear you got two of them," I said.

His face was all business, and on top of his normal police uniform, he was also wearing a black bulletproof vest and holding an MP-5 submachine gun in his hands.

"The plan worked smoothly until it came time to close on them," he said, his voice stern and powerful. "Those assholes were fast. The other boat got away."

"For now," Scott said, stepping out of the truck behind me.

Charles's eyes grew wide upon seeing Scott. "Senator Cooper?"

Scott stepped beside me and said, "We need to talk to you in private. We have information regarding where these guys are holding out at, and if we act fast, we can take them down before they find the wreck."

Charles listened intently and thought it over for a second. "So, that means you guys found it?"

I nodded. "And so did the Campos brothers." I moved towards the docks and added, "Join us for some coffee on my boat."

The four of us walked by the group of officers and headed down the mahogany steps towards the dock. I could see the two Coast Guard patrol boats Jack had referred to moored up against the temporary dock over by the fueling station. Three Coast Guardsmen were standing beside the cleats, dressed in full body armor and talking to Gus Henderson, the owner of the marina. The commotion had caused a handful of boaters to migrate out onto their decks, observing the goings-on while sipping a beer or smoking a cigarette.

Ange moved close to Charles and said, "You have the two men in custody, correct, Sheriff?"

"Yes, ma'am," he replied. "They're at the station right now, and first thing tomorrow, we'll be transferring them via armored vehicles to Homestead and then up to Miami. Both men have long criminal records, and we're confident it won't be long before we can lock them away for at least the next twenty years."

The four of us moved down the dock towards the Baia at slip twenty-four. I spotted Jack in the cockpit, talking to an officer who was holding a clipboard tightly in his hands and scribbling an occasional note. When we got close, I realized that it was Officer Kincaid.

"That's quite enough for now, Ben," Charles said as I stepped over the port gunwale.

The young officer turned around, wrote a quick note on his pad, then said, "I just have a few more questions, Sheriff."

"Then we will ask them later," he said sternly. "Now, head over to the parking lot, and have the guys head back to the station. Make sure Peterson stays for the night shift, and tell Howard to get some sleep and be standing by in the late morning for an update."

"Yes, sir," Kincaid said, then stepped over the transom and headed down the dock.

Jack was sitting in the rotating helm chair, staring into a flat screen that displayed a map of Spanish Harbor and portions of Big Pine Key as well as No Name Key. He smiled as he saw us step aboard, and when we asked him to join us in the salon for coffee, he told us he already had a pot brewing.

The five of us stepped in through the hatch, locked it behind us and gathered around the dining table. Under other circumstances, we'd be cracking open a bottle of champagne or going out on the town to celebrate. Finding a lost German U-boat was monumental, and this particular boat had disappeared completely from history, making the find even more spectacular. But we had a mission at hand, and until we took down the Campos brothers, there would be no cause for celebration.

As Scott opened his laptop and hooked it up to my flat-screen TV, I addressed the group. "As we've informed you, the clues my dad left me led us to the lost U-boat. And as he stated in his message, there was a torpedo stuck in the rock about a hundred feet ahead of its cone, jammed into a rocky ledge. Given the symbol etched into its metal casing, and the word *toxic* written in German, we have more than a good reason to believe that this torpedo is a biological weapon." I cleared my throat as I pointed to the map flattened out on the table. "We found it here, at the exact coordinates given, and after we surfaced and were being picked up by Ange, we spotted a blacked-out Cigarette cruising less than a quarter of a mile away from us."

"That's the same type of boats the guys following me were using," Jack said.

"And it's why one of them got away," Charles added. "As everyone here well knows, I'm sure, those boats were designed for speed and can easily hit eighty knots. Our patrol boats tried to catch it, but they lost it in Big Spanish Channel."

"So, that means they know where the wreck is," Jack said after thinking it over a moment.

"In all likelihood, yes," I said. "And while we were diving, we spotted something else wedged into the ledge on the ocean floor. A large metal box that was sunk much more recently and has nothing to do with the wreck. My guess is that the contents of this box are what these thugs are after, but I don't know for sure."

The salon went silent for a moment as Scott finished setting up his laptop. He sat down beside me on the white couch and set the HP laptop on top of the map on the table. Pressing a few keys, he brought up a satellite image on the flat-screen.

"Well, regardless of what's in that box, we need to take these guys down," Ange said.

We watched as Scott pressed a few keys on his laptop and zoomed in on what I instantly realized was Spanish Harbor, right where it met US-1. The image had a strange gray tinge, sort of like looking through a night vision scope. As he zoomed in a little more, I realized instantly what we were looking at.

"That's my boat," I said, staring at the top-down view of my Baia and a long white rippling wake behind it. Less than a mile behind my boat were two other boats.

"This was recorded earlier this evening," Scott said.

"How did you get this?" Charles said, amazed.

"I have contacts at Langley that specialize in global tracking and locations. I talked to them and had them watch and record everything that Logan's boat did from midnight until three o'clock this morning."

Sliding his fingers over a large trackpad, Scott eased forward on the recorded timeline, allowing us to see a fast version of Jack being followed by the drug runners. We watched as he piloted my boat under the bridge connecting Big Pine Key to West Summerland Key, cruising on a direct course for Big Mangrove.

"There!" Charles said, stepping forward and pointing at the screen. "You can see the Coast Guard and Navy boats spread out on the northern side of the small island."

"Yes," Scott said, slowing down the recording slightly.

The five of us kept our eyes glued to the screen, watching as Jack led the two boats around Big Mangrove and right into the trap the joint forces had set. Judging by the shape of the hull, the size of their wakes and the number of outboards clamped onto their transoms, it was easy to tell that they were both Cigarettes. One of them, however, was cruising a few hundred feet in front of the other as they maneuvered around the island, falling right into the trap.

Scott slowed the frames, playing it at normal speed as the two boats slowed and turned sharply upon realizing what was happening. The leading boat had no chance to make an escape. Before it had completed its dangerously sharp turn, two Coast Guard patrol boats had it surrounded. The drug runners raised their weapons but, quickly realizing that they had no chance of escape, they dropped them to the deck and held their hands high in the air. As the leading boat slowed to a stop, the third Coast Guard patrol boat and the Navy boat chased after the tailing drug runners, who had already completed their turn and were cruising full speed in the opposite direction.

"But what does this show us, other than what we already know?" Charles asked, shaking his head.

"Hold on," Scott said, punching a few keys. "I also told them to track any boats following the Baia in order to figure out where they're going."

"That's why you're the smart one," I said, grinning. "Now, let's see where these guys disappeared to."

The screen locked on to the trailing Cigarette, and we watched in real time as the boat sliced through the dark surface, flying across the water at well over eighty knots. In just a few minutes, the fleeing drug runners had tripled the distance between them and their pursuers. In the darkness of the night, it wasn't long before they'd escaped the patrol boats entirely, weaving around the numerous sporadic islands that litter the Lower Keys. We watched patiently as the boat continued, cruising along the southwest side of the Keys into the Gulf of Mexico.

"Looks like they're heading into the Contents," Jack said. "It makes sense. There're hundreds of uncharted islands out that way. It's a good place to hide. Mainlander boaters get lost out there all the time."

Ten minutes later, after zigging and zagging through narrow channels, the boat slowed and approached a small island, wrapping around and easing towards it from the southeast. The island, unlike most of the islands in the Content Keys, which were covered with nothing but thick mangroves and the occasional fishing camp, was surrounded by piles of large dark rocks. Zooming in closer, we saw the rectangular shape of a structure that, judging by its size, must have been a mansion.

The blacked-out Cigarette slowed into a narrow channel of deep water and cruised through a small gap in the rocks. A second later, it pulled up to a long dock alongside two other boats. The three men aboard quickly disembarked and headed inside the house.

"Wait a second," Jack said, focusing his eyes on the screen. "I know this place." The four of us looked at him intently, and he continued, "It's a private compound that belongs to Tom Steel."

Ange looked at him questioningly. "You mean, the Tom Steel? As in the famous movie star?"

"Yeah. He comes down here a few times each year, or so I've heard. Usually in the winter months, though. A lot of famous people own islands. It's a good way to get out of the spotlight for a little while."

"Wait a minute," I said, angling my head closer to the screen. "That's Blackett Key."

Jack nodded. "Yeah. It was originally owned by Ron Blackett, a multimillionaire businessman. Steel purchased it back in 2002, I believe."

"I've only ever seen it from a distance," I said. "Those walls surrounding the compound have got to be at least eight feet high. I've only ever caught faraway glimpses of the mansion beyond them."

"Looks like the perfect place for a group that wants to remain invisible," Scott said, searching over the satellite imagery of the compound. "It's close enough to reach just about anywhere in the Keys quickly with the right horsepower, yet almost completely hidden from civilization."

After examining the island compound for a few minutes, I turned to Charles. "We're gonna need the joint forces again on this one if we're gonna take them down. I mean, we could probably manage it on our own, but I know how much you hate it when people go and take the law into their own hands."

Charles smiled. "Tomorrow night?"

We all looked at each other and nodded in agreement.

"I suggest sending a few patrols over to the wreck site," Scott said.

"Already done," Charles replied.

Good, I thought. The last thing I wanted was for them to somehow get what they wanted, sweeping it from right under our noses before we had a chance to strike them in their heart.

"The Coast Guard has their men on shift work until we find these guys," Charles added.

"Working twelve-hour days and scouring the Keys for anything suspicious."

My resolve strengthened as I stared at the satellite image of the compound, my mind going to work instinctively, formulating an attack plan. These thugs had messed with the wrong guy when they'd killed my dad and tried to kill me back in Curacao. And now they were going to pay for that mistake.

We spent another hour and two more pots of coffee brainstorming ideas and coming up with a basic infiltration plan. The five of us had well-rounded knowledge that combined to plan and account for unexpected situations during a raid. It was almost zero four hundred when we finally decided to call it a night. Charles informed me that there would still be an officer in the lot as he left, walking down the dock and climbing into his sheriff police car.

As I walked alongside Jack towards the stern, he turned to face me. "I think your dad would be proud, bro."

I patted my old friend on the back. "I think he'd be even prouder after we bring these thugs to justice."

After locking the hatch and switching on my security system, I headed for the main cabin with Ange. With my mind racing with ideas and plans to strike the drug runners' compound, I hadn't realized just how tired I was. Moving into the main cabin, I collapsed onto the bed beside Ange and was asleep before my head hit the plush white pillow.

CHAPTER FIFTEEN

The following morning, I woke up with Ange sprawled out beside me, wearing only her panties. She had a long, lightly bronzed leg draped over my lower body, and her head rested against my upper chest. Her blond hair covered most of her stunning face, and it was close enough to smell the intoxicating scents of her shampoo and perfume.

Not wanting to wake her, I slowly reached over to my nightstand and grabbed my smartphone. Bringing the screen to life, I saw that it was just a few minutes past ten and I hadn't received any new messages. I brought up the weather forecast, and as if I'd summoned a tempest, I heard a few sporadic drops of rain hit the topside deck over my head, followed soon after a heavy tropical downpour.

The forecast predicted scattered showers all day and into the evening, with a high of ninety degrees. I'd made it about halfway into a Florida Keys summer, or rainy season, and could understand fully why most people only visited during the winter months. Though I didn't mind the rain and humidity or seeing a few extra millimeters of the mercury, I wasn't like most people.

I placed my phone back onto my nightstand and stayed in bed with my eyes shut, resting back on the pillow. I took occasional glances through a clear hatch over my head, watching as large raindrops hit the glass and flowed out of sight. I thought more about the Campos brothers and our plan to bring them down. I'd planned and executed attacks on enemy compounds before, both in the Navy and as a civilian, but this situation was different than all the others. To borrow the old cliché, this time it was personal.

Half an hour later Ange woke up, her face sliding up my body, stopping only when her lips met mine. She smiled as she blinked her eyes awake, revealing the crystalline shades of blue and turquoise behind her eyelids.

We took our time crawling out of bed and made our way barefoot into the salon for breakfast. The rains continued their torrent frenzy, pelting sheets of water into the windows and hatches and making it difficult to see much of anything outside. We sat around the dinette as we enjoyed a small fruit breakfast, talking over the events of the previous night.

"I think Sheriff Wilkes is wrong to have a large group storm the compound all at once," Ange said after taking a juicy bite of mango. "I read their files thoroughly, and these Campos brothers are notorious for booby traps and using explosives to take down their enemies. If we surround that place and just flood it with bodies, we'll take them out, yes, but we'll probably rack up a large body count of friendlies."

I nodded as I listened. Over the years, I'd learned that Ange was a brilliant tactician, and I agreed with her wholeheartedly. We both knew that a stealthy approach was the way to go about this situation. Taking down an enemy compound is good, but doing it without them even realizing that you're there until they have a gun aimed at their head is even better.

"But with these high walls and the flat landscape surrounding them, they'll be able to see approaching boats miles away," Ange said, staring at a map of the Content Keys and pointing at the small island where the drug runners were hiding out. "If someone were to sneak up on them underwater, they'd probably have to start from miles away to be safe."

Her words shoved an idea into my mind. "No farther than the Marquesas Keys are from Neptune's Table," I said with a grin, referring to the time when Scott and I had used powerful sea scooters along with our rebreathers to sneak up on Black Venom from six miles away.

She glanced up at me, then looked across the salon, biting her lip in that cute *I'm thinking it over* way that she usually did when mulling over an idea.

Her eyes drifted back to meet mine, and she smiled. "I think you just want an excuse to use your favorite toys."

I laughed and smiled back at her. "Of course I do. Those things are fun as hell. But that doesn't mean that I'm wrong."

By noon, most of the rain had abated, leaving behind patches of deep blue sky above the humid air. Stepping outside for a moment, I felt a nice ocean breeze blow against my face, bringing with it the scents of the Caribbean. I'd only been standing out in the cockpit for a few minutes when I heard the sound of flip-flops shuffling towards me down the dock.

Glancing in the direction of the sound, I saw Jack walking towards my boat, holding a small cooler in one hand and a black mesh bag full of spiny-tailed lobster in the other. Lobster season had just opened up a few months earlier, so I knew the bag would be full of bugs well beyond regulation size.

"Fire up the grill, bro," he said, handing the bag to me over the gunwale. "I'm starving after yesterday, and I'm betting on another long night tonight."

"You just woke up?" I asked, genuinely amazed.

He shrugged. "When you're born into a line of beach bums five generations back, you get pretty good at it." He winked, then climbed aboard.

Reaching behind the helm chair, I pulled out my grill that folded sleekly into the side. Then I opened the propane valve, pressed the starter button and had the grill hot in under a minute.

"Got these just yesterday afternoon after cruising over the wrecked U-boat," he said, grabbing them one by one from the bag. "We anchored down at Neptune's Table. Everybody always wants to see that wreck now. It's got to be the most popular dive site in the Keys ever since you found the *Intrepid*."

"You mean ever since *we* found it," I said. "And I'm willing to bet that in just a few short months, it won't be the most popular dive site anymore."

"Yeah," he said, killing each lobster as humanely as possible, removing the tails and handing them to me so I could douse them in Swamp Sauce and set them on the sizzling grill. "People will come from all over to see that."

The hatch door opened and Ange appeared with her head tilted upwards, clearly enjoying the smell of the fresh-grilled seafood as much I was. Of all the many reasons why I loved living in the Florida Keys, the supply of fresh seafood was right near the top of the list.

Before firing up the grill, I'd sent a text to Scott, and he arrived at the marina just as we sat down to eat. Ange and I told him the ideas we'd come up with, and he told us a few of his own, including his plan to use a government-issue advanced drone with a night vision camera to observe the compound during the strike.

"It's got a long range and is incredibly quiet," he said. "I've seen it flown within a hundred feet of people without them even realizing it was there."

I cut into a couple of lemons and squeezed the juice over my plate of lobster tails. It tasted delicious, and I ate four of them myself before calling it quits.

"The plan is set for tonight, then. I'll swim into the compound using my rebreather and sea scooter. Then, with Ange providing support from Cutoe Key, I'll take down the guards patrolling around the wall. Once the outside of the compound is clear of tangos, I'll take out their generator and radio in for support. Scott, you'll be on my Zodiac. Its draft is shallow enough to where you'll have no trouble cruising all around the rocks. Jack, you'll be on the Baia and cruise in with the patrol boats to provide backup and to extract us. Charles has informed me that he will have two police boats hidden from view to the north of the island that will be able to reach the compound in less than three minutes."

"Hooyah," Scott said. "These pirates won't know what hit them."

I nodded. "That's the idea."

"And how many bad guys do you think will be there?" Ange asked.

"Based on the satellite imagery I'd estimate around ten," Scott said. "But no more than fifteen."

"I agree," I said. "It's hard to tell for sure since we've taken out a handful already. But we've got to plan for the worst."

After we finished stuffing our stomachs full of all-we-could-eat grilled lobster, I called Charles and told him the finalized plan. I went over every detail, making sure he understood everything. One small misunderstanding or miscommunication can bring down an entire attack; I'd seen it happen before. After I finished, he thought it over for a moment.

"And we'll be on comms the entire time?" he asked.

"Yes. You, myself, Scott, Ange, and Jack will all be tuned in to the same frequency. I'll be in contact when I reach the compound and inform everyone once the outside is clear."

"Okay," he said. "I'll cruise over there with two police boats just after sundown. We'll approach from the northwest and remain out of sight until you contact me."

"Understood," I said. And once we were in agreement and he was about to hang up, I told him to hang on. "One more thing. Ange has been researching these Campos brothers pretty extensively. She found patterns of use of explosives and booby traps. We have to assume that they have the place rigged to blow sky-high."

"Great," Charles said. "I'll have the men informed. See you tonight."

By three in the afternoon, gray clouds again blotted out the blue sky and warm tropical sun. A few drops of rain hit the deck, and the four of us headed into the salon.

CHAPTER SIXTEEN

The distant sun sank down into the western horizon, glowing streaks of vibrant reds and oranges shining through the cracks in the cloud-covered sky. I try to make a habit of watching the sunrise and sunset every chance I can. There's something about watching the light disappear from the sky, watching the symphony of colors play their tune, bringing an end to the day.

With the help of Jack and Scott, I pulled my orange Zodiac up over the large swim platform jutting out the stern of the Baia and secured it tightly. Then I headed down the dock and along the waterfront towards the marina office. Glancing through the glass, I saw Gus lounging on a beanbag chair and staring into a boating magazine. Hearing my approach through the screen door, he came to his feet and walked over to me.

"Logan!" he said. "What can I do for you?"

"Just need to get into the shed, Gus."

He nodded, then pushed open the door and strode beside me. Grabbing a ring of keys from his pocket, he picked a small one and stuck it into a small padlock securing two large wooden doors beside the office.

"I should really make you a copy," he said as he pulled open the wooden doors with a loud squeak of their hinges. "Your kayak's right where you left it. Paddles are on top."

"Thanks," I said, using a small cart to roll it out.

"No problem. Pretty nasty evening for a paddle, though."

I smiled. "Maybe it will pass."

A few minutes later, I rolled it over to the Baia, where Jack and I lashed it to the deck at the base of the sunbed.

"Ah, I remember that kayak," Scott said, reminiscing about just a month earlier, when he and I had paddled to Monte Cristo Island and had taken down Benito Salazar, the notorious Cuban gang leader. I'd bought it at a garage sale and had always loved the sit-atop styles, which are easy to climb in and out of even on open water.

Glancing at my dive watch, I saw that it was just past 2000.

"Alright, everyone ready?" I asked, glancing around at the group.

I unhooked the power cable and the freshwater hose, then untied the mooring lines form the cleats. Starting up the Baia's massive twin six-hundred-horsepower engines, I eased us away from the dock and out of the marina. Once I'd cleared the no-wake zone, I quickly brought us up on plane, cruising through Fleming Cut and around Garrison

Bight Mooring Field. I put us on a course heading due northeast towards the Contents. Moments later, the final remnants of the sun vanished beneath the Gulf of Mexico.

By the time we reached National Key Deer Refuge, the sky was dark, the silver half-moon only visible through occasional breaks in the clouds. The rain had picked up while we'd cruised, but as I pulled alongside the southern end of Cutoe, there was only a faint drizzle. Since the Baia's draft is three feet and the waters surrounding Cutoe are just a foot or two deep, I'd brought my two-person kayak so Ange could paddle to the shore.

After being down in the salon for about fifteen minutes, Ange appeared through the hatch, wearing black all-weather pants, tactical boots, and a skintight long-sleeved camouflage shirt. Her blond hair was tied back and hidden behind a black beanie, and she had streaks of dark war paint across her face. I'd seen her dressed that way during operations before, but it always amazed me how such an innocent-looking blonde woman could transition into a warrior badass.

"I'll set up a sniper station just there," she said, pointing towards the western shore of Cutoe. She'd grabbed a plastic hard case that contained her collapsible Remington .338 Lapua Magnum sniper rifle, a weapon she was so proficient at firing that it was more like an extension of her own body.

"Call me on the radio once you're in position," I said, unlashing the straps from the kayak and easing it slowly down into the water.

The current was stagnant for the moment, so I was able to let it float beside the starboard side of the Baia while Ange loaded it up. Since she only needed one paddle, I left the second one stored against the inside of the gunwale, then offered my hand as she stepped over the side. She sat down in the rear seat, then secured all of her gear in front of her.

Grabbing the paddle, she glanced up at me, then smiled and said, "Good luck."

"You too," I replied, smiling back at her.

She dipped the paddles into the water, gliding across the surface in a sharp turn to starboard before heading straight for Cutoe. After watching her paddle into the darkness a few hundred feet, I turned around and went to work getting all of my gear. I already had my rebreather out on the sunbed along with my fins, mask, and snorkel.

While Scott performed the predive checks on my rebreather, I headed into the guest cabin and grabbed a large plastic hard case from the closet. Carrying it out onto the deck, I unclasped the hinges and pulled open the lid, revealing a top-of-the-line Aquanaut Pro sea scooter. It was one of the ones Arian Nazari, the billionaire oil tycoon who'd helped us with the Aztec treasure, had given to me, and it was capable of dragging someone through the water at over seven knots.

After checking that it turned on without a hitch and that the battery was good, I switched it off and set it beside the rest of my gear on the sunbed.

"Rebreather's all set," Scott said. "The tanks are about half-full but will be fine for this short of a dive."

"I have a full one down in the guest cabin," I said. "I don't want to take any chances."

Nodding, he headed through the hatch and came out a second later with the replacement. As he switched them out, I helped Jack untie my Zodiac and lower it off the swim platform and into the water.

"Just be wary of the currents in these shallow waters, bro," Jack said. "Tide's about to turn any second, and I've seen it push four knots in places around here."

I nodded and glanced over the starboard bow at the dark outline of Cutoe. We were a little over a mile from Blackett Key as the crow flies, and I decided that this would be as good of a starting point as any. We had cover from behind Cutoe Key, and I could follow along the reef line, swimming around the point before changing course and heading towards Blackett.

I knew it wouldn't be an easy dive. As if Jack had summoned the tides himself, I could already notice the water on the surface begin to flow by us ever so slowly. There are also hundreds of tiny islands, shoals, and sandbars scattered all over this part of the Keys, making underwater navigation difficult, especially at night.

Twenty minutes after Ange had paddled into the darkness, I heard her voice over my radio earpiece. I'd installed the earpiece so I could communicate in the compound without giving away my position and had been waiting for Ange's com.

"In position," she said, her voice calm.

"Roger that," I replied.

I set the radio down on the seat beside me, then grabbed my black O'Neill dry suit and put it on over my clothes. Once it was on and snug, I grabbed my rebreather from the sunbed and strapped it onto my back. I had my Sig, a silencer and an extra magazine sealed in a waterproof bag, along with a pair of tactical boots and a small towel.

Grabbing my fins, mask, and dive knife, I stepped onto the swim platform and plopped back onto the transom. Once there, I slipped into my neoprene booties and strapped my titanium dive knife to my inner right calf.

"You're all set back here," Scott said, and I heard the distinct low-pitched sounds of the rebreather starting up.

Jack handed me the radio, and I spoke into the mouthpiece. "Charles, I'm entering the water now."

"Understood," he said a few seconds later. "We're standing by."

I placed the radio inside the waterproof bag beside my Sig, then sealed it back up and secured it to my BCD using two carabiners.

"Hand me the scooter," I said, and a second later, Jack held it on the transom beside me.

He also handed me a long coil of nylon rope and said, "For the three Cigarettes."

I smiled, strapped the rope to the side of my BCD, and replied, "That's good thinking there, Jack."

I donned my fins and mask, then turned to them and said, "See you guys on the other side."

Then I gave them both a fist bump, positioned the mouthpiece between my teeth and stood up. Gripping tightly to the sea scooter, I faced my body aft and took a giant step out into the dark water.

CHAPTER SEVENTEEN

I splashed into the warm water and quickly sank to the bottom only five feet below. Still facing the same direction I had been when I stepped in, I flattened my body and kicked for about thirty seconds before reaching slightly deeper water.

Once I was in ten feet or so, I held my sea scooter out in front of me, switched it on and accelerated the propeller. My grip tightened to prevent the device from running away, and within a few seconds I was slicing through the water at its max speed of seven knots.

I couldn't help but smile as I navigated west through the channel with the shallows surrounding Cutoe just a few hundred feet to my right. In order to approach the compound unseen, I had to rely on the little moonlight that trickled through the clouds above instead of my flashlight. While in the Navy, I'd trained extensively at night and had learned to use my number of normal kicks in order to determine an approximation of how far I'd traveled. Using the sea scooter made determining my location more difficult, but I was able to navigate around the western edge of Cutoe without much trouble.

Turning the sea scooter to the right, I performed a long sweeping turn and put myself on a direct line with Blackett using my compass for guidance. I'd studied satellite imagery of the water surrounding the compound for a few hours the day before and had planned out my route, so I had a pretty good idea where I was going.

Jack had been right about the current. The longer I stayed underwater, the worse it got as the gravitational pull of the moon shifted with the rotation of the Earth. As I entered a shallower section of water past the tip of Cutoe, the current nearly forced my body into a barrel roll as it tried to pull me north out towards the Gulf. I countered this by aiming the tip of the scooter to the right, keeping myself on as straight of a line as possible.

Occasionally I'd have to adjust my course to deviate around a shallow section of water or a small patch of mangroves, but for the most part, I kept Blackett straight ahead of me.

As I glided through the dark water, I passed by hundreds of fish, their scales reflecting the little moonlight that trickled down from the night sky above. I swam right over a few large flounder that lay nestled in the sand and mud below, their flat bodies scurrying away as I moved passed them.

Roughly fifteen minutes after dropping into the water, I reached the opening into the channel that led straight into the compound on Blackett Key. The channel was only about ten feet wide and five feet deep at its shallowest point. The current in the channel was strong as water flowed down into it and swirled around, kicking up dirt and sediment from the bottom. The visibility wasn't great, but all I had to do was follow the channel and I knew that I'd eventually reach the compound.

Keeping my head aimed forward and my eyes focused through the swirling, shallow water, I spotted something dark ahead of me. A moment later, I realized that it was the rocks that surrounded the island, forming a complete circle aside from the small opening ahead of me.

Bingo, I thought as I eased back on the throttle. No longer requiring the sea scooter, I slowed to a stop and then turned it off, losing all forward momentum. It didn't take long for the shifting current to show me who was boss and push me up against the left side of the channel. Holding my arm out, I absorbed the shock and propped my back against the hard bedrock.

I set the sea scooter down under a small jutting rock, making sure that it was secure before forcing my legs into the side and shoving off as hard as I could. My body launched forward and I gave a few hard kicks until the current stopped and the water turned relatively still around me.

I'd just passed by the rocks and could see the moat surrounding the compound that stretched in both directions beside me. The water inside the rocks was only five feet deep, so I moved slowly and stayed as close to the shoreline as possible.

I moved past two rows of wood braces that held up the dock overhead and saw the three boats tied off, the dark outlines of their hulls bobbing up and down slightly. I grabbed the nylon rope strapped to my BCD, uncoiled it, and cut it into three separate lengths. Then I used each length to foul the props clamped to the stern of the three Cigarettes. *These guys aren't going anywhere*, I thought as I glanced in approval at my handiwork.

Finning a little farther along the bottom of the dock, I knew that I was getting close to the exit point I'd chosen. When I reached a point where the dock widened, I slid out of my rebreather and took one final breath before shutting it off and letting it rest against the seafloor.

My waterproof bag in hand, I unclipped the carabiners and slowly stood up, my six-foot-two frame easily breaking the surface. As my head broke out into the night air, I slid my mask down, then took a look around, getting my bearings and checking for any sign of movement. The only sounds I heard, however, were the rocking of the boats against the dock and the gentle flapping of a flag hanging atop a nearby pole.

As my ears adjusted, I heard what I thought was a television coming from the inside of the compound. I reached down into the water and slipped off my fins. Grabbing onto the wooden support braces, I pulled myself along the bottom of the dock and looked at the large concrete wall that surrounded the complex.

When I didn't see anyone nearby, I swam forward and pulled myself up onto the rocky shore. Moving in a crouching position, I kept my body hidden beneath a metal footbridge that led from the dock to a door built into the concrete wall. I moved across the few feet of white sandy beach between the rocks and the wall.

Once I reached a spot at the base of the wall beside two small palm trees, I slid out of my dry suit. Then I opened my waterproof bag, grabbed my small towel and put on my pair of black low-top tactical boots. After spending a few seconds drying off, I pulled out my Sig and holstered it to my right thigh, then strapped my dive knife to my calf just below it. Reaching for the radio, I inserted the earpiece and switched it on.

"Reached the island," I whispered. "No tangos outside walls. Stand by."

A second later I heard Scott's voice as he said, "Logan, we've spotted three tangos outside the house using the drone. One on patrol and two up on a second-story balcony."

"Roger that," I replied.

I slid the earpiece wire under my shirt and clipped the small radio to the inside of my pants. Then I gathered up my dry suit, booties, fins, and mask, stowed them inside my dry bag and hid it in a tight space between one of the palm trees and the wall, completely hidden from view.

"Alright," I whispered to myself as I shifted along the base of the wall, listening for any sounds.

I soon realized that the sound I'd thought was a television was actually a radio, though I couldn't see its source. I only knew that it was high up, probably coming from an open second-story window or a porch. Moving along the wall, I soon found a portion of the top that dipped down a little.

I took one final look around the outside, then moved away from the wall, turned around, and took two powerful strides back towards it. Forcing my left heel into the sand, I launched my body high into the air, gripped my right boot along the wall and kicked myself up. I extended my arms above me, easily reaching the top as I wrapped my fingers around the rough concrete edge. I waited in that position for a moment, with my elbows bent at ninety-degree angles and my head slowly rising over the crest to get a view of the inside.

The inside of the compound was mostly dark, with only a few dim lights glowing from inside the first and second floors of the house. The only movement I saw initially was two men on a second-story porch that was partly covered and separated from the main house, making it look more like a lookout tower than a place for a celebrity to get away and relax.

One of the guys was sitting inside a covered area, listening to the radio and the other was standing along a handrail and staring out over the ocean. The structure was almost hidden from view around the right side of the house and was surrounded on both sides by rows of coconut trees. The grounds were very well kept, and to the left I spotted a large swimming pool with a waterfall, though it wasn't flowing, and a diving board.

As I drew my gaze down towards the inside base of the wall, I spotted a guy slowly walking counterclockwise around the house. He took intermittent puffs of a cigarette in his right hand and had what appeared to be an AR-15 rifle hanging by a strap across his chest. I took one more look around, making sure that there was no one else in sight. As the guy below walked right underneath me, I pulled my body up quietly. Crouching on the top of the wall for a split second, I threw my body over the side and dropped towards my unsuspecting enemy below.

I slammed into his upper body, knocking him to the ground as I forced the tip of my elbow into the back of his head. His body went limp as I hit the grass, causing him to collapse onto his back. In less than a second, it was over. The guy didn't have time to realize what had happened, let alone make even the slightest sound.

I went silent and looked around the compound, making sure nobody had heard my attack, then grabbed him by his shins and dragged his unconscious body behind a large dried-up fountain with a cherub statue in the middle. He'd wake up in about an hour with a terrible headache, but other than that, he'd be fine.

Once he was out of view, I directed my attention back to the two guys up on the terrace. As I'd hoped, they hadn't moved at all, nor had they given any indication that they'd heard something happen. I moved in the shadows of the compound, stepping from a patch of green grass and onto a cobblestone pathway that weaved in and out of old-style statues, planter boxes, flowering bushes, and small koi ponds. I could hear voices coming from inside the house beside me, but they were too muffled to understand what they were saying.

When I reached the terrace where I saw the two thugs, I quietly jumped, grabbed hold of an overhanging support beam and pulled myself up. I kept my knees bent and my body low, my chest pressed against the wall. Just a few inches above my head was an open window with light bleeding out and the sounds of a Spanish radio station.

Peeking over the windowsill, which was only partially blocked by a fancy curtain, I saw one of the thugs seated in a white wicker chair. He was well built, with coffee-colored skin and a solid black goatee. He wore a blue polo shirt and a faded pair of jeans. In his lap was a radio, and on the end table beside him was what looked like a .44 Magnum revolver.

Leaning back into the chair, he closed his eyes and almost dozed off before jerking his head and blinking a few times.

"How in the hell does Pedro expect us to stay awake with only this damn radio?" the guy sitting down said. But the guy standing against the railing just outside the open doorway didn't respond. "Carlos, bring up more coffee."

I didn't have a good view of the guy outside the door, but he sounded younger.

"That's Manuel's job," the guy outside said.

"Well, then, go and tell Manuel to bring more coffee!" the man fired back.

The younger man sighed. "Fine. I'll try him on the radio."

Shit, I thought, assuming that Manuel was the man I'd encountered a few minutes earlier who was snoozing under a fountain. The guy outside was holding an assault rifle in his hands and I knew that the older guy could grab his revolver and have it trained on me in half a second. Reaching for my earpiece, I held the button and whispered into the small microphone.

"Ange, do you have a visual on the two guys on the sundeck?"

"I see only one guy," she replied. "He's holding what looks like a rifle and standing against a metal railing. Wait, he's reaching for something in his pocket."

I didn't have time to explain the situation. If he tried contacting Manuel, he could sound an alarm and screw up everything.

"Five-second countdown on my mark," I whispered. "Ready, mark."

Sensing the timer tick down in my head, I grabbed my silenced Sig from my leg holster and adjusted my footing. I had my boots planted firmly, each on a separate brace about three feet apart. Rising up, I'd just glanced over the windowsill when I heard a bullet strike the body of the guy outside.

His body lurched backward, and before he'd even hit the ground, I was standing with my Sig aimed straight at goatee's face. His eyes grew wide and he tried to say something as his right hand gravitated towards his revolver on the table beside him. Before a sound came out of his mouth, I squeezed the trigger, sending a 9mm round screaming across the room and exploding into the thug's forehead.

His head jerked backward in a mushy mess, blood and brain splattered along the wall behind him. Sliding my Sig back into its holster, I pushed myself up through the window and landed silently on the hardwood floor. I moved past the dead guy sitting in the wicker chair and found the other guy on the ground just outside the door. His body was bent awkwardly with his back against the wall and his legs dangling down the top two steps of a staircase.

Ange's sniper rifle had a top-of-the-line suppressor, allowing her to fire the .338 rounds while barely making a sound. Glancing in Ange's direction, I smiled and mouthed the words *thank you*. A second later, her voice came over the speaker in my earpiece.

"That's a case of Paradise Sunsets," she said.

I shook my head as I bent down and dragged the corpse into the cover of the room, placing him on the floor at the other guy's feet. Then I moved silently back outside and down the wooden stairs. I knew that it was only a matter of time before someone tried to contact one of the three incapacitated thugs, so I moved with purpose.

The outside looked clear of all hostiles, but I still kept to cover in case someone inside the house was watching through a window. Moving towards the northeast side of the compound, I came to a small shed, pressed my ear against the wall and heard a large rumble from within.

Grabbing the brass doorknob, I entered the shed, shut the door behind me and flipped on a small overhead light. The rumble I'd heard was exactly what I'd thought it was: the generator. It looked to be industrial grade and was about six feet wide and four feet tall. On its side it had a label plate that said that it was sixty kilowatts and also had controls for turning it on and off.

I glanced over the simple instructions momentarily, then pulled open a square of metal backing, revealing wires and hoses connecting to the engine. Reaching for my earpiece, I held down the small button.

"Stand by for securing power," I said. After hearing a quick reply from each of the four on the line, I added, "Securing power."

I removed my hand from the earpiece, then grabbed my flashlight from my pocket and switched it on. Removing the plastic cover surrounding the controls, I quickly depressed the red emergency shutoff button, causing the engine to sputter for a second and then go silent. As the light overhead went out, I shined the beam of my flashlight into the back of the machine.

With a firm grip, I ripped the power cord free where it connected to the generator, then did the same with the fuel line, causing a small amount of fuel to flow out onto the ground. It had only taken a few seconds to turn off and disable the generator, but I knew I had to move.

Switching off my flashlight, I shouldered through the door and exited back into the warm evening air. I heard a few shouts coming from inside the mansion, followed soon after by heavy footsteps moving in my direction. Charles had said it would take them three minutes to reach the compound, and I estimated it would take Scott around two. That meant that I had time to kick some ass before the cavalry arrived.

I saw the dark outline of two thugs stomping towards me just as I crouched behind a small Jamaican caper tree. They were both well built, and both carried a pistol in one hand as they moved confidently through the door and towards the generator shed. I waited until they were right beside me, then pounced on them from the shadows, grabbing the first guy forcefully by his gun hand and jerking his body around while simultaneously punching him square in the jaw.

As his body lurched and headed for the ground, I hit the second thug with a sweeping kick just as he was about to level his pistol at me. His legs flew out from under him and he launched backwards, his head slamming against the cobblestone path. In an instant, I grabbed a nearby potted plant and slammed the hardened clay against his forehead, causing it to shatter and his body to go limp.

With both guys down, I dropped the guy's pistol, then retrieved my Sig from my holster as I headed for the partly open door just a few big strides in front of me. Clearly someone had heard the commotion outside and was yelling just inside the door. Keeping my Sig raised, I ducked to the side and waited for the door to swing open wildly before taking a shot. A big-bellied guy with a white button-up shirt looked like a deer caught in the headlights as I put two rounds straight into his chest, causing him to fall backwards and drop the sawed-off shotgun in his hands.

Hearing shouts and the barking of orders coming from the center of the house, I stepped over the large dead thug and moved swiftly through the open door. Instead of a hallway or side bedroom, I walked right into the massive living room of the open-concept mansion. The emergency lighting had already switched on, illuminating only portions of the room and leaving the corners in darkness. There was a kitchen to my left, and beyond a sea of scattered sofas, recliners and tables was a wall of windows and a sliding glass door that led out to a swimming pool beyond.

I moved quickly along a side wall, keeping to the shadows as I heard the sound of footsteps coming from the second floor. Just a few seconds after entering the house, I spotted movement coming from a wide, fancy wooden staircase. The shadow materialized into a thug holding an Uzi and staring straight at me. He was running down the stairs, and as he spotted me, he sent a spray of bullets in my direction that splintered the furniture and shattered the glass doors of the kitchen cabinets behind me.

I dropped to the deck as bullets whizzed just a few feet above me, then fired off a round that struck him in the left knee. His left leg gave out beneath his weight as he moved down the stairs, and his body flew forward, tumbling violently before coming to a stop headfirst on the hardwood floor. In addition to multiple other bones, I distinctly heard his neck crack as he hit the bottom and watched as his body turned lifeless.

Rising to my feet, I ran for the stairs, keeping my Sig raised and ready to pull the trigger at the slightest sign of movement. I made quick work of the stairs, taking them three at a time until I reached the top. I came to a long, wide hallway with rows of white wooden doors on one side. As I moved towards the source of the sounds, I saw a door crack open in front of me. Sprinting towards the door, I fired off two shots into a thug as he appeared through the crack, then tackled him to the ground, shattering the door from its frame.

As his body slammed into the ground beneath me, I rolled into the room and raised my Sig. In an instant, I was greeted by a metal baseball bat that struck my right shoulder, causing my body to jerk sideways onto the hardwood floor. Intense pain shot through my body, radiating from my shoulder.

A thug kicked my Sig from my hands, then bent down and grabbed me tightly by my shirt collar. He was short but built like a bull, his muscles screaming out of a black tank top as he lifted me over his head and threw me onto a massive bed. I rolled to minimize the effect of the blow, slid off the silk sheets and gazed back at my opponent. He had dark skin and was wearing a backward ball cap as he snarled and moved towards me. As I searched for a weapon, I heard a loud, booming voice from a dark corner of the giant master bedroom.

"Stop!" a man growled from the shadows, causing the beast of a man in front of me to grudgingly freeze in his tracks.

It was a voice I recognized instantly, and a second later, two massive frames appeared from the far side of the room. Both men moved with powerful strides towards the center of the room, where a pair of emergency lights shined down from the ceiling. Pedro Campos was the first to enter the light. His gigantic frame and his jet-black Mohawk that streaked across his clean-shaven head were unmistakable. His dark brown eyes stared fiercely into mine, and he had a grotesque burn scar along his left cheek. A second later, his brother, Hector, moved into the light beside him.

At six foot five and at least 250 pounds, the twin brothers looked more like WWE fighters than MMA. They both wore jeans and thick-soled boots, making them look even bigger than they were.

"You just entered freely into the lion's den, Logan Dodge," Pedro said. He continued to step towards me alongside his brother, and I moved out from behind the side of the bed. Squeezing his hands into fists, he cracked his knuckles and shot me an evil grin. "Let's dance."

The short thug with the backward hat stepped out of the way, letting the two behemoths have an open lane as they stepped towards me at the foot of the bed. I remembered watching a few of their fights on pay-per-view, and they'd usually ended with a quick knockout. But while these two thugs were highly trained fighters, I was a highly trained killer. I hadn't trained to knock guys down or to make them tap out in the SEALs or in my recent years of employment. I'd trained to kill bad guys as quickly and efficiently as possible. My internal clock informed me that I had about sixty seconds before the others would arrive.

Yeah, let's fucking dance.

Since they'd both been professional fighters, I was surprised when neither of them shifted into an athletic stance. They just moved towards me, their heavy boots stomping into the floor. Pedro reached me first, swinging his left fist towards my face in a powerful hook. I bobbed my head back just in time to feel the wind brush by my face as his fist flew by.

Planting his left leg on the floor, he transitioned right into a sidekick, launching his right leg towards my chest. His leg shattered the bedpost between us, making contact with my left shoulder and hurling my body across to the other side of the bed.

I rolled to my feet, bracing myself against a chest of drawers just as Hector appeared beside me. He yelled violently as he threw two quick jabs my way, landing one square in my chest that almost knocked the wind out of me. I hadn't fought anyone with such a combination of speed and strength in a hell of a long time, and it forced me to heighten my senses and reflexes.

He jerked towards me and straightened his left leg, trying to hit me with a front kick. I weaved to the side, then grabbed his leg and twisted it back, causing him to grunt in pain. Gripping the back of his head with my left hand, I slammed it hard into the chest of drawers, smashing the wood to splinters.

As I reared my right fist back to hit him with another blow, my body was struck by Pedro, who appeared to my right and threw me against the wall. He forced his fists straight for my head in rapid succession, giving me only a fraction of a second to react as they flew by just inches from my head and broke through the sheetrock beside my face.

As I tried to counter his blows, he swept my legs out from under me, causing my body to fall backward onto the hardwood floor. In an instant, he jumped on top of me, sending punch after painful punch into my face before squeezing his strong hands around my neck.

"You look just like your father did before he died," he snarled, his lips contorting to form a sinister smile.

Rage burned within me, and I felt a surge of strength take over. Reaching over my head, I grabbed a wooden drawer, pulled it out and broke it over Pedro's head. As his grip loosened, I punched him in the nose, feeling the fragile bones crack beneath my knuckles. He yelled and tried to retaliate, but before he could, I threw him off me, grabbed a wooden shard from the broken drawer and stabbed him in the chest with it. Blood oozed out of his white tee shirt as I forced the splintered wood deeper, then ripped it out and slashed it across his face.

Forcing my body forward and flinging my legs under me, I landed on my feet in the blink of an eye and hit him with the strongest front kick I'd ever hit anyone with, catapulting his body backward and launching him off the ground. As his massive body fell onto the bed, the frame collapsed under his weight and crashed to the floor. Hector yelled and ran towards me, holding the metal baseball bat the short guy had hit me with when I'd entered. Before he could rear back to swing at me, I surprised him by lunging towards him and tackling him to the ground.

We tumbled a few times before I managed to knock the bat from his hands. Rolling me over with my back against the floor, he tried to hurl his meaty right fist into my face. But I countered by digging my heels into his chest and leg pressing him as hard as I could. I launched his body backward, and he slammed to the floor with a loud, ground-shaking thud.

As I jumped to my feet, I heard yelling coming from the first floor. A second later, the short muscular guy stormed back into the bedroom, his face filled with anger as bullets rattled against the door frame just inches behind him.

"There's fucking more of them!" he snarled, looking at the two Campos brothers. "They have the place surrounded."

Hector was still shaking off the blow, but Pedro was on his feet and moved towards the short guy, who met him in the side of the room. He didn't hesitate or waste a second thinking over the guy's words. Instead, he grabbed the short guy by his shirt collar and said, "Get to the Jet Ski!"

Then he pushed the guy aside towards the nearby open window, and the guy jumped out onto a balcony. I jumped to my feet and hit Pedro in his head with a powerful side kick that for any normal-sized man would be a knockout blow. He fell sideways and tried to shake it off as footsteps echoed up from the stairway. As I reared back to kick him again, he rolled to the side and reached for my Sig, which was still resting on the floor.

Gripping it with his strong hands, he turned to aim it at me. But before he could fire, I took a powerful step and dove in his direction, forcing the barrel of the weapon aside as I tackled him onto a fancy silver couch. His finger squeezed the trigger repeatedly, causing a barrage of bullets to explode out and scream across the room.

In my peripheral vision, I watched as the rounds riddled holes up Hector's back as he struggled to his feet, causing him to lurch in pain and topple forward onto a small end table. The table shattered, and he hit the floor hard as blood oozed out of his massive lifeless body. As Pedro stopped firing and forced me aside, he realized what he'd done.

"Motherfucker!" he snarled as he turned and stared back into my eyes.

Veins bulged out of his neck and arms as he tried once more to aim the barrel of my Sig at me. I grunted and gritted my teeth, using all my strength to keep it drawn away from me. Our arms shook as he squeezed the trigger, exploding a succession of 9mm rounds just inches away from the top of my head. The bullets whizzed past, splintering into the door frame behind me and causing the guys out in the hallway to stop and move back for cover.

After what felt like an eternity, the slider on my Sig locked back and the hammer clicked audibly a few times but didn't strike a round. The magazine was empty, and as I tried to break free of his grasp, he yelled wildly and struck my forehead with my Sig's handle, jerking me back in a haze.

As the footsteps grew louder just outside the doorway, Pedro knew that he was surrounded and turned and lunged for the open window. My legs wobbled as I struggled to rise to my feet and shake away the stars that were swirling around my head. I stepped towards Pedro, but before I could reach him, he'd already jumped through the window and disappeared into the night air.

CHAPTER EIGHTEEN

I ran over to the windowsill as fast as I could and searched the darkness. Pedro was nowhere to be seen on either the balcony or the roof, and a second later, I turned around to see Scott standing in the doorway. He had a Glock 19 gripped with both hands and raised chest height out in front of him. As he stepped into the bedroom, he took a quick look around at all the destroyed furniture, the shattered glass, and Hector's bullet-riddled body lying facefirst on the floor in a pool of blood.

"Holy shit, Logan," he said as he stepped towards me.

"Pedro's getting away," I said, my voice intense as I reached for the radio still clipped to the inside of my pants.

No longer needing to be stealthy, I ripped the earpiece plug free and held on to the rubber side button.

"This is Logan," I said, speaking as loudly and as articulately as I could with my heaving chest.

"Pedro Campos and another thug are trying to make an escape on a Jet Ski. He just exited the second-story bedroom window heading north."

Scott appeared beside me at the window and stared out. Just as he started to climb up onto the windowsill, we heard the unmistakable sound of an engine starting up, followed by a loud roar as it cut through the water, heading northwest.

"He's already out of the compound," I said, watching as their thin silver wake glowed behind them in the moonlight.

I grabbed an extra magazine from my holster and quickly exchanged it with the spent one. As I watched the Jet Ski speed up, cutting through the water, I spotted a faint flicker of light coming from Pedro's lap.

Scott was quickly followed into the bedroom by a group of three police officers, who entered like a SWAT team with their submachine guns raised and scanned every inch of the room.

"Shit," I said, realizing what the light was and staring back at the group. "We need to get out of the house now!" As the three guys turned to head back for the door, I added, "This way! There's no time."

Hearing the seriousness in my voice and seeing the stone-cold expression plastered across my face, Scott and the three others moved alongside me as I ushered them out onto the patio. We climbed over the railing, our boots slamming against the metal roof as we sprinted for the edge of the compound. Up ahead, I saw a gap of about ten feet between the roof and the wall surrounding the compound. A second later, I heard a deep rumble resonate from inside the house and knew that my instincts had been correct.

"Jump!" I yelled as I reached the edge of the roof in a full-on sprint.

Digging my right heel into the metal, I launched myself into the air with reckless abandon. I landed on the wall, then rolled over, grabbed onto the edge and eased myself down onto the other side. Just as my soles hit the sand, I looked up and saw the others dropping down beside me. The night air suddenly shook as an explosion boomed from inside the house. The sound was deafening as it rattled across the air, causing the ground to rumble beneath my feet like an earthquake. The explosion lit up the night sky with a bright yellow flash, and shattered pieces of the mansion rained down around us, splashing into the water and smashing against the rocks. The three-foot-thick wall acted like a bunker, shielding us from the flames and the shockwave as we crouched down beside its base.

In seconds, the explosion stopped, and all I could hear was the occasional pieces of shattered wood hitting the ground and the roar of the inferno as what remained of the mansion went up in a blaze. Standing up from the base of the wall, I could see the tops of the flames as they flickered powerfully high into the night sky. The smell of smoke and napalm dominated the air.

"Did everyone make it out?" I asked while moving down towards the water and scanning the outside of the compound.

Scott nodded. "We were the only ones inside," he said, motioning to the five of us. "Everyone else is still aboard their boats."

I reached for my radio. "This is Logan. We all made it out of the house. What's the status on Pedro?"

After a brief silence, I heard Ange's voice. "I only caught his shadow as he vanished on the other side of the compound," she said.

I hadn't expected Ange to be able to take him out. The window he'd climbed out of faced northwest, the opposite side of the compound from where Ange was posted.

"He hopped on a Jet Ski and turned east," Charles said. "We chased after him but were already heading into the compound when you informed us he was on the move." After a short pause, he added, "I still have contact with a patrol boat that has a visual, but it looks like he's gonna get away."

Moving along the water beside Scott and the three police officers, I saw that all three boats I'd sabotaged were still tied off to the dock. From the looks of things, Pedro and that short muscular guy had been the only two to make an escape. As the massive flames pierced the blackness behind us, I grabbed my gear bag and we headed onto the dock.

A second later, I heard the sound of a familiar pair of engines, then spotted the Baia cruising in our direction over the water surrounding the compound. The beach, waters and rocks surrounding the mansion were littered with broken pieces of wood, sections of the metal roof and various other remnants.

Jack eased the Baia right up alongside the dock beside the three Cigarettes, and I tied her off to just one cleat, then climbed aboard, changed into a pair of swim trunks and jumped down into the water to retrieve my rebreather from under the dock.

Once I had my gear aboard and stowed, Jack looked me over. "You alright, bro? You've got a nasty cut on your forehead."

As the adrenaline from the ordeal wore off, I felt pains all over my body from my encounter with the Campos brothers. The blood dripping down from my forehead was no doubt from when Pedro had hit me with my Sig. But what hurt the worst was my right shoulder, which felt like it had almost broken when the short guy had hit me with the baseball bat.

"I've had worse," I said as I grabbed my first aid kit from a storage compartment just inside the salon.

I spent a few minutes patching myself up, then headed back out into the cockpit.

Scott moved beside me and patted my left shoulder. "Hell of a job," he said. "It looked like we arrived just in time."

He shot me a grin and I shook my head. "I had those big assholes right where I wanted them."

Scott chuckled, then replied, "Charles wants us to clear out and meet him outside the compound."

I nodded, and Scott jumped onto the dock and moved with the three officers along the beach towards my Zodiac, which was beached about a hundred feet away.

Jack untied the line and I started up the engines. As I eased us away from the dock, the night sky was still lit up by the fire behind us and the flames showed no signs of slowing. I idled us momentarily as we left the compound, then dove down into the channel and surfaced holding on to my sea scooter. Handing it to Jack, I climbed aboard, toweled off again, then cruised out through the channel towards a cluster of three police boats that were gathered about a quarter of a mile from Blackett Key.

I saw Charles standing on the bow of his police interceptor as it pulled out of the group and headed towards us.

"Permission to board, Captain?" Charles said as his boat crept just a few feet from mine.

I nodded. "Come on over, Charles."

A second later, he jumped the gap separating our boats with the agility of a man much younger than his years.

Landing on the swim platform just aft of the transom, he stepped towards me. "We've got a beat on where he's headed, and we've got people on the lookout for him." Then, turning to look at the massive fire still blazing in the center of the compound, he added, "What in the hell happened in there?"

"As we suspected, they had the place rigged with explosives," I said. "Only two of them survived. Though they may have others who were out on the water when we attacked."

After dropping off the three police officers on one of the patrol boats, Scott brought the Zodiac up against the swim platform, and the four of us pulled it up and secured it with ratchet straps.

Charles thought it over for a moment, then said, "If there are any others, we'll find them."

"Update me on what's going on," I said. "I'll be at the marina if you need anything. For now, there's a beautiful woman waiting patiently for me to pick her up."

Charles said that he'd come by my boat for a debrief of the attack the following morning, then stepped onto the gunwale.

"Hey, Logan," he said, turning back to me. "You did good tonight." After taking in a deep breath, he added, "And we'll find him."

With a powerful push, he launched himself back onto his police boat, gave a tip of his cap and cruised back towards the small cluster of boats. Putting the engines back into gear, I accelerated past the group, heading southwest towards the end of the channel and into deeper water. Turning to port, I banked around the tip of Cutoe and slowed to a stop at roughly the same place where we'd dropped off Ange on the kayak. I knew Ange wouldn't be very long, so instead of lowering the anchor, I kept the bow facing into the current and kept us stagnant by throttling to three knots.

Even from over a mile away, the brightness from the burning mansion shone like a brilliant beacon across the dark sky. Listening in the stillness, we could hear the distant low roar and the occasional crackling of the fire. Using my night vision monocular, I spotted Ange as she climbed aboard the kayak with her gear and quickly paddled towards us.

Within a few minutes, I could hear the paddle slipping into the water and splashing as she propelled herself. A few moments later, I moved along the port side and held the kayak steady as she handed up her gear. Offering her my hand, I helped her up onto the swim platform.

"You look like you had fun," she said with a smile as she looked me over from head to toe.

Even with black paint splattered across her face, she managed to look sexy as hell.

"A blast," I replied with a grin. "Good call on the booby trap. Maybe I should listen to you more often."

She laughed as we reached over the gunwale, pulled up the kayak and secured it to the transom just ahead of the Zodiac.

"Any word on Pedro?" she asked, looking out over the dark horizon and the distant burning house.

"He's long gone," Scott said.

She shrugged. "I'm not surprised. Looked like a Yamaha FX, which has an engine with over eighteen hundred cc's of supercharged power. That thing flies across the water. Maybe we'll get lucky and he'll hit a sandbar."

"It's just the two of them," Scott said. "And even if they manage to escape, what then? If they're stupid enough to attack again, everyone down here will be ready for them."

Though I heard his words and they made a lot of sense, there was a big part of me that wished I hadn't let them get away. That I'd finished all of them off tonight and ended their entire operation. Instead, one of the thugs responsible for my dad's death had managed to escape. And I knew that if his motives had been strong before, they were amplified exponentially now that his brother was dead.

The three of them could see that I was lost in thought, and Jack stepped towards me.

"What are you thinking, bro?" he asked.

Bringing myself back from my thoughts, I looked at him and said, "I think it's time we do some salvaging."

Stationing myself at the helm, I accelerated to twenty knots, then turned sharply and entered Harbor Channel. Less than a minute later, I had us up on plane in the Gulf, weaving around the various small islands and heading back towards Key West. Cruising through the darkness, we soon heard the unmistakable sound of sirens as the fire department boats from Key West passed by in the distance, heading for the ever-dying glow on the horizon behind us.

As we cruised past Great White Heron National Wildlife Refuge, I couldn't help my mind from drifting back to Pedro and his goon. I knew deep down that I hadn't seen the last of him. And part of me wanted him to come back so I could face him once more. I made a firm resolution that if that did happen, he wouldn't get away again. His fate would be the same as his brother's.

CHAPTER NINETEEN

Back at the marina, I pulled the Baia up against the dock, controlling both engines separately to ease her in close, then tied her off. The clouds had moved on, leaving behind a dark blanket covered in sparkling stars that stretched from horizon to horizon. The mercury had just crept below seventy degrees, and with a calm breeze sweeping in from the Gulf, the night air felt good.

After washing down and stowing all of the gear, we cracked open a couple of Paradise Sunset beers and plopped down on the cushioned seats and sunbed. With every swig, I could feel the alcohol taking more and more of the edge off and taking my mind off my sore body.

When the four of us decided to call it a night, I thanked Jack, then he walked barefoot and shirtless down the dock towards the *Calypso*. I offered Scott the guest cabin but realized that he had his bag at his feet and was reaching to grab it.

"I have a flight to catch," he said.

"Tonight?"

"Yeah. I was going to leave tomorrow, but I'd rather sleep on the flight up and arrive early in the morning."

I wasn't surprised. He'd always been a very busy guy, but ever since he'd become senator, his time had grown even more precious, and I rarely saw him for more than a few days at a time.

"Thanks for coming down," I said, rising to my feet and wrapping an arm around him.

One of the things I'd always loved most about our friendship was the fact that we always had each other's backs. It didn't matter the time, day or location, if one of us needed the other, we were there as fast as possible, willing to risk our lives, no questions asked.

"Of course," he said. "I can't let you have all the fun." Then he wrapped his arm around my shoulder and added, "Just be careful with that damn torpedo. I'm gonna call a few of my contacts. See if they can help out with getting rid of it."

It was a good idea. I'd dealt with explosives many times before, but pulling a biological weapon up out of the ocean that had been down there for sixty-plus years didn't exactly sound appealing.

As he stepped from the swim platform onto the dock, he turned back and said, "If you guys need anything else, or if that idiot decides to show his face again, let me know."

I told him I would, and then he disappeared down the dock, heading towards the parking lot, where he told me he already had a ride waiting for him. Turning back around, I saw that Ange had disappeared from the cockpit.

Assuming that she must have turned in after the long night we'd had, I rounded up the empty beer bottles and threw them into a plastic recycle bin on the dock. We'd pushed the Zodiac from the swim platform and it was now in its usual place, tied off to the starboard side of the Baia. I placed the kayak on the dock beside the port gunwale for now and would return it to the storage shed when Gus arrived in the morning.

After taking a final look around to make sure everything had been stowed, I headed for the hatch into the salon. Just as I swung it open, Ange appeared in front of me, wearing her white bikini bottoms and nothing else. She smiled at me seductively, and I could barely shut and lock the hatch behind me before she jumped into my arms and pulled me towards the main cabin.

As we moved forward, our lips locked together, I turned on the security system and turned off the outside lights. A few steps later, we were falling onto the queen-sized bed, our bodies pressed against each other and our hearts pounding.

The next morning I woke up to the smell of sizzling sausage, eggs, and freshly brewed coffee wafting into the stateroom as the door opened. A second later, Ange was on top of me, her long tanned legs straddling my waist as she looked at me with her sparkling blue eyes and smiled. Her blond hair was tied back, and she was wearing her bikini bottoms and a tank top. The morning sun bled through the hatch overhead as I smiled back at her.

"Something about you taking down bad guys," she said. "And bringing down a drug-smuggling operation. It really turns me on."

Not able to control myself, I pulled her close, pressed my lips to hers and twisted her onto her side.

"After breakfast," she said in a cute stern voice as she crawled out of my grasp and tiptoed towards the kitchen, her perfectly shaped butt swinging exaggeratedly from side to side to torture me.

It wasn't until I tried to sit up that I realized just how sore my body was. It ached all over, forcing me to ease over onto my side and slip my legs out sideways onto the deck. The Campos brothers hadn't made it easy on me, and neither had Ange when we'd hit the sack late last night.

I pulled on a pair of workout shorts and walked shirtless and barefoot out into the salon. Ange was plating the food as I arrived, and she set it on the dinette along with a small pitcher of fresh orange juice. I filled my Rubio Charters mug with coffee, added a little bit of cream and sugar, and sat down beside her.

The food was delicious. Freshly baked croissants with sausage, over-easy eggs and pepper jack cheese. She told me that she walked along the waterfront to a local bakery, arriving just as they opened to get the croissants as they came out of the oven.

While eating, I made a quick phone call, dialing the number I'd kept in my wallet. It was the number Alice Pierce, from the Curacao Police Department, had written on a napkin for me while we were eating at the Green Iguana in Willemstad.

I gave her a quick rundown of everything that had happened, ending with Pedro's escape.

"He's gonna try and recoup his losses," she said in her island Dutch accent. "He has associates all over Miami. My first bet would be he'd try and go there."

We talked for a few more minutes, then I thanked her and hung up the phone.

"What's up?" Ange asked as she dipped her last bite of croissant in runny egg yolk.

I stared off into the distance for a few seconds, then turned to look at her. "If Pedro makes it out of the Keys somehow, we might have a problem."

After breakfast, we returned the kayak to Gus's storage shed and made a few phone calls to local salvagers. I'd had good experience dealing with Blackbeard Salvagers out of Marathon while salvaging the *Intrepid*, so they were at the top of my list. They agreed to let us use the *Queen Anne's Revenge*, a forty-six-foot research vessel fitted with a crane at the stern. The owner assured me it would be large enough to haul up thirty-three hundred pounds, the typical weight of a Nazi torpedo, as Professor Murchison had informed us.

Just after noon, we met Jack and Charles for lunch at the Greasy Pelican. It was only about a minute's walk from my boat, so I went there often, especially for their lunch special, which always featured the catch of the day. Today it was cobia, and I ordered a large plate with plantain chips on the side, coconut shrimp for an appetizer, and lemonade to drink. Charles had met us just after we sat down, and we had a table out on the veranda, overlooking the ocean and marina.

"I can't stay long," Charles said as he waved off being handed a menu. He was wearing his short-sleeved police uniform and his usual Oakley sunglasses. "I need to head up to Key Largo to interview a few witnesses."

That caught my attention, and as I chewed my coconut shrimp, Ange said, "Witnesses? Someone saw Campos?"

Charles nodded. "We received a report of a stolen vehicle this morning from a harbormaster in Vaca Key. As far as we can tell, Pedro and his accomplice took it late last night."

"Any idea where they went?" Jack asked.

"Miami," Charles replied. "The Miami police found the vehicle less than an hour ago. They're doing forensic analysis as we speak, but I have no doubt that it was stolen by our guys."

"Miami?" Jack said, shaking his head. "You think the bastard's trying to rebuild his little army?"

"It would appear that way," Charles said. "Though I'm hopeful they'll bring him down before he has a chance to retaliate. Regardless, we should be ready for anything."

I listened intently and thought over their words. Ms. Pierce had warned me that he might head to Miami, and she was right. I didn't know much about Pedro, but I knew that he wasn't someone who let things go. Ever.

Charles left, and after we finished our food, we drove down to Marathon in my Tacoma and picked up *Queen Anne's Revenge*. It was a beautiful day, and I wasn't about to let it go to waste, regardless of the fact that I was still sore as hell and Pedro was on the loose. Jack canceled his charters for the next couple of days, allowing the three of us to spend all day every day out on the water.

We put priority on getting the torpedo up carefully and disposed of properly, but were waiting for Scott to get ahold of different joint force agencies. So, in the meantime, we devoted all our time to exploring and identifying the wreck. We strove to ensure that no part of the wreck was touched or tampered with, as any minor detail could be incredibly helpful in determining the reason she had gone down. Given the massive crack near the centerline of the hull and the damage to the cone, it was clear the U-boat had run aground. Why she had run aground, however, still remained a mystery.

We spent a few days surveying the entire wreck, filming every inch of her hull and capturing intricate details of the conning tower, hatches, rudder, stern planes, and screws. Since the crack in the centerline was too small for us to swim through, we used an underwater drone to explore the inner workings of the boat, the same one we'd used to discover the *Intrepid* wreck, which had been covered by thirty feet of rock.

Piloting the drone into the wreck for the first time was incredible. The high-powered LED lights and the three built-in cameras allowed us to get a great view of the inside while sitting comfortably on the surface.

Taking control using the joystick, I eased on the downward thrusters and the three of us watched as clusters of wires, pipes, valves, and various electronic and mechanical equipment came into view. We all went silent as we stared in awe at something that hadn't been seen by human eyes in over sixty years. The water was surprisingly clean, and I did my best to maneuver the ROV slowly so as to avoid stirring up the layers of silt that coated everything in view.

We returned to visit Professor Murchison, who lit up with excitement when we told him we'd found the wreck and showed him the pictures. Wanting to do all that he could to help us, he gave us an entire folder dedicated to the model XXI, which included design sketches of the entire inside, detailing the different sections.

Based on the drone's orientation to the conning tower and the long metal tubes that we'd clearly identified as the periscopes, we surmised that the drone was in the control room. Using the sketch, I maneuvered around the helm and plane controls, doing my best not to get the tether tangled on any of the jutting metal pipes and wiring.

Every now and then, one of us would gasp as the remains of a German soldier came into view. Regardless of who they'd fought for and the propaganda that had fueled their military's resolve, these young men had died for something they'd believed in. They'd died with the hope that they could give their families and their countrymen a better future, which is more than most people die for.

I had a tremendous amount of respect for all of them and was careful not to disturb their remains as I piloted my way through the inner workings of their old boat. As I moved the drone forward, we discovered that most of the forward section was inaccessible, even for the small drone. The bulkhead leading forward out of control had been crushed, causing the door to be less than a few inches tall.

Back aft, the door leading into the engine room was blocked only by minor amounts of debris, allowing us to explore and get good footage of the radio room, the electric engine room and the aft torpedo tube. After three days of exploring, we'd learned a lot more about the wreck and had hours of film that could be used to help discover how and why she had sunk.

I talked to Scott every day, and he informed me that he had contacted various groups to help us with the recovery of the torpedo. One group he'd contacted was Mobile Diving and Salvage Unit Two, an expeditionary mobile unit that was homeported in Little Creek, Virginia, and was known as the experts of salvage. They had participated in many salvage and recovery operations, including TWA 800, the ironclad USS *Monitor*, and the space shuttles *Challenger* and *Columbia*. Scott also contacted Vice Admiral Gears, the director of joint force development, to send a team of explosive ordnance disposal technicians to help handle and dispose of the torpedo.

CHAPTER TWENTY

On October 14, just five days after taking down Hector along with most of his organization, Scott called and told me that the joint force would be arriving in the Middle Keys the following day aboard the USNS *Grasp*, a 255-foot Navy salvage and rescue ship.

The *Grasp* was one of the most versatile salvage vessels on the planet and had been utilized by many of the Navy's Mobile and Salvage Units in various operations around the world. Though she had been decommissioned in 2006, she had been transferred to the MSC for continued use. The MSC, or Military Sealift Command, is an organization that works in unison with the United States Navy to provide a full spectrum of support to our nation's warfighters during peacetime and while at war.

The USNS *Grasp* appeared on the northeastern horizon at zero nine hundred the following morning. The large salvage vessel was painted in the typical dark gray of US Navy ships, a color chosen to reduce the contrast of the ship with the horizon and therefore reduce the vertical patterns in the ship's appearance. On the horizon, it looked very similar to an Arleigh Burke–class destroyer, with a long, narrow body and a large bridge that rose fifty feet into the air. The ship had two cranes, the smaller one up forward and the larger back aft.

The massive and legendary salvage vessel cruised towards our position as we sat anchored just above the wreck. Brilliant white numbers painted on both the port and starboard sides of the hull indicated its hull number of 51. At five times as long as *Queen Anne's Revenge* and with a bridge nearly three times as tall, the *Grasp* cast a shadow over our boat as she motored close.

The pilot and crew put the *Grasp* in a three-point moor, utilizing its port, starboard and stern anchors to orient the large ship in a stabilized position from which dive operations could successfully take place. Due to the depth of the water and strong currents, the crew let out a considerable amount of chain to keep the ship in place.

A few minutes after the crew had finished mooring the ship in place, they lowered a blacked-out Zodiac Hurricane into the water. We watched as three men climbed aboard, started up a pair of two-hundred-horsepower Mercury engines, and motored over towards the *Revenge*. The small boat pulled up alongside the stern, and one of the guys stood, staring straight at me.

"Request permission to board," he called out.

My mind went to work as I heard something familiar in the guy's voice. I stared at the guy as he stood on the bow of the inflatable for a moment, then said, "Come aboard."

The guy instantly climbed up over the transom and landed on the deck beside me. He was about five foot eight with a dark Pacific Islander complexion. He was sporting a pair of tan UDT shorts and a faded dark blue tee shirt, along with a gray ball cap and sunglasses. As he stepped closer to me, I instantly realized who it was.

"Chief Dodge," he said with a big grin on his face.

I smiled back, then threw an arm around his shoulder. "Oh, it's like that, is it?"

Though calling each other by your rank is typical among many communities within the Navy, Special Forces, divers, and EODs were almost always on a first-name basis. Usually ranks were only brought into the conversation when higher-ups were present, or when you just felt like messing with each other.

I laughed and added, "Well, Seaman Wade Bishop, it's good to see you."

"Hey, it's Petty Officer First Class Bishop now. You're not surprised, are you?"

"A little. I'm surprised they let you reenlist."

"It's amazing how far a bribe can go," he joked.

The truth was, I was surprised that Wade hadn't made chief himself yet. The energetic and incredibly intelligent Hawaiian had always been a top-notch sailor and an even better friend. We'd first met back in 2000 after I'd just finished a six-month-long operation in Nigeria. I'd been assigned to be a temporary Underwater Ordnance Division Instructor at EOD school at Eglin Air Force Base in Fort Walton Beach, Florida. Wade had been in my unit and had been one of the top students in the class. He was one of only a few students I had gone diving with in my free time once he'd finished training, exploring the Emerald Coast. Though I'd only seen him once since then, during an operation in the Mediterranean, it would be hard for me to forget him.

Turning back to Ange and Jack, I said, "Wade, this is Angelina Fox and Jack Rubio."

After the introductions, we hopped aboard the inflatable and motored over to the *Grasp*. It was a calm day, with only a slight breeze blowing in from the east and patches of clouds covering about half of the sky. The small skiff pulled alongside the port side of the stern, where an opening in the gunwale allowed us to climb up onto the ship.

There was a lot of activity on the deck. Service members and civilians worked in preparation for a long day of diving, bringing out dive suits, metal cage structures, hoses, cabling, and various other pieces of equipment.

Wade introduced us to a few members of the crew, including the lead civilian project managers and a few of the divers, including the lead diver, Master Chief Snyder. He was about my height, well-built and with a clean-shaven head.

"I knew your father, Logan," Snyder said. I wasn't surprised, since most everyone in the US Naval diving community had known him or known who he was. "I was sad to hear of his passing. He was a damn good sailor and the best diver I ever met."

I thanked him for his condolences, and after meeting most of the crew, Wade took the three of us up to the bridge and introduced us to Commander Sprague, the temporary commanding officer of the *Grasp*. He looked to be in his mid-forties and had a lean, athletic build, tanned skin and thinning black hair. After meeting him, Master Chief Snyder met up with us for a brief.

"We really appreciate all of you coming down," I said to the small group assembled. "I know how hard it can be to be away from family."

"Don't mention it," Commander Sprague said in his Southern accent. "We should be thanking you. I'm not sure I could handle another northern run right now. We've had three trips up to the Arctic in a row, and we're happy to be down in paradise for a few days. Now, tell us about this U-boat."

We told them everything we knew about the wreck, including depth, size, condition, and of course mentioning the torpedo we had good reason to believe was a biological weapon. I also showed them pictures, sketches and digital scans showing details of the wreck and how it sat on the bottom.

"These are great," Sprague said, looking them over with awe. "Are you some kind of professional salvager?"

I laughed. "More of a treasure hunter. The truth is, it's been a while since I did much salvaging."

"Don't let him fool you," Wade said. "Logan here was a SEAL, and a damn good one at that. He still holds the record for the highest grade in Improvised Explosive Devices at EOD school. That's right, he's that guy whose name's on that plaque in the Kauffman Training Complex. He was also one of my instructors when I went through the training."

"I see," Sprague said, thinking it over for a moment. "Well, from what I hear, you've been diving the site for a few days now. What do you recommend?"

I gave a quick rundown of how I would go about bringing up the ordnance if I was them, keeping short, concise and articulate, the way hardened Navy men usually communicate. But I made it clear that they were simply my opinions and that I encouraged them to use their judgment and experience to make the call.

While in the SEALs, I'd been trained heavily in explosive ordnance disposal and had utilized my training many times in combat. I was good at disarming and handling explosives, but these guys were the best. The most highly trained divers and EODs in the United States military, masters of their craft. The best in the world. With that being said, I was happy to have them team up with us and happily deferred to their judgment regarding how to go about raising and disposing of the torpedo.

"We agree with your line of thought completely, Logan," Commander Sprague said. "Which is why we must strive to execute with minimal contact to the ordnance. As you said, we don't know what kind of weapon it is or how exactly the firing mechanism operates. We also must take the toll of the ocean over the years into consideration. But based on these surveys you've shown us of the outside of the casing, we concur that it appears to be a biological weapon of some kind."

"Professor Murchison predicts that it's probably a chimera virus," I said. "A hybrid modified biological weapon containing variations of viruses such as anthrax, plague, and smallpox. Which means it could spread through the air, making isolation of the package before it exits the water a priority."

The commander nodded. "Let me show you what we have in mind. If you'll all follow me, we have a briefing room just down the passageway."

Sprague led us down the main passageway, into a room with dry-erase boards and a projector screen covering the far wall and littered with those chairs with built-in fold-up flat surfaces for writing on. It was eerily familiar and made me feel like I was back in the Navy again, awaiting the brief for our next mission along with the rest of my team. The talk didn't take long. Sprague and Snyder wasted no time and, using a dry-erase marker, they sketched out the basis for how we would bring up the payload.

"We used a similar technique when we brought up the USS *Monitor*'s steam engine back in 2001," Snyder said, describing a metal cage that they planned to lower and clamp around the torpedo. "That old hunk of metal was so fragile you could practically tear it apart with your bare hands."

"What about the fact that it's stuck in the rock?" Jack asked. "How can we get it out without potentially detonating it?"

Sprague nodded. "It's a good question, and one we've been thinking about these past few days while cruising down the coast from Virginia." He grabbed a marker and drew the rocky surface nearly half of the torpedo was buried in. "We've welded a set of hydraulics here and here," he said, pointing to the drawing of the metal cage, "and attached flat metal surfaces to the end of the plunger so we can carefully ease it out of place."

"Then once it's out, you'll cover it?" Ange asked.

Snyder nodded. "We've rigged an inner shell to the cage that's rubber-coated. Once the torpedo's out and resting on the shell, we can enclose it and bring it up to the surface, perfectly contained."

As I'd expected, they'd arrived more than prepared, and we all sat silent for a moment, thinking over the plan.

"It really is an incredible find, Logan," Sprague said. "How did you manage to discover it?"

"I didn't," I said, surprising him with my answer. "It was my dad who found it. He left me clues that led to it before he was murdered."

"Murdered?" Snyder said gravely after a brief moment of silence.

I nodded. "By the same assholes that are after this site."

The room was quiet for a moment as the men realized the entirety of the situation.

"We also wanted to discuss that with you, Logan," Sprague said calmly. "Senator Cooper has informed us of the situation and, as of earlier this morning, Pedro Campos is still at large."

"That's right," I said. "We ambushed his compound last week, but he managed to escape. Sheriff Wilkes of the Key West Police Department informed us that he stole a car, which was later found just outside of Miami."

"The main priority is securing this weapon," he said. "Though I'm told that isn't what Campos is after."

"Right. As far as I know, Campos doesn't even know about the U-boat. He's after this." I set a picture on the table of the metal box lodged into the rock beside the wreck. "My guess is its filled with cash. They murdered my dad after he'd done a large run for them while working undercover to take them down."

Sprague thought it over a moment. "Okay. Once we have the ordnance topside and secured, we'll take care of this as well." Then, turning to Snyder he added, "Make immediate preparations. I want three divers in the water using surface-supplied air down at the bottom, examining the wreck and handling the rigging. I want two more divers with nitrox alternating in shifts to oversee the lowering of equipment. Let's take our time and do this right." Then, turning to the three of us he said, "I'll have eight guys armed and ready, monitoring the horizon, and I have a team of radar techs aboard. If anyone comes within five miles of this site, we'll know it."

"Sir, I'm very familiar with the wreck," I said. "Since I'm one of the three guys who have dived the wreck before, might I request to be one of the guys on the bottom?"

Sprague glanced over at Snyder. "His dad was the best diver I ever knew," Snyder said. Then turning to me, he added, "If the apple fell anywhere close to the tree, then we could use you."

"Right at the trunk," Wade said confidently, patting me on the back.

Sprague nodded. "Get suited up, Logan. This concludes the brief."

As Sprague and Snyder walked out of the room, I turned and smiled at Wade.

"Well, all the talking and pictures in the world won't do this U-boat justice," I said. "Let's get you guys in the water so you can see her for yourselves."

"Sounds good, Chief," Wade said with a grin.

I hadn't been called chief in years, unless you counted Scott's occasional slips. And though I was proud of what I'd accomplished and the people I'd worked with, I much preferred to go by my real name. And boy, did Wade know that.

I grinned back. "If you keep this up, don't be surprised if you find a bug in your dive helmet."

He laughed, and the four of us headed back out onto the deck.

CHAPTER
TWENTY-ONE

Thirty minutes later, I was fully geared up for surface-supplied diving, donning a three-millimeter wetsuit complete with neck lining, weights, and a tank of air strapped to my back just in case. I donned a Kirby Morgan stainless-steel dive helmet with a built-in two-way communicator, as well as mounted lights and video cameras so everyone topside could watch what was happening below. Three lines led into my helmet: the main air hose, the communicating line and a bailout hose supplying oxygen in the event the main hose failed. Military and commercial divers always have a backup for everything whenever possible.

Checking the pressure gauge, I saw that I had just over two hundred bar, or about twenty-nine hundred PSI. A bar is a unit of pressure equal to roughly 14.5 PSI, or slightly less than the atmospheric pressure at sea level. Utilizing an air compressor topside, MDSUs pump a special blend of eighty-five percent helium and fifteen percent oxygen, allowing divers to stay down much longer and avoid experiencing nitrogen narcosis, also referred to as the bends.

Once the other two divers were ready and we'd verified that all of our gear was functioning properly, we stepped towards the starboard railing. From the outside looking in, a highly technical dive operation such as this one can appear chaotic. But every hose, wire, tank, and all of the various pieces of equipment scattered about had a purpose. The sound of diesel engines, metal gears, and massive cables unraveling filled the air as the crew slowly dropped the massive metal cage into the water. The surface was relatively calm, and though clouds filled most of the sky, it was a nice day out on the water, with very little wind.

I moved to the edge in my fins and was the first diver in the water, splashing down and floating on the surface. The two other divers, Wade and a first-class diver named Hartigan, held on to the metal cage and were lowered into the water by the massive aft crane. Slowly and cautiously, the three of us released air from our BCs and began our descent.

Soon, the incredible visibility of the water allowed us to see the ledge below, its dark rocks extending as far as you could see to the northeast and southwest. I'd been down to the wreck many times over the past few days, but it was still difficult for me to pinpoint exactly where the different sections of the U-boat were from afar. It was easy to see how, given the depth and massive amounts of coral, rocks, sponges, anemones, and silt covering the wreck, it could go unnoticed for so many years.

"There she is," I said into the com, pointing to a spot about thirty feet beneath us where the top portion of the U-boat's hull rested against the ledge.

Using the grid and coordinated imagery I'd created over the past few days, we were able to position the *Grasp* with its stern right over the location where the torpedo was lodged into the rock. The crane could rotate and extend, allowing some versatility, but as I looked down, I could see that we were descending almost perfectly right above the torpedo.

"Alright, Snyder," I said. "We're about one-five feet above the target. We're gonna drop down to the rock beside the ordnance and direct the cage."

"You're gonna drop down and direct the cage, aye," Snyder said, giving a typical Navy verbatim repeat back. "Standing by at the crane control station."

Surface-supplied diving is all about trust. If one person messes up, it can mean the end for a diver. Each and every time they drop down into the water, they're counting on those that are topside, trusting them with their lives.

Wade and I descended down onto the rock just a few feet away from the torpedo, leaving Hartigan with the cage. I watched Wade's eyes light up as he gazed upon the barnacle-and-algae-covered shell with its old rusted propeller sticking out of the back. I moved closer and carefully pointed to the markings on the side.

"Here's the word and the symbol," I said.

"This is incredible, Logan," he said as he finned slowly over to where the front of the torpedo was lodged into the rock. "Sure looks stuck, though."

The process of lowering and carefully setting up the metal cage, clamps and hydraulics was slow and methodical. The last thing we wanted was to work too fast and cause accidental shock to the ordnance that might cause it to detonate after all these years. Once the cage assembly was in place and the torpedo was clamped securely, we carefully fired up the four hydraulics, forcing the flat metal pistons against the rock face with gradually increasing pressure at a slow and controlled rate.

As we brought the hydraulics to just below full strength, I noticed the front of the torpedo start to move.

"Ease back," I said. "She's coming loose."

A second later, the torpedo slid out of the rock, moving in a slow and controlled manner backward and resting against the rubber-edged round clamps. *Damn, these guys are good*, I thought as the three of us went to work setting up the metal enclosure that would prevent the biological weapon from releasing any of its toxins into the atmosphere. It made me proud to watch Wade and see a former student handle his work with such expertise. After four hours of work, we had the torpedo dislodged, secured and ready to be raised.

Once on the surface, the three of us removed our dive helmets and posed for a picture with our haul, grinning from ear to ear. But the job was far from over. The next few hours were spent transitioning the torpedo into a storage device capable of containing it in the event of detonation. EODs went to work, examining it and preparing it for its trip to the Anniston Chemical Agent Disposal Facility located in Alabama, where it would be taken apart and disposed of properly.

There were occasional times when I missed my days in the Navy. Hanging out with the other guys on the *Grasp* made me reminisce about those days. I'd have been less than six years away from retirement by now and probably would have had a gold star or two to give the anchor on my uniform company. But I love what I do. Having freedom both financially and occupationally and living in the Florida Keys is a life I wouldn't trade for any other.

"Hell of a job," Snyder said after I'd removed all my gear and changed and was toweling off beside the starboard railing, watching the technicians go to work alongside Ange, Jack, and Wade. "The CO wants to speak with you up on the bridge. He says he has news."

Wade stayed behind to finish helping out the crew, but Ange, Jack, and myself headed up to the bridge. Commander Sprague was hovering behind a row of sailors seated in front of monitors and turned as we arrived.

"Nice work," he said, walking over and patting me on the back. "You three handled that perfectly."

I shrugged. "It helps when you have the right gear and the greatest crew in the world. Snyder said you had news for us?"

He nodded. "I just got off the phone with CIA Deputy Director Wilson, and there's been an update on Pedro Campos's movements. Apparently, he was spotted in Fort Hancock just a few hours ago. They even got a credit card swipe from a Visa in his name."

"Texas?" I said with raised eyebrows, making sure I'd heard him right.

"That's right," Sprague said.

Jack shook his head. "You guys think he's making a run for Mexico, don't you?"

"It appears that way. And a guy with his kind of reputation probably won't have a hard time making it across the border." Sprague looked down at the floor and sighed. "I'm sorry, Logan. But it looks like he won't be caught anytime soon."

I was silent for a few seconds. Something wasn't right here. A credit card swipe? I knew that Pedro would never be careless and stupid enough to pay with anything except cash.

"And what about the metal box down by the wreck?" I asked, changing the subject.

Sprague shook his head. "An armored truck will be waiting at zero seven hundred tomorrow morning, along with Key West Police vehicles for escort. It will be taken up to Homestead and then transferred to the US Treasury Department building in Birmingham."

"Why not just take it with you guys on the *Grasp*?" I asked, confused as hell.

"With Campos leaving the country, it's not a priority," he said. "Right now, we have to get this ordnance up to Savannah, then put on a train to be taken to Anniston and be disposed of as soon as possible. Your ship's crane will have no trouble bringing the box up."

"We could bring it up in less than an hour," I said.

"I follow orders. And right now, my orders are to leave as soon as possible. You were a military man, so I know that you understand."

I did understand. All too well. I'd had to follow bad orders before. The kind that were given by men thousands of miles away, sitting comfortably behind a desk, who oftentimes had little to no interest in the opinions of the men on the ground. It was one of the major reasons I'd gotten out after eight years and refused government employment. The red tape, procedures, and unwillingness to change had driven me away.

"It's a mistake," I said. "And it puts law enforcement at risk. Campos wouldn't dare try and strike a ship like the *Grasp*. But a small convoy and an armored truck are well within his capabilities."

Sprague sighed. "I agree with you, Logan. But as I've said, I have my orders, and we have it on good authority that he's nowhere near Florida."

"You're all underestimating this guy," I said, shaking my head. "He's been doing this successfully for years. He knows what he's doing."

Sprague assured us that he was doing everything he could to help the situation as we headed back down to the deck. The *Grasp* was already making preparations to get underway, wanting to take care of the ordnance as quickly as possible. By the time we reached the small inflatable skiff, the orders were already going out to raise the anchors.

We said our goodbyes to the crew, wished them good luck with the rest of their trip, and jumped onto the small boat alongside Wade and two other crew members. It was now just after fourteen hundred and the winds had picked up a little, creating a good amount of chop on the surface. The small boat bounced up and down as Wade pulled us up along the stern of the *Revenge*.

As the two other crew members held on to the transom to keep the inflatable relatively steady, the three of us climbed up and over the transom.

"It was nice to see you still got it," Wade said, standing behind the helm and staring over at us. "You better call me if you're ever up north."

"Likewise," I said. "You should take some leave and come down to the Keys. The islands are a lot more enjoyable when you don't have to work the whole time."

He laughed and said, "I'll do that. Just save some lobster for me to catch, Logan."

With that, the two crew members let go and Wade punched the throttles, sending the inflatable bouncing over the surface as it cruised back towards the *Grasp*.

CHAPTER
TWENTY-TWO

"I don't like this, Logan," Ange said. "The report was that they believe they saw him, but he's yet to be captured or identified. It just makes no sense. Why would he travel to Texas?"

"I'm with you guys," Jack said. "This doesn't feel right."

"It doesn't feel right because it's not," I said. "Campos isn't in Texas. It's all a ruse to make everyone think that he is."

After a few seconds of silence, Jack said, "So what do we do? There's only one road in and out of the Keys. Do you really think he'd be stupid enough to come down here, bro?"

I shrugged. "All I know is I'm not letting that convoy out of my sight. As for tonight, I'll take the first watch, and we'll all be up by four in order to haul up the box. I for one am curious as hell to find out what's inside of it."

We watched as the *Grasp* started up its two massive Caterpillar diesel engines and performed a wide turn to starboard before reaching their desired heading of due northeast. Designed with towing capability in mind rather than speed, the *Grasp* could only hit about fifteen knots, so it took a while to disappear on the cloud-covered horizon.

The three of us decided to stay the night on the boat, and at twenty hundred, we ate some lobster rolls while watching the sunset. The dying sun illuminated the cloud-covered sky with unique shades of dark purple just before it dropped down behind the Lower Keys. At twenty-two hundred, Ange and Jack hit the sack, and I moved out onto the deck with my cell phone. Punching in a few numbers, I called Scott and was quick to tell him how I thought we were playing with fire on this one.

"Look, Logan, we've received intel that a terrorist organization has learned of the biological weapon," he said. "Getting it taken care of was the most important thing. As for the money, trust these guys to do their jobs and bring it up north safely."

I sighed. "Right."

He paused a moment. "But you and I both know you can't do that."

"Yes," I said. "We do both know that."

After ending the call, I stood against the railing and stared out over the dark ocean. It wasn't cool by any means, but the breeze coming off the water and the absence of sunshine was a nice relief from the heat of the summer days. I let my mind drift, thinking about my dad, and about the Campos brothers and how they'd murdered him. This was a job my dad had started years ago, and I wasn't about to sit by now. If Pedro was still in the States and he decided to try something stupid, I was gonna be there to stop it.

At twenty-four hundred, Jack showed up on the bridge and poured a cup of coffee. I hit the rack and woke up four hours later to the sound of the alarm on my phone going off. I got dressed in a pair of swim trunks, tee shirt and flip-flops, then headed out into the salon. After eating a quick breakfast of blueberry muffins and a banana, washing it down with coffee, the three of us went to work.

I used a crowbar and the crane to dislodge the metal box, and we had it up on the surface in less than an hour. Climbing up onto the deck, I removed all my gear, leaving only my wetsuit on as Jack eased the metal box down onto the stern with a loud thud. The once-shiny metal was covered in a thin layer of grime and riddled with dents. The lid was secured by a large padlock.

"This thing's heavy as hell," Jack said. "I'd say around four hundred pounds."

Grabbing the crowbar, Ange handed it to me. "I think you should do the honors."

I gripped the crowbar with both hands, wedged the tip into the space between the hasp and broke it free with one strong motion. As the broken lock rattled onto the deck at my feet, I set the crowbar aside and pushed up the lid.

The grime and corrosion from being at the bottom of the ocean for so long caused it to stick a little, but once I got it loose, the entire lid swung open. The three of us stared in awe for a moment as we gazed at the contents of the box. We riffled through it and realized that the bottom half was covered in stacks of gold bars, and the top was filled with bags of diamonds and bundles of US hundred-dollar bills.

"Damn," Jack said, then knelt down and sifted through the loot. "How much do you think is in here?"

"Hard to say for sure," I said. "What are those, one-kilo bars?"

Jack nodded. "And there's got to be well over a hundred and fifty here."

"And that's over two million in cash," Ange said. "But these diamonds are the real moneymaker here." She had one of the bags of diamonds in her hands and was sifting through them. "These are big and great quality. I'd estimate there's tens of millions of dollars' worth here."

We spent about five minutes going through the box, then shut it back up. All told, we estimated that the haul was worth somewhere around fifty million dollars. I glanced at my dive watch and saw that it was zero five thirty, which meant we had an hour and a half before the scheduled time to meet with the convoy in Bahia Honda.

Dark black clouds swirled in over the eastern horizon, and as I rattled up the anchor chain using the windlass, raindrops began to splash against the topside of the salvage boat. Jack stood on the bow and communicated with me as the anchor broke free of the surface, letting me know when it was in place and securing the safety strap.

I fired up the two 375-hp John Deere engines and we cruised northwest, a strong wind building and flapping against the starboard side. Whitecaps formed on the surface, causing the boat to rock up and down. Bahia Honda Key didn't appear behind a blanket of dark clouds until we were less than a mile from shore.

Bahia Honda is nestled between Ohio Key and Summerland Key, and about twelve miles west of Marathon. The entire island is a state park and is known for its pristine, secluded beaches and some of the best snorkeling around. The National Oceanic and Atmospheric Administration, or NOAA, has a private dock near Calusa Beach on the western side of the island. That was where we were informed the convoy would meet us.

We cruised around the southwest corner of the island, motoring right between a hundred-foot-long removed section of the old Bahia Honda bridge. Cruising past Calusa on the starboard side, I eased us slowly into the private channel, then up against the NOAA dock. The NOAA dock and small sand-covered driveway were adjacent to the boat ramp and main parking lot for the state park. The area around the dock is flat and mostly white sand, aside from a few palm trees and a patch of purple-flowered morning glory bushes. Since most of the small dock was being used by two other moored boats, I backed the stern in, which would also make it easier to unload the box.

We spotted the armored truck and two police vehicles idling beside a boathouse when we pulled in. I glanced at my dive watch and saw that it was zero seven hundred on the dot. Shutting off the engine, Jack and Ange tied us off as I took a quick look around. To my surprise, other than the convoy and a few trucks over in the parking lot, the place was empty. I guess it was still pretty early in the morning and the poor weather most likely turned off a lot of people. Though it had been barely sprinkling when we left the wreck site, it was pouring now and showed no signs of dying down anytime soon.

Before meeting the convoy, I stepped down into the main cabin and quickly changed clothes. Removing my cargo shorts, I pulled on a pair of black tactical pants and boots. Then I tightened a thin bulletproof vest over my body and hid it beneath my tee shirt. I stowed my holstered Sig and extra magazine to the back of my waist. Then, grabbing my dive knife, I strapped it to my right thigh, then threw on a rain slicker and headed back up into the cockpit.

Glancing towards the convoy, I spotted the tall, dark frame of Charles as he walked towards the *Revenge* alongside two other guys. Charles, along with the guys beside him, was wearing a bulletproof vest and tactical pants and had an MP5 SD6 strapped across his chest. He was also wearing a Key West Police Department hat. I didn't recognize the two guys he was with, but they both looked like they hit the gym on a regular basis.

"Right on time," Charles said, stopping when he reached the transom. He motioned towards the guys standing on either side of him. "This is Officer Walker and Officer Smith from the Homestead PD. They've come to help us move the package. Guys, this is Logan Dodge."

I shook both of their hands, then welcomed the three aboard. As the tropical rain soaked our bodies, Jack opened up the storage space, revealing the metal box below.

"I was glad to hear about the torpedo getting removed," Charles said. "I'll sleep easier knowing it's no longer in the Keys. What's in the box, anyway?"

"Diamonds," Ange said. "Extremely valuable ones. And about five million in gold bars and two million in US dollars. All told, we figure close to fifty million."

All three of their eyes grew wide in unison and in an instant.

I dropped down into the space that was filling with water and said, "Yeah, look, let's get this thing out of here. We can discuss what's inside later."

The men nodded and helped me heave it out of the space. Using a heavy-duty fishing net, we were able to distribute its weight easier, and the six of us carried it over to the armored truck. Loading it up into the back, two more men appeared, fully dressed in tactical body armor, and locked it up. Seconds later, everyone was climbing into their respective vehicles and preparing to leave.

"How many men do you have in all?" I asked as I looked around through the thick sheets of rain.

"Seven including me," Charles said. Then, seeing the look in my eyes, he added, "You've done enough, Logan. Let us take care of this."

Standing still for a moment with the rain beating against me and drenching my clothes and hair, I finally nodded. "Yeah. You're right. Just be careful, and keep me updated."

Charles looked surprised, then said, "You did good, Logan. All three of you did good."

He glanced at Ange and Jack, who were standing beside me, then turned around and hopped into the driver's seat of the lead police car. A second later, he had it in gear and cruising out of the driveway, followed closely behind by the armored truck and the trailing police car. Their tires sloshed through the puddles, and a moment later all three disappeared around the corner.

When I turned around, Ange and Jack were staring at me in confusion.

"Really, Logan?" Ange said. "You feel the same way we do about this, and you're just gonna let them go without trying to help?"

Just as the words came out of her mouth, my black Tacoma started up in the parking lot adjacent to us and cruised down the driveway, stopping right against the dock. Through the windshield wipers gliding back and forth, I could see Pete sitting in the driver's seat. Ange stared at the truck, then looked at me.

"Come on, Ange," I said. "You know me better than that."

CHAPTER
TWENTY-THREE

Despite all of my protestations, I knew that there was nothing I could do or say that would keep Ange on the boat.

"Your stubborn ass isn't going alone," she said.

I nodded, then climbed back onto the boat, entered the salon and came back out a few seconds later with my black CamelBak over my shoulder, a waterproof duffle bag in one hand and a bulletproof vest in the other. Everything was soaked after just a few seconds as I moved swiftly towards my Tacoma and threw everything onto the backseat.

Leaving the truck running, Pcte stepped out and said, "I sure hope you're wrong about this, Logan."

"Me too."

Pete nodded. "We'll take her back to the marina in Marathon."

"You sure you don't need another body?" Jack asked.

I shook my head. "Just take her back to the marina and be safe. You guys can take the Baia back up to Key West and we'll meet you there when this is over."

Without another word, Ange and I jumped into the truck. After a quick wave through the rain-splattered windshield, I put her in reverse and spun through the mud for half a second before the tires gained traction and shot us backward to the end of the driveway.

When I reached the main sandy road leading to the beach and parking lot, I turned the wheel sharply counterclockwise, skidding the tires, then put it in drive and floored the gas pedal. Within seconds we were on US-1, heading northeast through the heart of Bahia Honda.

"Put this on," I said, reaching to the seat behind me and grabbing the bulletproof vest.

Ange held it for a second, then said, "Where's yours?"

By way of an answer, I pulled down the collar of my soaked tee shirt, revealing the one that I was wearing underneath. As I accelerated us to over sixty miles per hour, Ange tore apart the Velcro with a loud crackling sound and strapped it around her tank top. Reaching behind her seat, she grabbed a fresh towel and dried off her dripping-wet hair.

"Hold on," I said as I hit the gas, passing a row of three cars before hopping right back into my lane.

Hitting a large puddle of water, the Tacoma hydroplaned a little, causing a momentary loss of control before I regained it.

"Jeez, Logan. You trying to get us killed?"

"Just gotta catch up. I can see them up ahead. They're about to get onto the Seven Mile Bridge."

The Seven Mile Bridge is the longest bridge in the Keys and would be the best place for Campos to make his move—that was, if he was even in the Keys. Seven miles of two-lane road with nothing but a small railing and water on both sides is a good place to ambush someone. My mind instantly jumped back in time to when Black Venom had done just that, ramming Sam and me off the road and taking us captive.

A loud lightning strike snapped me from my thoughts, and I saw that Ange was shuffling through the duffle bag.

"Just my MP5N and an extra Sig, firepower-wise," I said as I slowed to match the speed of the traffic in front of me.

I was only two cars behind the convoy by now, a good distance to watch without drawing attention to myself. The drive across the Seven Mile Bridge was slow, as there appeared to be some kind of congestion heading into Marathon. As I stared through the windshield at the torrential rainstorm, I let my mind drift to what Scott and Commander Sprague had said. Maybe I was wrong about Campos. Maybe he was thousands of miles away and had never intended to come back for his loot. I knew that tracking down a guy like him in Mexico wouldn't be easy, but what choice did I have? The guy had murdered my dad, and he'd tried to kill me too. It would take a while, but I would find him wherever he was and rain painful justice upon him.

"What in the hell's going on up there?" Ange asked, snapping me from my thoughts.

Looking forward through the waterfall that cascaded over my windshield, proving too great of a task for my wipers, I saw that traffic up ahead, about half of a mile from the end of the bridge, was at a standstill. As we drove closer, I saw a big white truck blocking half the road and about five construction workers wearing bright orange vests and helmets directing traffic. There were eight vehicles ahead of us, including the convoy, as we came to a stop.

I didn't make the drive up north in the Keys very often. If I had to make a trip to Key Largo, the Everglades or Miami, I almost always took the Baia. Cruising offers more freedom, and I've always preferred piloting a boat to driving a car. But I'd heard that traffic could be terrible at times, and though I'd never been caught in construction in the Keys before, I'd heard many stories from the locals.

"Looks like they're just letting one lane go at a time," Ange said, as a row of cars moved slowly towards us in the opposite lane.

As we waited, I took a look around and watched as a center-console fishing boat passed just beneath us, cruising north under the Florida Keys Overseas Heritage Trail, which ran right alongside US-1. Through the rain, I could see the dark outline of Boot Key to my right and a few buildings on the outskirts of Marathon ahead of us, including the Sunset Grille, one of my favorite seafood places in the Middle Keys.

"I think this is the last car," Ange said as a few straggling vehicles passed by.

One of the construction workers spoke into his radio, then twisted a sign in his hands, replacing the word stop with slow. Traffic ahead of us turned into the left lane and inched forward. As the leading police vehicle reached the construction workers, they twisted the sign and held up a hand.

"What the hell?" I said, my mind racing as I looked around.

Seeing motion behind me, I glanced through my rearview mirror and saw a truck flying towards us through the rain-splattered rear window. I quickly put my Tacoma in gear, floored the gas and jerked the steering wheel to the right, trying to get out of its path. The truck hit my bumper, sending us into a powerful spin that slammed us both against our seat belts.

A second later, we came to a stop against the railing and I watched as the semitruck continued forward, crashing into the trailing police vehicle from behind. The back of the police car collapsed and slammed into the back of the armored truck ahead of it.

I drew my gaze forward and watched as a second truck slammed into the leading police car, hitting it so hard it almost flew over the bridge and into the water below. I shook myself from the haze of the collision and reached for my Sig. Reaching for the door handle, I pulled it down and shouldered the door open.

Just as I stepped out into the rain, I heard the sound of gunfire erupt over by the convoy. The five construction workers had thrown their equipment to the ground and grabbed Uzis, handguns, and submachine guns that they'd hidden beneath their orange vests. I moved forward and saw that both police cars appeared to be totaled and the officers inside were motionless.

The thugs dressed in construction attire went straight for the armored truck, forcing the two officers inside to get out at gunpoint. Ange appeared beside me, my MP5N clenched in her hands. We moved quickly towards the armored truck but kept our bodies low. When we were about a hundred feet away, we crouched behind a car, then popped up and opened fire. I hit one of the thugs just as he was climbing into the armored truck, causing his body to spin sideways and splash onto the wet pavement. Ange took down another, catching him off guard as he ran around the back of the truck.

The three other thugs let out a stream of automatic gunfire in our direction, forcing us to take cover. By the time we popped back up, the three remaining thugs were climbing into the armored truck. We fired a few rounds in their direction but hit only the thick metal doors as they slammed shut behind them, sending sparks flying wildly into the air.

Shooting the truck would be useless, as I knew that it was plated with thick steel capable of withstanding even high-caliber rifle rounds. Instead, I took aim at the tires, sending a few bullets into the rear left rear one before it accelerated around the construction truck. But even that did little but slow it down as it barreled down US-1, heading towards Marathon.

Inside the red Camry I was taking cover behind, I saw a young woman with her body bent down, trying to stay out of sight.

"I need you to call 911," I said, yelling through the shattered windows.

Her body was shaking, but she looked up at me and I knew that she'd heard me. A second later, she reached for her phone, which had been resting in the passenger seat.

Glancing up, I saw that the armored truck had almost disappeared from view.

"Shit," I said as I jumped from my cover and ran over towards the police vehicles. I headed for the leading one first, knowing that was the one Charles was in. As I moved closer, I saw that it was smooshed in on the side where a truck had hit it and the windshield was shattered. Charles was sitting on the pavement, rain beating down on him as he leaned against the driver's-side door. His right hand was holding a radio, and his left was pressed against his chest, where I saw splotches of red mixing with the rainwater. His eyes were wide as he glanced up at me, barking orders into the radio.

"Charles, are you okay?" I asked as I knelt down beside him and examined the bullet wound to his left shoulder.

"I'm fine," he said, shaking me off. "I've ordered a roadblock set up in Marathon." The words struggled out of his mouth. "These fucks won't make it far, and they sure as hell aren't getting out of the Keys."

I glanced up at the officer sitting unconscious in the passenger seat of the cop car. "Where's your first aid kit?"

"Center console."

As he answered, I was already opening the driver-side door and reaching for it. I grabbed a roll of gauze, alcohol pads, and an Ace bandage and handed them to Charles, then checked the other officer. He was hunched over the dashboard and was breathing, but was bleeding out from a cut on his forehead.

I wrapped the guy's head enough to slow the bleeding, then turned back to Charles and said, "We shot three of them."

He nodded. "There's nowhere for them to run."

Ange, who had been tending to the officers in the other car, ran over to us, her shoes splashing through the water. As she stood over us, I noticed something through the heavy rain out of the corner of my eye. I turned my head to the north, and my eyes grew wide as I saw the armored truck, barreling west on the Florida Keys Overseas Heritage Trail at over seventy miles per hour.

CHAPTER
TWENTY-FOUR

Seeing the expression on my face, Ange turned her head to see what I was looking at. From where we were standing on the Seven Mile Bridge, the old heritage trail bridge was only a few hundred feet away, allowing us to hear the roar of the armored truck's engine as it drove away from us. Ange took aim with the MP5N, but I shook my head and waved her off.

"You'd be wasting your ammo," I said. Then I drew my gaze ahead of the truck, my eyes following the old bridge to a small speck of land a little over a mile away. "They're heading for Pigeon Key!"

Without waiting for a reply, I holstered my Sig, moved around the police car and sprinted back towards my Tacoma. A few seconds later, I jumped into the driver's side door, which I'd left open, and then slammed it shut. The seat, dashboard and center console were soaked from the rain, but I didn't care.

With the engine still running, I put her in drive and floored the gas pedal, causing all four tires to spin freely over the soaked asphalt for a fraction of a second before catching and propelling the truck forward. I kept my eyes focused ahead as I weaved in and out around the two police cars, the other cars that had been stopped and the two trucks that had crashed into the shoulder after finishing their tear of destruction.

Once past the mass of vehicles, I quickly accelerated up over eighty miles per hour. The storm rumbled and lightning cracked just ahead of me as I reached the end of the bridge. Easing off the gas and hitting the brakes slightly, I took a sharp left, sliding in between two guardrails and almost running over a small palm tree. I did a full U-turn, my tires screeching as I straightened into a small parking lot and hit the gas once more. The concrete barrier blocking traffic from entering the old bridge had been removed, and the metal gate was bent to hell and lying sideways on the side of the road.

I picked up speed again, wanting to traverse the two miles of bridge to Pigeon Key as quickly as possible. In the back of my mind, I knew that I might already be too late. I knew that there was a section of the old bridge that had been removed just west of Pigeon Key, which meant that they would be loading the metal box onto a boat. I knew it wouldn't take them long to move it and try to make their escape, which caused me to push my Tacoma's engine harder than I'd ever pushed it before.

I calmed my breathing and maintained focus. They had me outnumbered and outgunned, which meant I would have to make each and every shot from my Sig count. I kept my eyes trained forward, trying to focus on the small island ahead of me through the darkness and thick sheets of unrelenting tropical rain.

Pigeon Key is only five acres and is known primarily for its Institute of Marine Science. Like most every island in the Keys, it's flat and littered with patches of coconut, gumbo-limbo, and palm trees. I knew that there was a ramp that led down from the old bridge, allowing authorized vehicles to enter. I'd expected to have to search the island's shore for signs of the truck and was surprised to see it idling directly in front of me, right where the bridge dropped off.

A moment later, as I cut the distance between us to less than a quarter of a mile, my question as to what in the hell they were doing was answered. Beside the armored truck was a lifted SUV that was backed up right to the edge. Two thugs stood beside it, and as I drove closer, I realized that they were operating a winch. As the water beneath the bridge transitioned to land, I eased off the gas and coasted across the island. When I reached the SUV with the two thugs operating the winch, I rolled down the window, grabbed my Sig, then turned the wheel and hydroplaned sideways.

The two thugs spotted me, but it was too late. I already had my window down and my Sig locked on them as I did a full one-eighty, screeching over the rain-splattered asphalt. Time slowed as I hit the brakes, then squeezed the trigger of my Sig, sending round after round into the first guy and then the second. Blood sprayed out from their shirts as they jerked backward and crashed onto the pavement, their lives ending in a flash of hot lead.

Just as I finished firing, my Tacoma slid to a stop, its two rear off-road tires less than a foot away from the edge. I put her in park, then killed the engine and shoved open the door. As I stepped out into the rainstorm, I could hear yelling coming from the water below.

With my Sig still clenched in my hands, I peeked over the edge and spotted a dark blue Cigarette idling on the choppy surface. The metal box hung lifelessly less than ten feet above the deck, nylon straps securing it to the cable that hooked up to the winch. Three guys stood directly below it. They reached up and tried to get it free while a fourth guy stood beside them, barking out orders. Even through the thick veil of rain, I recognized the fourth guy instantly as Pedro Campos, his massive frame and short Mohawk unmistakable.

Even though I only glanced over the edge for a second, it was long enough for one of the guys to spot me. Pedro yelled out violently, and I stepped back from the edge just as a symphony of air-rattling gunfire erupted through the air. Bullets whizzed by just a few feet away from my face, causing me to take an extra step back. As the automatic gunfire continued, I spent a fraction of a second thinking up a plan. They were seconds away from releasing the box, so running for the SUV and gunning it forward would most likely take too long.

No, I had to take them out. But I was pinned down by a stream of automatic gunfire. Four bad guys with Uzis and assault rifles against me, my Sig, and eleven 9mm rounds.

Suddenly, I heard gunfire erupt from behind me and turned around in an instant. Through the rain I could see Ange crouching behind the wall on the side of US-1, firing rounds from my MP5N at the Cigarette below.

This was my chance. As the bullets heading in my direction stopped momentarily, I reached into the backseat of my truck, grabbed my sweatshirt and sprinted for the edge. Kneeling down, I leaned over the edge and fired off two rounds just as the guys got the metal box free. It fell hard, its bulky weight slamming against the deck. Ange and I sent two of the guys to their bloody deaths, but that still left Pedro and another guy who I recognized as the short, muscular thug from the compound. The short guy ran for the controls, and I knew that I had no choice but to go for it.

Wrapping my sweatshirt around the metal cable that now dangled loosely over their boat, I held on tight and slid down. Holding myself with my left hand, I aimed with my right, covering myself as I rushed down the cable, my hand burning from the friction even through the fabric. One of my rounds hit home, exploding into the back of the short thug as he manned the controls. He lurched forward suddenly, roaring the engines to life just as I let go. I fell about ten feet above the Cigarette, landing on top of Pedro at the stern and almost sending us both tumbling over the side as it accelerated.

I grabbed onto the gunwale with a firm grip as my lower body dangled freely in the churning water, just inches starboard of the spinning propellers. Pedro was on the deck in front of me, his back having slammed hard against the transom. In a daze, he struggled to his feet and towered over me, breathing heavily and giving me an evil sneer. As he reached for me I pulled myself up as hard as I could and swung my right leg over the side, knocking him savagely across the face. His head jerked sideways and a combination of spit and water sprayed out over his shoulder.

As he gathered himself, I swung my left leg over and jumped to my feet in front of him. The boat was slicing through the whitecapped water like a rocket, bouncing violently up and down with every passing crest. Glancing forward, I saw the short thug leaning over the console, his body pressing against the throttles, accelerating us to the engine's max speed. He struggled to keep control of the boat as blood gushed out of his back, and he looked like he was gonna pass out any second.

As the strong winds and torrential rains beat against our bodies, Pedro and I faced off. He lunged his massive frame towards me. With his right hand clenched into a fist, he hurled a powerful haymaker straight for my face. I arched back, barely avoiding the blow as he whipped his body around and shoved his knee up into my chest. I grunted in pain, then returned with a sidekick of my own, striking him in the hip. As his body lurched sideways, I punched him square in the chest, knocking the air out of his lungs.

He grunted loudly as we cruised under the Seven Mile Bridge, heading southwest and narrowly missing the concrete pillars. Giving out a menacing battle cry, Pedro came at me like a wild animal, throwing punch after punch and striking me in the jaw and shoulder. I ignored the pain, deflecting his punches as best as I could and hurling my fists back at him in retaliation.

Suddenly, he grabbed a bowie knife from his waist, tackled me to the deck and tried to force the blade into my chest. The steel blade shook just inches from my sternum as the massive thug put all of his weight into it. I yelled out and struggled to keep it from stabbing through me, knowing that I couldn't keep it off me forever. My strength was giving out, and this guy was a monster, the kind of guy who knocked out professional fighters in the first round.

Suddenly, the sound of gunfire rattled the air, drawing Pedro's attention away from me and towards the source of the sound. The Cigarette turned sharply to port, causing us both to roll and slam into the starboard gunwale. Holding on tight to the handle, I forced the blade to the right, causing Pedro to fall and stab it through the fiberglass deck.

With the knife off me, I reared back my left fist and punched him in the cheek. As he jerked sideways, I pushed him off me and jumped to my feet. He tried to sweep me back down with a kick, but I avoided it, stomped his calf into the deck and kicked him in the head.

As he fell backward, I glanced up and saw the short thug lying dead under the console. Scanning the water around us, I spotted the *Revenge* motoring just a few hundred feet away. Jack was standing on the bow, his compact Desert Eagle clasped with both hands.

"Logan!" Jack shouted, pointing forward.

I turned around swiftly, thinking that Pedro had come to his feet and was trying to take me out while I was distracted. Instead, I saw that the massive thug was still on the ground and realized what Jack was pointing at. As the short thug had collapsed to the deck and turned us port, he'd put us on a direct course for Molasses Key, the largest of a small trio of islands that rose just a few feet above sea level.

I only had time to crouch down and pin myself against the cushioned seat in front of me, holding on tight as the hull crashed against the rocky shore. The boat jerked into the air and crashed down onto a flat sandy beach covered in mangroves and lush green grass. My body was thrown forward into the seat, then tossed to the side as the boat's momentum rocketed it almost across the entire island. As it slowed, the bow slammed against a palm tree and cracked as the boat twisted onto its side, launching me out of the cockpit. I landed in the grass and sand, my body rolling to a stop right by the southwest shore.

My body hurt all over as I sat up, and I was lost in a daze. I pressed my hand against my burning forehead, then pulled it away and saw blood covering my fingertips. The blood washed away with the rain within a few seconds, and I turned to look at the wrecked boat.

It was upside down, its cracked and scratched-up hull facing towards me as it lay propped against the rocks. The engine was still running and loud as hell. The propeller spun wildly, cutting through the rain and air and making noises that were painful to my ears. I knew it would only be a matter of seconds before the engine would overheat. There was already a small plume of smoke billowing out, and soon the powerful engine would kill itself.

Forcing my battered body to move, I rose to my feet and stepped towards the totaled boat. Wiping the bloody streaks of rain from my face, I squinted as I scanned the beach, trying to find out what had happened to Pedro. A moment later, I saw him appear from the other side of the boat. He was limping, his face contorted to show all the pain he was feeling. His left hand was pressed against his right shoulder, and blood dripped down from his nose. Upon seeing me standing on the beach about thirty feet in front of him, he froze.

He stared at me and gritted his teeth, his face consumed by a powerful and desperate rage. His eyes strayed down towards the beach, and he struggled to breathe for a few seconds before his body went motionless, his eyes staring at the beach in front of him. Suddenly, I wiped the water and blood from my face and realized what he was staring at. My Sig was lying in the sand just a few steps in front of him.

He looked up, shot me an evil smile and said, "You're fucking dead!"

An instant later, he moved for the weapon. In one quick motion, I reached behind me and grabbed my dive knife, which was sheathed to the back of my leather belt. Taking a step towards Pedro, I reared it back, then threw it straight at him. The titanium knife sliced through the rain and hit Pedro right in the chest as he was bending over and wrapping his left hand around the pistol. The sharp five-inch blade stabbed deep into his tissue, bone and internal organs. He grunted and his massive body fell backward, his hands dropping my Sig back onto the sand. As his back hit the beach, he pressed his hands to his bleeding chest and gave out a loud and painful cry.

I moved towards his dying body, my boots sinking into the wet sand. As I got closer, I realized that my knife had sliced straight through his heart and that he would only have a few more seconds before it was all over. He struggled for every breath. Blood spilled out from his mouth. His eyes looked at me one more time before he took one final breath and closed them forever. His shaking body went limp, and his head dropped back onto the sand.

I stepped towards him, knelt down beside his corpse and removed my knife. As I rose back to my feet, I looked off in the distance at the sheets of rain and whitecapped ocean. The *Revenge* suddenly appeared into view, cruising around from the northern side of the island. Jack was still standing on the bow, his Desert Eagle raised and aiming my direction. When he realized that I was still alive and that Pedro was dead at my feet, he lowered the weapon.

I looked one last time at Pedro's corpse and thought about my dad and the countless others Pedro had murdered. *No more*, I thought. Their entire drug-running operation was over, and neither he nor his brother would hurt anyone else ever again.

CHAPTER
TWENTY-FIVE

"This feels like déjà vu," Charles said, smiling up at me as he lay on a hospital bed with a stack of three white pillows behind his back. "You know, except this time it's me in the hospital."

I laughed. "I made off pretty lucky this time around. Dr. Patel just gave me a few stitches and then that was it. I'm glad to see you're healing up well."

Fortunately, the bullet had lodged into Charles's chest without hitting an organ or an artery, so the doctor said he should be out of the hospital in just a few days.

Charles shook his head. "It's not luck, Logan."

"Well, if you need anything, just give me a call," I said, patting him on the shoulder. "Jack, Ange, and I will be going to work exploring the U-boat."

As I moved for the door, he said, "Thanks for taking down Pedro." I turned around and he added, "You were right, and he'd probably have gotten away without you."

My eyebrows rose high into my forehead and I said, "I was right? I might need to get that recorded." He laughed and I continued as I turned back for the door, "Just get back on your feet. Key West needs its sheriff."

After a few days of late-night celebrating, we went back to work on the wreck, further exploring and striving to identify it. Professor Murchison proved incredibly helpful as both a source of knowledge and as a diver, joining us on our expeditions at least once every week. He encouraged me to get in contact with the divers who had identified U-869. After getting ahold of them and spending a few hours on the phone, I learned how they'd identified the wreck by finding a small box of spare parts in the engine room. It was this information that soon brought a successful end to our quest.

Using the ROVs to explore the insides had been informative, but we hadn't been able to bring any artifacts to the surface. Though there were ROVs with robotic arms and carrying capabilities, none of them were small enough to fit inside.

After spending weeks down at the wreck, Jack and I had found a way to swim inside the hull. The aft escape trunk had been damaged to the point where it was inoperable, and the forward trunk was too small for us to enter with all our gear. However, based on the diagrams, the trunk built into the conning tower would theoretically be just big enough for us to swim through—provided it too hadn't been seriously damaged.

It took us a few days to clean off all of the grime and sediment from the trunk. Professor Murchison showed us design plans for the model XXI, showing us how the trunks were designed to be able to be opened from the outside of the hull in the event of an emergency.

Less than a week after penetrating the hull, we searched the engine room and found a small metal box of parts. Returning to the surface with it, we gathered around and washed it off.

"There it is," I said, staring at a series of numbers that were visible after the grime was washed away. "U-3546."

The stern of the *Calypso* erupted into a chorus of loud cheers as we celebrated the milestone. Pete came out of the salon with bottles of champagne, and the rest of the evening was a wild blur after we returned to the marina. The celebration continued long into the night, and when it was over, Ange and I crashed together in the main cabin of the Baia.

It had been two months to the day since I'd killed Pedro on Molasses Key, and we had our wreck. Professor Murchison did heavy research on our new discovery, even traveling to Germany and parts of France, but could find very little information about the U-boat or its mission. Nowhere in all of the Nazi records and volumes that remained since the war was there any mention of U-3546 ever being commissioned.

Finding a lost German U-boat doesn't happen often, and it always gets global attention from news outlets. But finding one that nobody even knew existed was another thing entirely. I'd received more attention than I desired from the discovery of the *Intrepid*, the ship that had sunk south of the Marquesas Keys while transporting the Aztec treasure. And I was determined to ensure that any article written about the U-boat mentioned Owen Dodge and Joseph Campbell as the discoverers and Mobile Diving and Salvage Unit Two as the salvagers. Few people outside of some of the locals in the Keys knew that I'd been involved at all, and I preferred it that way.

As for the metal box and all of its contents, it eventually did reach the US Treasury Department building in Birmingham. Once there, all of the diamonds and cash were assessed and then appropriated by the US government. I never got an exact figure as to how much the loot was worth, but Scott told me that he'd learned that it was pretty close to the fifty million dollars we'd estimated.

Ange and I spent Christmas and New Year's in the Keys, which marked the first time I'd celebrated the holiday season in the Keys since I was thirteen years old. Key West is a wild and crazy town, and the holiday season is no different. The city transitioned into a colorful and festive tropical paradise in the weeks leading up to December 25.

Coconut trees and palm trees were decked with Christmas lights and holiday cheer. Bright red stockings hung from fence posts, wreaths strung with ornaments covered doorways, and ribbon-wrapped bicycles pedaled by in the busy streets. The Beach Boys' "Little Saint Nick" and Bing Crosby's "Mele Kalikimaka" echoed across the air, combined with the happy laughs and glees of carefree, alcohol induced pedestrians. Ange and I especially enjoyed watching Coast Guard boats cruise by and illuminate the tropical night sky with brightly-colored lights in the annual Lighted Boat Parade.

For New Year's, we moored just off Islamorada, watched the fireworks show and listened to the live music from Pierre's Restaurant and Morada Bay Café. Ange and I sprawled out on the Baia's sunbed and drank tequila out of the bottle while watching the vibrant explosions light up the night sky. We stayed out in the sunbed long into the night, talking about everything and anything for hours after the final fireworks went off. I thought about the previous year and how so much had changed in my life. Looking forward, I couldn't help but wonder at the adventures that 2009 would bring.

Near the end of January, Ange and I ran the Key West Half Marathon. The popular race starts right beside the Conch Harbor Marina, runs south through downtown, cuts east at the southernmost point marker, then runs along the waterfront to the turnaround at Cow Key, where the course loops back to the starting point.

I'd spent months leading up to the race following an intense training regimen alongside Ange, and I was confident that I had a shot at winning. Unfortunately, a few professional long-distance runners from Kenya had signed up at the last minute. I kept up with them for the first nine miles before they broke away from me, their lean bodies gliding across the pavement effortlessly.

I met them after the race, and they told me that I'd put up a strong fight. I knew that they were just being polite though, given how I'd finished in third place. I ran across the finish line a solid five minutes behind them, with a final time of one hour, twenty-three minutes and thirty-six seconds. Ange, however, finished first among the women with a time of just under an hour and thirty minutes. I didn't hear the end of it for over a week.

The race took place less than a week after US Airways Flight 1549 landed in the Hudson, in an act that quickly became known as the "Miracle on the Hudson". After the race, we headed over to Pete's place and watched as our country elected its first black president into office. We were still in January, and the year had already kicked off with an interesting and historic start.

On February 12, Ange and Jack surprised me with a party at Salty Pete's to celebrate my thirty-second birthday. He had a buffet of my favorite seafood sprawled out on tables on the balcony, including seemingly endless lobster, grouper, and shrimp cocktail. Scott even made it down for a few hours, and we all enjoyed the food and drinks while listening to live music by the Wayward Suns, a band I'd heard live a few times and was quickly becoming one of my favorite bands.

After getting everyone's attention, Pete and Oz rolled out a cart with a massive U-boat cake, covered in what seemed like too many burning candles. After blowing them out, I gave a toast to all the lost sailors aboard U-3546 and every other submarine lost to the sea. The heroes entombed by the sea on eternal patrol.

After the food and dessert were finished and it was well past midnight, I thanked Pete and everyone who'd showed up and then Ange drove my intoxicated butt back to my house on Palmetto Street. A few trips to the local hardware store and a week's worth of sweat had returned my home to its formal glory. Due to the happy trigger fingers of Campos's goons, I had to replace two of the living room windows and patch up the walls, which had been riddled with bullet holes.

Once we arrived, I chugged three large glasses of coconut water, the best hangover remedy I'd ever tried, and met Ange out on my terrace. We sat on the hammock together and watched the stars and their reflections on the calm water below.

"Well, what's next, Captain Dodge?" Ange said, shooting me that sexy smile that always managed to take my breath away.

"What do you mean?"

"I mean, it's been four months since we found the U-boat and took down the Campos brothers. So, what's next?"

I laughed. "You make it sound like I go looking for trouble. The truth is, it usually finds me. At least, ever since I moved here."

"Well, I hope something happens soon. We could use a little more excitement around here."

I shook my head. "We live in a tropical paradise. We go diving on the reefs, wrecks and ledges every week. We catch fresh lobster, spearfish and enjoy some of the best restaurants in the country." I took in a deep breath of the fresh Caribbean air and let it all out, emphasizing my relaxed island mood. "I think I'm enjoying this laid-back lifestyle we've had these past months. And I think I could sure as hell get used to it."

I took a few sips of my coconut water, then looked out over the dark ocean and the star-covered night sky above.

"Yeah, right," Ange said. "The Logan Dodge I know doesn't stay still for long." She stood up, looked out over the water, then placed a hand on my shoulder. "Let's just not lose the edge, okay? I've got a feeling something's coming on the horizon."

I smiled as she wrapped her hands softly around my neck and leaned in close. "Maybe you're right, Ange."

EPILOGUE

A few days after my birthday, I was sitting on the sunbed on the Baia, reading a book and enjoying the afternoon sun, when I spotted a familiar boat pull into the marina. It was early afternoon, with the sun shining down from directly overhead and a nice steady breeze blowing in from the east.

It was seventy-five degrees with not a cloud in the sky, and the marina had been bustling with activity all day. It seemed that there was a never-ending stream of pleasure boaters, fishermen, jet skiers, paddleboarders, and the ferries running to and from Dry Tortugas. But this boat was the first to cause me to lower my book down onto my lap, drawing all of my attention.

It was a sleek, fancy-looking yacht with a shiny dark blue hull and brilliant white trim. It had a similar design to my Baia, though it was bigger and much more expensive. Before it had even cruised close to a temporary mooring space at the end of the dock, I knew that it was a fifty-two-foot Regal. An extremely high-end yacht.

I folded the corner of the page I was on, then set my book aside. Reaching into my nearby Yeti, I pulled out a coconut water and sat up on the sunbed. As I took a few sips, I watched the yacht ease up against the dock and tie off. A woman and a young girl jumped over the gunwale and tied the mooring lines around the cleats.

I smiled as I watched them, unable to believe that it could be the same yacht that I'd last seen on Loggerhead Key, crashed against the beach with her hull covered in bullet holes and cracked to shreds from the nearby reefs.

Less than ten minutes after pulling in, Chris, his wife and their two daughters walked down the dock towards me, heading for the shore. Chris Hale was an attorney from Miami whose family had been hunted down by Benito Salazar, following his escape from prison. Salazar was a notorious Cuban gang leader, and Chris had played a pivotal role in making sure he was sentenced to life in prison.

His yacht had crashed against Loggerhead Key, and I'd just happened to be cruising by the island when I had seen the wreck and heard gunshots. After fighting off all of Salazar's thugs on the island, coming inches away from biting it multiple times, I'd managed to get the young family out of it alive. Scott and I had tracked down Salazar a few days later, killing him as he tried to shoot us and sending his corpse to a watery grave in over three hundred feet of water.

I hadn't seen Chris or any member of his family since the incident over six months earlier and was surprised when they pulled into the marina. The four of them walked briskly over the cypress planks. Upon seeing me, the two girls ran for the boat.

"Logan!" Alex screamed.

She was the youngest of the two at thirteen but was already taller than her mom. Both girls had their mother's brunette hair and hazel eyes. They were wearing sunglasses, shorts and flip-flops.

"Girls," Chris said, quickening his pace to catch up to them. "Remember proper boating etiquette."

The two girls froze and smiled at me as I rolled over onto the deck.

"Captain Dodge," Alex said. "Request to come aboard."

I laughed and said, "Come on over."

The two girls jumped onto the swim platform, then up over the transom with light steps. I held my arms open and they ran into me, laughing and telling me how good it was to see me.

"It's good to see you too," I said as we came apart and I got a good look at them.

I was amazed at how much older they looked since I'd last seen them. Jordan, who I later learned had recently turned sixteen, looked more like a young woman than a young girl. "Alex, how much taller are you gonna grow?"

She smiled and said, "Hopefully a few more inches. I'm a middle hitter now."

"Volleyball," I said, nodding.

"She's very good," Chris said, having reached the boat alongside his wife. "They both are."

Chris was wearing one of those nice ball caps, the kind you usually see golfers wear, along with a pair of sunglasses, a blue polo shirt, plaid shorts, and a black backpack over one shoulder. His wife Cynthia was wearing a vibrant purple sundress and stylish but simple brown sandals.

"Well, we should play sometime," I said. "I'm not terrible myself."

I'd enjoyed playing beach volleyball while I was stationed in California and had been looking to get a group together on occasion.

"It's good to see you, Logan," Cynthia said, smiling as I stepped onto the dock and greeted her and her husband.

"It's good to see you all too," I said. Then I glanced over at their yacht and added, "I see you replaced your Regal."

"It's the same one, actually," Jordan said.

I smiled and shook my head, turning to Chris, "Exactly how much money do you make, anyway? Must have cost more to fix her than replace her."

He laughed. "Actually, the insurance covered most of the damage."

"Well, what brings you to Key West?"

The girls chimed in, telling me how their great-uncle had died and they were on their way back from Pensacola, where his funeral had taken place.

"We had to fill up the tank," Chris said.

"We were hoping we might see you too," Jordan added.

"Well, I'm glad you pulled in," I said. "I'll get Gus to fill her up. You guys hungry?"

The five of us headed down the dock, then along towards the Greasy Pelican for lunch. On the way there, I popped my head into the office and asked Gus if he could fill up the Regal over at temporary slip three. Chris handed him enough money to handle a day's moorage and enough diesel to top of his yacht, but Gus only took the money for the fuel.

"A friend of Logan is a friend of mine," he said. "The moorage is on the house."

Chris thanked him, and we made our way to the large covered outdoor patio that extended right over the water in front of the restaurant. Lucy, my favorite waitress at the Pelican, came out and got our orders, and we were soon enjoying each other's company while feasting on some of the best seafood in the Keys.

I texted Ange, who'd been running errands in town, and she showed up just as the main courses were being set on the table. She was wearing a pair of skintight jean shorts that complemented her legs well and a white tank top. Her hair was tied back, and she was wearing a pair of aviator sunglasses and flip-flops on her feet.

The two girls stared at her as she stepped out onto the patio. It was the usual response people gave when they saw her for the first time.

I stood, greeted Ange and made the introductions as I pulled out a chair for her.

"Are you a supermodel?" Alex asked, still staring at Ange.

Ange laughed and hit it off instantly with the two girls. By the time we'd finished eating, they were begging their parents to spend more time with their new friend.

"You know we have to be back in Miami tomorrow," Chris said.

"I could just quit school and move down here," Alex said enthusiastically.

We all laughed at that, then headed back down to the dock. After we said our goodbyes and let them know that they were welcome to visit anytime, Cynthia walked alongside the girls back up towards their yacht. I was surprised to see that Chris had stayed behind.

Turning to me, his face grew serious and he said, "Logan, is there any way the two of us could talk in private?"

I looked him in the eyes for a few seconds, then nodded and turned to Ange.

"Don't mind me," she said, sprawling out over the sunbed and closing her eyes. "I'll be right here, relaxing."

I motioned towards the cabin door and Chris followed me down into the salon. I shut the door behind us and we sat down, facing each other on the half-moon dinette seat.

"What's going on, Chris?" I asked.

He'd sparked my curiosity, and I hoped that he wasn't in trouble of some kind.

He unzipped his backpack, which was now resting on the deck between his legs. Glancing up at me, he said, "As Alex told you, we're on our way back from the funeral for my Uncle Ken." He leaned back in the chair, lost in thought for a moment. "He was a good man, and he practically raised me." He paused for a moment. "He'd risen to be a successful business owner in Pensacola but had actually spent the majority of his life as a shrimper here in the Keys."

I nodded, listening intently and wondering where he was going with all of it.

"You see, when I was young, he would always tell me stories about things he found while shrimping. You would be amazed at the things he would catch: tires, toilet seats, and even televisions. But it was something he caught during his last year on the water that interested him more than anything else."

Chris reached into his backpack and pulled out an old leather pouch. He reached inside the pouch and pulled out an antique dagger. My eyes grew wide as I examined it closely. It was incredibly intricate in its design, with a solid gold handle. But it looked like it had been through hell. Judging by how faded and banged up it was, it was clear that it had spent hundreds of years under the ocean. My interest grew the more I looked at it.

"It looks really old," I said.

Chris nodded. "There's a name and date here," he said, pointing to an old and barely legible set of letters and numbers.

"It looks like 1665," I said, reading it aloud.

"That's right, and look here."

My heart nearly stopped beating, then raced with excitement a second later as I read the words etched into the hilt.

"Beatrice Taylor," I read, then looked up at Chris and saw the same serious expression, though tinged with excitement as well. "He found this in a net?"

Chris nodded. "My uncle used to tell me the story of how he found this all the time. He said it must have come from some lost shipwreck, and he has written a good description here of where it was found. Never inclined to go searching for the ship himself, given his age and physical ailments, he'd decided to make it a part of my inheritance."

"That's quite the gift," I said. "Well, if you'd like help trying to find it I'd be more than happy to oblige."

Chris went silent for a moment, then took in a deep breath and let it out. "Logan, there's no way I could ever repay you for saving me and my family's lives, but I want you to have it. From what I've heard about you, you've got a knack for finding treasure." He held the dagger out in front of me. "Please. With how busy my work keeps me, I have no use for it anyway."

I shook my head, "It's too—"

"Please," he said, cutting me off and setting it on the dinette. "It's the least I can do."

A few minutes later, I agreed, and we walked up out of the salon into the cockpit. Ange was still sunbathing and glanced over at us as we passed by.

"It was great to meet you, Angelina," Chris said, smiling at her after stepping onto the dock.

She smiled back and said, "You ever need a babysitter, let me know."

He laughed. "After an hour or so, I think you'll be whistling a different tune."

Before he turned to leave, I said, "Thanks, Chris. And again, you and your family are welcome in my house or on my boat anytime."

"No, thank you, Logan. For everything."

He turned and walked up the dock towards his yacht. Turning around, I placed my hand on the roof and leaned over Ange.

"You don't like kids," I stated with a grin.

She shrugged. "Usually, yeah. But something about those girls... I don't know." She blocked the midafternoon sun from her eyes and added, "What was that all about, anyway?"

I looked up at the distant ocean, the brilliant blue that stretched on as far as the eye could see beyond the bay. Feeling the warm tropical breeze against my face, I smiled and said, "You were right, Ange. Something has come from the horizon."

THE END

Logan Dodge Adventures

Gold in the Keys
(Florida Keys Adventure Series Book 1)

Hunted in the Keys
(Florida Keys Adventure Series Book 2)

Revenge in the Keys
(Florida Keys Adventure Series Book 3)

If you're interested in receiving my newsletter for updates on my upcoming books, you can sign up on my website:

matthewrief.com

About the Author

Matthew has a deep-rooted love for adventure and the ocean. He loves traveling, diving, rock climbing and writing adventure novels. Though he grew up in the Pacific Northwest, he currently lives in Virginia Beach with his wife, Jenny.